Duncan Delaney
and the
Cadillac of Doom

by
A. L. Haskett

JonLin Books
PO Box 1109
Pasadena, CA 91102-1109

JonLin Books, Third Printing, June 2006

Published in the United States by
JonLin Books, PO Box 1109, Pasadena, CA 91102-1109

Library of Congress Catalogue Card Number: 00-100697

ISBN 0-9678833-0-X

Cover photograph © 2000 by JonLin Books.
Cover Design by Pierce Palmer

Printed in the United States by
Morris Publishing
3212 East Highway 30
Kearney, NE 68847
1-800-650-7888

Duncan Delaney
and the
Cadillac of Doom

For my children

One

On the clear blue Saturday of Duncan Delaney's twenty first birthday, not long before he had first seen the Cadillac of Doom, his mother, Fiona Delaney, saddled her horse and rode out to deliver an ultimatum to her son. At the time Duncan still thought himself an artist.

Which was what Fiona wanted to speak to him about.

She was a trim widow of forty with apple red hair, eyes blue as summer glaciers, and an accent green as her native Ireland. Fiona stood a head shorter than Duncan, but they shared strong Irish bones and fair skin. She had searched for her son well into the afternoon over most of the Circle D's ten thousand grassy acres, and by the time she tied her horse to a post outside the bunkhouse, her patience was lagging. She walked to the rear of the old splintered building and stopped cold.

"Sweet Jesus preserve us!" she screamed.

Duncan's best friend, a lean, full-blooded Arapaho answering to the name Benjamin Lonetree, knelt in the dirt above the bloody body of Woody McCune, the Circle D's foreman and Fiona's covert lover. Benjamin was naked except for stained moccasins and a ragged loincloth which just about covered his privates. His long hair fell in black braids along sienna painted cheeks. He gripped Woody's shirt in one hand and a Bowie knife in the other. He looked up at Fiona and, grinning an evil grin, ran the blade across Woody's throat. The foreman fell to earth in a dusty cloud, his eyes surprised and terrified. Benjamin held his bright wet knife to the sky and howled an Arapaho war cry.

Fiona fainted.

Woody sat up and anxiously shook his head. "I sure wish you hadn't done that, Benjamin."

Duncan stepped out of bunkhouse shadows away from his easel and set his brush and palette on an old redwood picnic table. He was tall and thin with trusting green eyes, an easy smile full of straight white teeth, mostly clear skin, and a mane of hair red as Fiona's falling about his shoulders. He knelt beside his mother and cradled her head in his lap.

"And you wonder why she doesn't like you," he said.

"I know why." Benjamin wiped the phony blood from his knife and sheathed it. "She's a damn bigot."

"You watch your mouth," Woody said as he rose from the dirt.

Woody was tall and lanky, with a permanent squint and scorched leather for skin. More than one traveler had mistaken him for the Marlboro Man. He helped Duncan lift Fiona and set her on the picnic table bench. Duncan softly slapped his mother.

"Mom," he cooed, "hey, mom."

Fiona opened her eyes and looked about. Woody nervously wiped fake blood from his neck and brow with a handkerchief.

"Hi, Fiona," Benjamin said when her gaze fell upon him. He winked. "How's the girl?"

Fiona stood and picked up an axe that lay in golden leaves beside a woodpile.

"Uh oh," Benjamin said.

He backed away as Fiona advanced. He stumbled into Woody and they fell together in a nervous heap. Woody scrambled away like a crab. Duncan grabbed Fiona from behind as she hefted the axe above her head.

"Woody," he yelled, "get him out of here!"

"Come on, you moron." Woody dragged Benjamin into the bunkhouse while Fiona struggled in Duncan's grip.

"Go suck a potato, Fiona!" Benjamin shouted as he vanished inside.

"Let me go!" Fiona commanded.

Duncan released her and jumped back. Fiona paced the grass by the picnic table, her face flushed and nostrils wide, the fury in her eyes as sharp as the axe in her hands. Duncan kept a wary eye on her. He did not think she would come after him with the axe but he wanted to be sure. Fiona was unpredictable and dangerous when her temper flared. The night before, when she could not find one of a pair of silver earrings Duncan's father had given her long before, she had thrown a crystal perfume bottle through her bedroom window. Woody spent the morning replacing the glass and now the confused roses in the garden beneath her room reeked of violets. Fiona buried the axe in the picnic table with a loud *thunk*. She turned and glared at Duncan.

"I hope I didn't disturb you," she said.

"No ma'am." Duncan pried the axe from the table. "We were just finishing."

He sidled over to the bunkhouse door where a hand reached out and took the axe. Keeping his eye on Fiona, Duncan removed the painting from his easel and leaned it against the wall. The canvas depicted Benjamin murdering Woody in front of a burning covered wagon, all on black velvet. Fiona regarded the picture and shuddered.

"It's time you got a real job," she declared.

"I'm a painter," Duncan said. "I don't know how to do anything else."

This was not strictly true. Duncan could ride and brand and castrate cattle and do random jobs about the Circle D. But when it came to business he was without a clue. He did not even own a bank account. He kept his share of the money he and Benjamin earned peddling Duncan's cowboy and Indian paintings to tourists in a shoe box beneath his bed.

Fiona sighed and gazed across her ranch. The Delaney house stood on a green hill above a creek that ran the length of the Circle D to the highway. There was a white picket fence around the house, and a barn and stable near it, all big and well built with a fresh coat of white paint applied each spring.

"You can't eat canvas," Fiona said. "When you marry Tiffy and take over the Circle D, you'll be glad you heeded me."

Duncan thought back to that sky blue afternoon when they were both fourteen and Tiffy Bradshaw took him behind the stable to prove, she said, *that the universe was truly expanding.* Roughly fifteen seconds was all it took to convince him. Tiffy was blond and beautiful with breasts the size of softballs, though much softer and not as white.

Duncan was pretty sure he was in love with her.

"I don't want the Circle D," he said. "I want to be an artist."

"Horse shit!" Fiona cried.

Duncan had not heard Fiona curse since his father's funeral, when she wept over Sean Delaney's casket, repeating *you asshole* like a litany. She did not stop swearing until Father Fay wrested her from the coffin and the pall bearers conveyed what remained of Sean Delaney away from the tears and the flowers into a hearse whose tail fins sliced through the air like twin black sharks. Now, like then, Fiona's face was scarlet and her fists were clenched. Duncan thought she might smack him a good one across the jaw.

"It's time to quit playing cowboys and Indians and grow up!" Fiona hissed. "I'm going to Denver for the weekend." She pulled her gloves on. "When I return Monday, you will either have a job or you will be living on the street." She flipped a thick red lock from her eyes and fixed Duncan with cold, sapphire orbs. "And tell your stinking friend to call me *Mrs. Delaney!*"

3

She mounted her horse and galloped away. Benjamin and Woody came out of the bunkhouse. They had washed and put on clean blue jeans and cotton shirts. Woody had shaved and put on a silver and turquoise bolo tie and a quart of cologne. He calibrated his Stetson and sketched a circle in the dirt with the toe of a lizard skin boot.

"Sounds serious this time." Woody's voice twanged like a bass guitar. "She set a date. She never done that before."

"I know."

Duncan filled a mason jar with turpentine and cleaned his brushes. He spread newspaper on the picnic bench and laid the brushes out to dry.

"Fuck her and fuck her threats," Benjamin proclaimed.

"Benjamin," Woody said, "I told you to watch your mouth."

"Fuck you too, Woody."

Benjamin was twenty-two, five foot six on a typical day and one hundred thirty pounds of bone and muscle and fierce shadow eyes beneath long raven hair. He could fight like a mountain lion when provoked, a faculty which earned him two weeks in jail, to be served on alternate weekends, for beating the bejesus out of two drunken cowboys outside the Cheyenne Club the month previous. Benjamin stuffed his gear into a leather gym bag with the words *CUSTER HAD IT COMING* stenciled in white on the side.

"Let her kick you out," he said. "You can stay with me on the reservation. We'll paint your face red and dye your hair black and stick an eagle's feather in it. We'll paint all day and fornicate all night. Not with each other or domestic animals, of course. With women I mean."

"Why not just try a job?" Woody asked. "Make her happy."

"Still banging her, eh Woody?"

"Benjamin," Woody said, "one day I'm going to take a tire iron to the back of your head and see if that doesn't cure your foul mouth."

Woody stalked off. Duncan frowned.

"Well, he is you know," Benjamin said.

"I don't care. I like Woody and what he and Fiona do is their business."

Benjamin studied the finished canvas. "Not bad. I bet we get a hundred for it."

He put the painting in the cab of his forty-nine Ford. The truck was a pile of dents and rust held together by primer and bondo, but it had a four hundred horsepower V-8, a four-speed Hurst transmission, and fat tires. Duncan had seen it take a Corvette through a quarter mile. They called it the Purgatory Truck, because Benjamin did not believe in Hell.

4

Duncan picked up another canvas. "How about this one?"

He had painted it from a photo Benjamin's mother took years before on a family trip to Yellowstone. Their car had broken down and they were obliged to camp by the highway, while hundreds of more affluent families motored by, staring straight and uncaringly ahead. In the picture Benjamin's father toiled beneath the hood of his battered sixty-three Chevy wagon. Benjamin's grandfather sat in the dirt next to the car, a frayed and faded cavalry hat on his head and a half empty bottle of Jack Daniels in his hand, staring at the camera with a despair as long as the continental divide, wrinkles like dusty rivers running down his withered face, a cigar wedged between cracked, tired lips. If hope were gold, the old man's eyes were as bereft of it as were the mountains behind them, and the only one who did not know it was Benjamin. Seven years old, he sat with his hands on the wheel, grinning like hell as he pretended to drive. The sun behind him painted the clouds above the Tetons in pastels of orange and violet. Benjamin's grandfather had complained of vertigo after the sun set. Benjamin's father, thinking him drunk, ignored him. Benjamin fell asleep in his grandfather's arms. When help arrived with the dawn, the old man was cold as the Chevy's engine, and they were required to pry his stiff arms from the crying boy with a crow bar in order to set him free.

"It won't sell," Benjamin said. "The white man likes his savages, not unlike his women, on black velvet. This is too depressing."

"It's the best thing I've ever done."

Benjamin sighed and tossed the painting in the truck bed. He got in behind the wheel, rolled his window down, and leaned out.

"I'll see what I can do," he said as he pulled away. "But don't get your hopes up. And happy damn birthday!"

Duncan sat on the redwood bench and looked west at the shriveling sun. A tender wind pushed the grass towards him in waves across the range, touching his face with a wet green smell of cattle. The sun scattered a deep red through atmospheric dust until it was too dark to see anything but stars like distant candles above Wyoming and headlights on the highway. He waited there in the dark until he saw Fiona's Lincoln head down the drive and pass through the gate. He collected his paints and brushes and folded his easel. He headed for home, wondering as he walked what he would tell Fiona come Monday.

Duncan found a box wrapped in gold paper on his bed when he went to his room to put his easel and paints away. An envelope was slipped beneath the ribbon. *Waited until two,* the card inside read, *Happy Birthday, Tiffy.* He had forgotten that she was coming over. He picked up the phone and dialed. After seven rings he hung up and opened the box. The boots inside were soft and well tooled and smelled of olives. The tags said *Made in Italy.* Duncan laughed. Leave it to Tiffy to buy Italian cowboy boots. He took off his old boots and dropped them in the trash. The new boots fit his feet like twin Lamborghinis. Duncan had never been in a Lamborghini, but he imagined it would fit something like the boots. He took his new footwear on a test walk to the kitchen. He grabbed a cold beer and settled at the table.

A cake with twenty-one candles sat there beside a box wrapped in silver paper. Inside the box was a card from Fiona and a black Stetson with a wide brim and a woven green ribbon. He put the hat on and looked in the mirror behind the table. He looked ridiculous. He loved it.

Just when I'm convinced she's the world's biggest bitch, Duncan thought as he fiddled with the hat, *she does something to remind me of how much I love her.*

He lit the candles and blew them out. He forgot to make a wish. He got a plate and a fork and cut a thick slice. It took three swallows before he realized it was graham cracker cake, his childhood favorite, and he knew Fiona had baked it from scratch, like when he was a child. Duncan stopped smiling.

The last time Fiona had baked graham cracker cake was two months short of twelve years before, on the day that, for no good reason, Sean Delaney had allowed himself to be blown to pieces so small that what was finally found of him and put in a seven-foot brass casket could have just as easily been buried in an Italian boot box.

Duncan dreamed a nine-year-old boy playing in a haystack behind a barn beneath a moist August sky filled with clouds and thunder. He dreamed he was that child. He dreamed his father drove up to the barn in a white sixty-five Cadillac convertible.

"Hey, Duncan," Sean Delaney said as he got out of the car.

"Hi, dad! Nice car."

"Hi, Mr. Delaney," Tiffy said.

Duncan was surprised to find her in the hay beside him. Tiffy was a big, beautiful blond with chocolate eyes and strawberry lips and, in the dream, she was twenty-one and naked except for a pair of Italian boots and the black Stetson on her head. She winked at Duncan.

"Hey!" Duncan said. "That's my hat!"

"Forget about the hat, boy," Sean said. "We need to talk."

Tiffy grabbed Duncan and pulled his head between her breasts. "Don't listen to him, Duncan! He's dead!"

Duncan pulled free. "He is not!"

Sean smiled and took Duncan's hand. He was a wide, red-haired man with jackhammer arms and hydraulic lifts for legs, barely as tall as Fiona, but he was young and strong and clearly alive. He had left Ireland at sixteen, made a fortune in Wyoming uranium by twenty, married that year, and saw Duncan born the next.

"Actually," Sean said as he led Duncan to the creek, "I am dead."

There had been a dearth of precipitation that year and, despite the clouds and the threat of rain, the ranch was mostly brown. But the Delaney's creek was fed by a spring and the bank where they sat was green and cool. Sean plucked a blade of grass and put it between his teeth.

"You've got hard times ahead, son," he said. "Take Tiffy back there."

Duncan looked. Tiffy jumped up and down in the hay. She was still naked and her breasts swayed in a much more than simple harmonic motion. She appeared to be stomping on his Stetson.

"Hey!" Duncan jumped up. "That's my hat!"

Sean Delaney slapped the back of Duncan's head.

"Ouch," said Duncan.

"Never mind your stupid hat, boy. I'm trying to tell you something important."

Duncan sat. "Sorry, dad."

"Tiffy doesn't love you," Sean said, his voice a soft Irish breeze. "She never really has."

"Sure she does!"

Sean squeezed Duncan's shoulder and smiled sadly. "I don't expect you to believe me, lad," he said in the dream. "Not yet. But when it happens, remember I warned you. And remember this, too: you will love again."

A jet from the Air Force base in Cheyenne broke the sound barrier above the ranch and Duncan looked up to watch it pass. When he turned back his father, Tiffy, and the Cadillac were gone.

Duncan awoke to rain and thunder. He lay in bed and wondered what Sean Delaney would think of him now. The only worthwhile things he had done in his twenty-one years were paint with Benjamin and fornicate with Tiffy. His father would probably be proud of the first and impressed with the second. But what would he think of Fiona's ultimatum?

He would spit in the dirt.

All his life Sean Delaney had asked for nothing and expected less. But Fiona preferred the safe way, and Duncan was as much her son as he was Sean's. He lay in bed, fears chasing hopes through his head like dogs after rabbits. He watched lightning strike through his window. He listened to thunder and the rain against his roof. He closed his eyes.

It took him a long time to fall asleep again.

Duncan spent the next morning doing chores. He mended fence on the west end and dug out a drainage ditch clogged with branches and mud after the hard rain of the night before. At one o'clock he read the help wanted ads as he ate a grilled cheese sandwich and drank a beer. None of the ads interested him and he threw the paper in the trash. He called Tiffy three times but she never answered.

After lunch he cleared brush from around the stable and tended the horses. He saddled his mare and rode out to the Circle D's lone oil rig, where he greased the pump and checked the motor. The well produced less than ten barrels a day, but Fiona wanted to do her part to reduce America's reliance on foreign oil. Duncan was glad to tend the pump. He wanted to do his part too. He was riding back to the stable when a flash of sun on metal caught his eye. He reined his horse and circled until he saw the glint again. He followed the reflection across the grass to the edge of what was once a good-sized crater.

It was not much now, maybe seventy feet across, a shallow, grassy soup bowl in the earth with a rainwater puddle in the middle. Duncan got down from the mare and plucked a silver earring from the grass. It was an inch long and shaped like a jumping trout with small sapphire eyes. He knelt and looked around him, the wet grass soaking unnoticed into his jeans.

The air force people did a good job cleaning up after the crash, but in the twelve years since, Duncan had found numerous jagged metal pieces and plexiglass shards and lengths of melted wire. When he was ten, he found a tooth there. He had cried until Woody convinced him it was a buffalo molar. That took some time, because it was a big tooth, and Duncan remembered his father as a giant. He had not gone there for a long time after because of the things he might find.

But the scorched earth had grown back green and twelve winters had washed the rocks clean and neither grass nor rocks had been black for years. All that remained of the crash was a grassy rut where the jet had plowed the prairie, leading to a dent in the earth where it finally exploded in a brilliant, futile burst. Duncan dropped the earring in his pocket, mounted the mare, and started back to the house.

Duncan had just walked through the front door when he heard the Purgatory Truck turn off the highway. He popped two beers and stepped onto the porch. Benjamin braked in a dusty whirlwind and leaped out. He stopped when he reached the porch steps.

"Jesus God!" Benjamin declared. "And Fiona says I stink!"

Duncan gave him a beer and went to his room. The earring fell from his pocket when he took off his jeans. He set it beside a picture of him and Tiffy taken at the rodeo when they were high school seniors. Neither had changed much since, though Duncan shaved twice a week now instead of twice a year, and Tiffy spent more on clothes. He went into his bathroom, turned on the water, and stepped under the shower. He soaped and rinsed and dried himself with a thick, lavender-scented towel. He called Tiffy but she still did not answer. He put on clean jeans, got his beer, and went outside. Benjamin sat on the porch, his lips stretched and showing teeth like a hungry coyote.

Duncan sat beside him. "What are you so happy about?"

Benjamin laid six one-hundred dollar bills on the porch.

Duncan looked up. "Who'd you rob this time?"

"Nobody. That's for your painting of my family!"

Benjamin handed a card to Duncan. *Angela Moncini, Artists' Agent,* it said in a fine black script. The address above the phone number was on Wilshire Boulevard in Beverly Hills.

"She wants you to call her." Benjamin closed his eyes. "She is beautiful as the night and smells like rain." He opened his eyes and his smile faded. "I think I love her."

Benjamin threw his beer high into the yard. The bottle hit the dirt with a thud and rolled in the dust. It stopped in a beetle's path. The oppressed insect tarried and contemplated this new impediment in the immutable course of its existence.

"But I do not wish to speak of it," Benjamin said.

"All right."

Duncan picked the bottle up. The beetle slowly and with vast dignity went on its way.

"I would, however, like another beer."

"These were the last."

"So what are you going to do about it?"

Duncan thought hard. He considered what would happen if he left and what would happen if he stayed. The first prospect terrified him and the second was depressing.

"It's not a trick question," Benjamin said.

Duncan made up his mind. "Go to Los Angeles."

"What I meant was what are you going to do about the beer."

"Oh." Duncan stood. "Well, go get some, I guess."

He went inside and put on his new Italian boots, a t-shirt, and a brown leather jacket. He stopped at the door and went back to get his Stetson.

"Nice hat," Benjamin said when Duncan got in the truck.

"Birthday present from Fiona."

"No kidding." Benjamin slipped the truck into gear. "The bitch did something nice for a change, didn't she?"

"Yup." Duncan pulled the hat down over his eyes. "She sure did."

"I parked on Highway Thirty a few miles east of Medicine Bow," Benjamin told Duncan on the way to town. "It's always been a good spot to catch tourists heading for Cheyenne. I set the cowboy painting against a fender and sat in a folding chair in the shade of my truck. No one stopped the first hour, so I leaned the painting against the other fender and moved my chair. No one stopped the second hour, so I set the painting in the chair and leaned against the fender. When no one stopped the third hour I began to worry. Your work always sold within thirty minutes. Then it came to me. It was karma. I told you I would sell both paintings. The lie worked against me. I smacked myself on the forehead. It hurt, but I deserved it."

"Don't think I don't appreciate that," Duncan said.

"I leaned the picture of my family against my bumper," Benjamin continued. "Just as I sat down a woman in a Mercedes roared past. She wore dark glasses, but from her profile I could tell that she was beautiful. Brake lights came on. I sat up. She made a U-turn. I stood. She stopped across the highway. I carried your paintings to her.

"She was tall and her hair was dark. Her lips were thin but her mouth was wide and her bones supported a body bordering on amazing. She looked to be forty, but a good forty.

" *'My penis is a rattler striking in the night,'* I told her.

" *'One of those Zen Indian sayings no doubt.'* Her voice was wind across a deep lake.

" *'Arapaho,'* I told her.

" *'Gesundheit,'* she said.

10

"She pointed at the painting of my family. She told me she only had six hundred, and asked me if that would do. I took the money and gave her the painting. I swam in her gray eyes.

" *'I want to be your love slave,'* I said.

" *'Thank you,'* she replied, *'but that won't be necessary.'*

"She gave me her business card and told me to have you come see her in Los Angeles. I stood in the center of the highway and watched her drive away. Death in the form of a semi hauling melons from California to Nebraska missed me by inches, its horn a blast of hot wind. I took the hint and got out of Death's way and went back to the Purgatory Truck.

"I doused your black velvet painting of me and Woody with gasoline and threw it on the asphalt. I touched a match to it and watched it burn. Then I got in the Purgatory Truck and headed for the Circle D." Benjamin shrugged. "Now you know as much as I do."

"Wrong," Duncan said, "I finished high school."

Benjamin pulled into the parking lot of a Lazy Rancher Market and shut off the engine. They got out and went inside. Benjamin stood by the door and stared at the clerk, a fat, balding man of forty-five with a raw neck and a tattoo of a snake on his forearm. His name was Leroy Kern, and ten years before he had accused Benjamin of stealing a Milky Way, beating him with a yardstick when he could not find the candy bar. Nothing came of it. Benjamin had been picked up for shoplifting before.

If he didn't rate a beating today, the sheriff said, *he'll rate one tomorrow.*

"What's his problem?" Leroy Kern asked Duncan. He had forgotten about the Milky Way a long time past.

"Beats me."

Duncan was not feeling particularly verbose. He was upset that Benjamin had burned the cowboy and Indian painting. He took a case of beer from the cooler and a cheese pizza from the freezer. He grabbed a bag of corn chips and went to the counter. Leroy Kern rang him up.

"Tell him I got a gun," he said, one eye on Benjamin.

Duncan took a box of miniature chocolate donuts from a rack beside the counter and put it with the beer. He glanced at Benjamin.

"He's got a gun," he said. Benjamin kept staring.

"I'm not afraid to use it neither. Killed a punk who came in here four years ago."

He held up a yellowed newspaper clipping containing a photograph of Leroy Kern behind the counter, a smirk on his gap-toothed face and a forty-five Colt in his hand. *Blood Bath at the Lazy Rancher,* the caption said.

"Did I ever show you this?"

"Only about twenty-seven times."

Leroy Kern put the clipping back under the counter and held up the chips. "You see how much these were?"

"One ninety-nine."

Leroy Kern rang up the chips. "He was a heroin addict from New York on his way to lotus land to play guitar in a rock band. He pulled a knife and I blew his brains across the dairy section. Three rounds between the eyes. You tell him that."

Duncan looked at Benjamin. "He heard you," he said, "but he doesn't seem to care."

"Well, he ought to. That'll be twenty-nine thirty-five."

Duncan paid and took his change. Benjamin left and got in the truck. Leroy Kern looked miserable.

"Every time he comes in here he stares like that. It bugs the hell out of me. One day I'm going to put a stop to it. You tell him that."

Duncan picked up the beer and groceries. He stopped at the door. "That wouldn't be smart."

"You think I'm scared of him?" Leroy Kern's breath came in ragged bursts. His eyes were wide and his face cherry red. The artist in Duncan appreciated the color. *You tell that shit-ass punk the next time he comes in here I'll blow his head off!*"

"Ok," Duncan said as he left, "your funeral."

Two

"Sure it has a lot of miles," Smiling Jack Sweeney said, "but that just means the engine's wore in proper."

Duncan and Benjamin stood beside a white sixty-nine Volkswagen mini-bus beneath a cool morning sun. A diverse multitude of used cars in various states of repair were parked about them. A flaking billboard manifesting Smiling Jack's face soared over them. The Smiling Jack keeping vigil from above had manhole sized nostrils, most of his original teeth and hair, and looked thirty years younger than the worn and wrinkled gnome in the cowboy hat beside them.

"How much?" Duncan asked.

They had spent the previous night celebrating his first real sale, and he had a hangover twice the size of his Stetson. Smiling Jack kicked a wheel with the steel tip of a shiny white snake skin boot.

"Brand-new radials," he said.

Benjamin examined the tires. "Retreads."

"How much?" Duncan repeated.

His brain hurt and a foul taste resided beneath his tongue. He was in no mood for haggling. Smiling Jack pushed his white cowboy hat back. The act deviated his toupee an inch.

"Look here." He opened the engine hatch. "Rebuilt engine."

Benjamin contemplated the oil dripping onto the asphalt. "Needs a head gasket."

"Damn it," Duncan said, "would you please tell me how much?"

Smiling Jack grasped the lapels of his white coat and looked thoughtful. "I see your friend knows cars, boy. Tell you what." Smiling Jack hawked up something green and spat. "Seven hundred and it's yours."

"Seven hundred!" Duncan exclaimed.

"And that's one hell of a deal."

Duncan despaired. The night before, somewhere between the last ding dong and the third six-pack, he had extracted the shoe box from beneath his bed. When he finished counting, he had clutched less than half the three thousand he had expected to find. He had forgotten about a ski trip to Jackson Hole he treated Tiffy to the previous winter.

"We'll give you five." Benjamin said.

"I like your people." Smiling Jack smelled a deal. He took a half-smoked cigar from his pocket and proceeded to re-ignite it. "So I'll let it go for six."

Benjamin smiled back. "Four."

Smiling Jack frowned. He normally did not do that, and he did not want to set precedent, but he felt he must impart to these young men the seriousness of their error.

"You got the concept wrong, boy. I set a price, you make an offer, we meet in the middle." Smiling Jack smiled again. *"Understandee?"*

Benjamin took out his Bowie knife and commenced cleaning his fingernails. Smiling Jack stopped smiling. Smiling Jack went pale.

Here we go, Duncan thought.

"Three," Benjamin said.

Smiling Jack swallowed hard. Conroy, his other salesman, was on the far end of the lot showing a forty-seven year old middle school teacher a seventy-two Volvo. Conroy carried a single-action Beretta semi-auto, but even if he were standing there Smiling Jack would have a hard time defining the threat, and you could not just launch bullets at an Indian for nothing anymore anyhow. A shimmer of sweat grew on his upper lip. He considered the fact that he paid one hundred and fifty for the van three weeks ago and that it had sat on his lot oozing oil since.

"Fine," Smiling Jack said. "Three. And I'll throw in a case of thirty weight."

"And a tank of gas," Duncan said. It was to be his car. He wanted to participate.

"Sure," Smiling Jack said. "Why not?"

A mechanic loaded the oil and filled the tank. Duncan traded cash for pink slip and key and started the bus in a smokey blue cloud. Benjamin got in the Purgatory Truck and followed him off the lot. Smiling Jack fanned his face with his hat as he watched them drive away. Conroy came over and took a pewter flask from his jacket. He removed the cap and held the flask to his lips, then proffered it to Smiling Jack. Smiling Jack took a long pull and screwed the cap back on.

"And they say we stole from the Indian," he muttered.

Tiffy was sitting on her porch swing next to Danny Carpenter when Duncan pulled into the Bradshaws' yard. Danny had loved Tiffy ever since that incident in kindergarten when she kissed him in the coat closet during nap time. After that, Danny made sure Tiffy never lacked graham crackers or milk, but to his abiding frustration, nothing else ever came of it. Or so Tiffy maintained. Duncan trusted her. Duncan trusted everyone, though some, like Danny, he liked to keep one eye on.

Tiffy's blond hair was lightened, but her enormous brown eyes were real, and her teeth were responsible for three of her orthodontist's most recent nocturnal emissions. Her face and smile were all Wyoming but her body was pure Hollywood mud wrestler. Duncan held that opinion because once, when he was sixteen and a run away from the reservation, Benjamin had mailed Duncan a postcard from the Hollywood Tropicana. Duncan had studied the card intently before Fiona confiscated it with a long, sad commentary on Benjamin's abundant lack of character. The card depicted numerous tanned and oiled women whose synthetic breasts strained the limits of string bikinis. Tiffy resembled that, but without the oil and silicon.

"Hey, Duncan," Danny said.

Danny was five ten in boots and pushing two hundred and fifty pounds. He had bad skin and a round, not quite ugly face, but his daddy liberally shared his thick wallet with his son, and that went a long way to equalize his social standing. As usual, he looked nervous.

"Take a hike," Duncan said.

"Sure." Danny got up and left.

"That was rude," Tiffy said.

"I get tired of him sniffing around you all the time."

She turned her head when he bent to kiss her. His lips brushed a surprisingly cold cheek. He took Danny's place on the swing.

"Sorry about Saturday," he said. "I got wrapped up painting."

Tiffy aimed a neon pink nail at the van. "Whose is that?"

"Mine. What do you think?"

"Well, I think you better move it. It's leaking oil. Daddy will be mad if you stain the driveway. He's proud of his concrete."

Duncan moved the van to the street. He returned to the porch and took off his hat. A picture of a cowboy holding a hat full of water for his thirsty horse was screened onto the Stetson's white satin lining. He had not noticed that before. The portrayal's humanity made him smile.

"What the hell did you buy that thing for anyway?"

"Fiona gave it to me."

"Why on earth would Fiona give you a wreck like that?"

"What?" Duncan spotted the misunderstanding and moved swiftly to rectify it. "No. Fiona gave me the hat. I bought the bus."

"Whatever for?"

"I'm moving to Los Angeles. To paint."

Tiffy laughed. "And fish have testicles."

That threw Duncan. He was not sure if fish were so equipped.

"I'm serious, Tiffy," he finally said.

"Let's see if I have this right," Tiffy said. "You're moving to California, despite the fact that if you do your mother will cut you off but good."

Duncan put his hat back on. "That about sums it up."

"Duncan Delaney, you're not going anywhere least of all California. So just get that idea out of your head. I suspect you'll die in Cheyenne like the rest of us."

"Which would be fine if that was what I wanted. I love you, Tiffy, but I'm going. I want you to come with me."

Tiffy initiated a laugh, but something in Duncan's eyes stopped her cold.

"You're really serious, aren't you?"

"Yes," Duncan said. "Yes, I am."

Tiffy punched him with such authority that his hat flew off and he fell backwards over the swing into a bed of posies. He had not been sucker punched in a long time and, coming from the girl he loved, it was a revelation. He shook his head and looked up. Tiffy stood over him, a terrible Valkyrie with retribution flashing like strobe lights in her eyes.

"You pitiful bastard!" She grabbed his shirt and shook. "If you think I'm moving to L.A. to be some nobody waiting on tables in a Bob's Big Boy to support a no talent painter like you well you've got another thought coming! To think I wasted seven years on you!"

She released him and he fell back into the posies. She grabbed his feet and tugged off his new Italian boots. Duncan lay back in pain and amazement. He slowly sat up. Tiffy kicked his hat across the porch.

"Hey!" Duncan said, overcome with *deja vu*, "that's my hat!"

"Screw your hat!" Tiffy screamed. "Screw your painting!" She flung the boots at his face. Duncan caught them. *"And screw you!"*

She wrenched the boots from his hands, ran into the house, and slammed the door after her. Duncan stood and slapped a dirty cloud from his jeans. He dusted off his hat and straightened the brim. He walked down the drive to the sidewalk. Tiffy's words bit into his heart like the gravel bit into his bootless feet. He looked back. The front door remained shut and cold. He got in his van and drove to the corner where Danny skulked. He rolled down his window.

"Go on back, Danny," he said. "We took care of business."

"You don't care?"

"Any reason I should?"

"None comes to mind."

"Go on, then."

"Well," Danny said, "see you."

As Duncan drove away he saw Danny in his rear view mirror, sprinting as best he could back to the Bradshaw house. Duncan stopped at the corner and closed his eyes, afraid to feel anything lest the feelings overwhelm him, until a restless motorist honked behind him. He opened his eyes, took his foot off the brake, and drove slowly back to the Circle D.

Benjamin was waiting on the porch with his toolbox handy beside him when Duncan arrived home. He looked at Duncan's feet, but said nothing. Duncan fished his old boots from the garbage can by the back porch and put them on. He got two beers from the kitchen and returned to the van. Benjamin had changed into greasy overalls and was already swapping spark plugs. Duncan gave him a beer.

"I take it she's not going with you," Benjamin said.

The enormity of Duncan's loss commenced to demand notice. He took a deep breath and a profound pull off his beer. A lone tear, a clear dew drop condensed on a cold window to his heart, spilled from his eye and ran down his cheek. He brushed the tear away with the back of his hand.

"Doesn't look like it," he finally said.

Duncan packed while Benjamin labored on the van. He crammed a suitcase full with jeans, sweaters, and t-shirts. He loaded another with socks, underwear and tennis shoes. He put his toothbrush, toothpaste, and a cake of soap into an overnight bag along with a razor, deodorant, and a bottle of shampoo. He dismantled his easel and put his paints in a case with his pallet and brushes. He packed his stereo and took his sleeping bag down from a shelf in his closet. He packed like a sleepwalker, and when the Volkswagen was full and he stood dazed beside it, he could not remember having loaded it. Benjamin slid out from beneath the van and wiped the grease from his hands with a rag.

"It runs better," he said. "It still leaks oil, but if you check it every hundred miles or so you'll be okay."

"Thanks, buddy." Duncan felt overpowering afraid and lonesome. "Why don't you come with me?"

"I still have six days to serve."

"Right. I forgot." Duncan kicked dirt. "I'll write when I get settled."

Benjamin faltered, then clumsily hugged Duncan. He let go and got in his truck.

"See you, buddy," he said. Then he was gone.

Duncan walked through his room one last time. He picked up the photograph of himself and Tiffy at the rodeo. For the first time, he saw that she did not really smile. Her lips were turned up, and you could see white teeth and pink gums, but her eyes were distant and cold. Duncan's smile should have been wide enough for them both. But that was not how it worked. He set the picture face down on the dresser and picked up the earring beside it. He found a pen and a slip of paper and wrote. He left the note on the kitchen table and the earring on top of the note.

Gone to California, the note said, *love Duncan.*

Half a mile down the road he saw his mother's Lincoln coming towards him. Woody was piloting, his arm around Fiona and her head against his shoulder. Fiona smiled as she slept and Woody smelled her hair. Neither spied him. Duncan watched the Lincoln in his rear view mirror until it sank behind a hill. Then he fixed his gaze on the road before him and drove on toward California.

Benjamin parked in front of the Lazy Rancher Market right about the time Duncan passed Fiona and Woody. He sat in the Purgatory Truck and listened to a country station on the radio. He rolled a cigarette and let it hang unlit from his mouth. He had not smoked in years, but he found it easier to forsake the actual act than to give up the associated rituals. Through the window he watched Leroy Kern serve a woman. He waited until she left and Leroy Kern was alone. He got out and spit the cigarette onto the asphalt. He adjusted his hat and walked slowly inside.

Leroy Kern, one hand beneath the counter, warily watched Benjamin lift a six-pack of beer out of the cooler. Benjamin selected a turkey with potatoes and gravy frozen dinner from the freezer. *Microwavable,* the package said. He resolved to one day get himself a microwave. He dropped the beer and the frozen dinner on the counter. Leroy Kern was pale and sweating and his hand remained beneath the counter.

"How much white man?" Benjamin asked.

"I got a gun."

"And I got a dick. Who do you think has the bigger balls?"

"I ought to . . ."

"Yes, but you won't." Benjamin was enjoying this. "Now get off your fat ass and ring me up."

Leroy Kern looked miserable but he punched the requisite buttons on the register with his free hand.

"That's eight ninety-five," he said.

Benjamin laid eight one-dollar bills on the counter. He took a handful of change from his pocket, counted out ninety-five cents, and dropped the coins on the counter a half a foot to the right of Leroy Kern's outstretched hand. Quarters rolled off the edge and hit the linoleum with a sound like metal raindrops. Benjamin smiled.

"Sorry," he said. "Now bend over like a good boy and pick those up."

Leroy Kern pulled the gun. Benjamin knocked his arm aside and boxed him hard in the face. The gun went off and Leroy Kern went down. Glass fragmented in the dairy section as the bullet pierced the cooler and a one-gallon jug of skim milk before coming to rest in a quart carton of low-fat cherry yogurt. The discharge was deafening, and Benjamin's ears commenced to ring. Leroy Kern shook his head and slowly stood. It was then Benjamin noted that he still held the gun.

"Uh oh," he said.

Benjamin dove behind the chip display as Leroy Kern fired a second round. The bullet whispered a lethal song beside his ear and a Fritos rain fell around him. Leroy Kern jumped the counter with adrenaline assisted agility. He fired again as Benjamin ducked around the magazine rack. A woman opened the door, screamed, and ran out. Leroy Kern chased Benjamin through the narrow aisles, firing a fourth and a fifth time as Benjamin ran through the frozen foods, only to discover he had reached a dead end. He reached into the freezer and grabbed something small and hard and cold. Leroy Kern came around the soap aisle and smiled when he saw Benjamin trapped beside the poultry.

"Say goodbye, red-skin," Leroy Kern said as he raised his gun.

That's when Benjamin threw the frozen Cornish game hen.

Back when he and Duncan were growing up and playing ball, Benjamin was the Cheyenne Dodgers' star pitcher, until he was thrown out of little league for beaning Whitey Carpenter, Danny's brother, three out of three times at bat. Whitey was two years older than Benjamin and forty pounds heavier, and for no real reason had regularly trounced Benjamin. Benjamin always was deadly accurate, and even at that age he brushed back little leaguers with such skill that he could impart a greasy coat to the ball by running it through the part in the batter's hair. So no one believed the three bean balls were accidental, and Benjamin's mother drove him back to the reservation during the bottom of the seventh, and he had not pitched again.

He threw the bird with all his might. It hit Leroy Kern center forehead with a sharp *crack*. The gun dropped from his hand and clattered to the floor. Leroy Kern's eyes rolled up into his head. He did not quite fall. Benjamin grabbed the fat man's shirt and gangster slapped him ten times fast. He let go. Leroy Kern crumpled to the floor. Benjamin picked up the gun, took out the clip, and racked the round from the chamber.

"Drop it, Lonetree!"

Two deputies stood at the end of the soap aisle, pistols drawn and pointing. Benjamin dropped the gun. One deputy holstered his weapon. It was Billy Masterson. Benjamin and Duncan had attended high school with Billy.

"Hey, Billy. About time you got here." He pointed at Leroy Kern's unconscious body. "This asshole nearly killed me."

"Turn around and put your hands behind your back, Ben."

"Sure, Billy." He did so, felt cold steel encircle his wrists.

Billy put him in the back seat of a patrol car and belted him in. Two more deputies arrived and went inside. One revived Leroy Kern. Benjamin began to see how this thing looked. The other deputy went behind the counter and took a surveillance videotape out of a VCR. He came out and put the videotape in the trunk of his car.

"Hey, deputy," Benjamin called out just before Billy Masterson shut the door, "you take good care of that tape!"

They drove him to the county jail where they strip searched him and took his picture and put him in a cell with a drunken rodeo clown. They did not bother taking his fingerprints. They had several copies on file already. Benjamin sighed deeply and sat on one of the cell's two bunks. The rodeo clown looked up and promptly vomited.

"Ain't this some shit?" he asked miserably.

"Yup," Benjamin allowed. "It sure is."

Three

Duncan topped off his tank in Fort Collins and put in a quart of thirty weight. He stopped at a diner and bought a burger and a coffee. He put another quart in when he reached Denver. He slept beside the van, rose with the sun, gassed up, and bought a case of oil at an auto parts store. He crossed the Rockies that afternoon. He stopped only for food or gas or to put oil in the engine or to relieve biological demands. He was a driving fool. He would have driven non-stop, but the bus blew a tire at four a.m., and Duncan pulled off the road in the heart of the Mojave Desert. It was then he determined that the Volkswagen had no spare. He wrapped a blanket around his shoulders and slumped against the van. He watched his breath and listened to the wind in his hair. He waved at passing cars but none stopped. He tensed when a coyote yelped nearby. But the moon and stars revealed nothing but Joshua trees so ultimately he relaxed.

Half an hour later, a star close to the horizon became two stars hurtling towards him. Duncan's head whipped from west to east as a Porsche raced by in a cold rush of desert wind. A coyote stood transfixed in the middle of the highway, its eyes reflected red in the Porsche's lights. The car jerked left. Duncan heard a dull thud and the coyote sailed into the desert. The Porsche's wheels lost traction with a nauseating screech. The car spun cartwheels end over end, impacting the asphalt in a flurry of sparks like electric snowflakes, finally coming to rest upside down in the dirt by the side of the road, headlights bright and horn sounding sickly flatulent in the otherwise silent desert night.

It took Duncan a minute to run to the Porsche. He knelt beside the inverted vehicle and looked inside. The driver was twenty-five years old, her head bent in an unlikely angle, her blond hair wet and red. The steering wheel was broken and the post impaled her chest. He knew she was dead, but she did not look it. She just looked disgusted. He tried both doors but they were jammed shut. The engine caught fire. Duncan backed away. He heard something wail.

Oh my god, he thought, *there's a baby in there.*

Duncan saw movement in the back seat. He kicked out a window and pulled something warm and hairy out. He staggered from the burning car and collapsed in the brush beside the road as the gas tank exploded. He looked at the squirming bundle in his arms and groaned. He had risked his life for a bright orange cat.

"One down," he said to the cat as the Porsche burned like a bonfire among the Joshua trees, "eight more to go."

"Judging by the skids," the Highway Patrolman told Duncan after the fire burned itself out, "she must have been going over one-twenty."

He gave Duncan hot coffee from a thermos and radioed for a tow truck. He measured the skid marks and filled out a report. Then he wrote Duncan a ticket for having two bald tires and a burned out brake light. Two coroners arrived and took the woman, now reduced to a stick figure in charred crepe, out of the smoldering car. Her blond hair was gone and her clothes were melted to her skin. They put her on a gurney and covered her with a white sheet. An arm broke from the corpse and fell to the ground. A coroner tossed it back on her chest beneath the sheet. Duncan threw up.

"You okay, bud?" the man asked.

"Just great," Duncan replied. "Thanks for asking."

He picked up the cat and wandered into the desert. Not far off the highway he stumbled across the coyote. One leg was gone and there was blood across its matted fur, but it was alive enough to snap at his leg. Duncan dropped the cat and walked up to the Patrolman's car.

"The coyote's out there. It's hurt pretty bad."

The Patrolman considered Duncan from behind the mirrors of his glasses. "What do you expect me to do?"

"Take care of it, I guess."

He followed Duncan into the desert. They stopped beside the coyote and regarded the dying animal. The Patrolman was not much older than Duncan, though he was bigger in the arms and chest, with a black crewcut and baby fat in his cheeks. He looked like a life size Ken doll in a tan uniform. He sighed and drew his pistol and shot the coyote in the head. He holstered his gun, picked up the cat and handed it to Duncan.

"Consider it taken care of," he said.

The tow truck dropped Duncan off at a garage in Baker where he bought a retread and a spare. He bought two hamburgers and a chocolate shake at a diner and cat food at a market. He bought a map of Los Angeles and charted a course to Angela Moncini's office. He reached Los Angeles at dusk. He exited the freeway at Sunset Boulevard when the van began to lurch and sputter. He parked in a lot in front of a mini-mart just as his engine died. He got out, opened the engine hatch, and pulled the dipstick. It burned his hand and he dropped it. He had forgotten to check the oil. He sighed and stared at the engine. But it looked as it should and no amount of staring could make it run again. A small, dark man came out of the mini-mart and tapped Duncan's shoulder. He was five and a half feet tall, slim, with Hindu skin, a sharp nose, and a lone thin eyebrow across his forehead. He spoke perfect English with an accent that spoke of opium fields in his native Pakistan. He had been a lawyer in Islamabad until his religion made him the target of an extremist group who butchered his wife and five year old son and set fire to his house while he lay bleeding from a gut shot beside the front door he had innocently answered. Once healed, he went straight from hospital to airport to Los Angeles, and had never looked back.

"Excuse me," he admonished, "you cannot park here if you are not patronizing my store."

"My girl dumped me," Duncan said. He was not making sense but he found it difficult to care. "My van just died, I have no place to stay, and I really need a beer. Can you understand that?"

The small man nodded and smiled. His teeth were bright and clean and a gold cap sparkled to the left of his incisor.

"My name is Assan, my friend. I will help you."

He led Duncan to a stairway behind his mini-mart. A rag pile lay beneath the steps. It moved and Duncan realized the rags contained a human. Assan led him up the stairs. At either end of a dark hallway lay two doors. A pipe crossed the hallway at head level. Assan walked under it but Duncan had to duck. Assan threw open the door on the left.

"Your new home, my friend."

The room was half the size of the store below, with a small kitchen and a bathroom beside it. The floor was dirty hardwood and the walls peeling gray. A couch sat by a wall, a rip in its red vinyl cushion revealing foam the color of Assan's skin. An old typewriter sat atop an older metal desk. Two lights hung by rusty chains from a water-stained ceiling. It was a dingy room that smelled of dust and mildew. Assan had tried to rent the studio at two fifty a month, with no luck because of the noise from the bar across the street. But what Duncan noticed were the windows facing east, with all the morning sun he could want. He looked out. Across four traffic lanes and next to a hardware store stood the Hollywood Bar and Grill. There were no windows in front, just a steel door set in a dirty, brick wall and the name spelled out in blue and red neon. Three Harleys were parked in front between a BMW and a Toyota truck. Rock music drifted from the door as three men sporting leather and long hair emerged from the bar. They got on the Harleys and thundered away.

"For you, my friend," Assan said, "three hundred dollars a month."

Duncan sighed. It was not much, but it was his only prospect, and the windows and open space appealed to him. Plus his van was dead and he had nowhere to go and no way to get there.

"I'll take it."

"Very good. But no pets."

"Sure," Duncan said. "No, wait a minute. I have a cat."

"One cat then. But no dogs. Dogs are very messy."

"They're not nearly as bad as horses."

"No horses!"

"I was kidding."

"Horses are messy. Cats are clean. Have you ever given a cat a bath?"

"Can't say I have."

"It is not necessary. They clean themselves."

Assan went downstairs. Reality slowly but thoroughly slapped Duncan with meaty fingers about his face and head. The walls needed paint and the floor required sanding. He turned the taps in the kitchen. The water ran rusty. The refrigerator and water heater worked, as did the toilet, but the tub was a disaster, the shower head needed replacing, and the lock on the front door was broken. Assan returned with a lease, a pen, and a beer. Duncan twisted the cap off and downed the beer without stopping. He could not remember a beer ever tasting so good. He belched quietly and set the bottle down. Consigning himself to an uncertain fate, he took the pen.

"Where do I sign?" he asked.

"Hey, Roscoe," Misty said to the bartender the next afternoon when she reported for work at the Hollywood Bar and Grill, "some guy across the street wants me to come up to his studio and pose for him."

Roscoe was a huge biker of a man with a black rose tattooed on the back of his bald head, a fu-Manchu mustache hanging down to the gold nipple rings piercing his pectorals, and tattooed muscles built up over ten years pumping iron in and out of prison. Misty dropped her bag and sat at the bar. She was a naive young peroxide blond from Ohio with artificially enhanced breasts and big brown eyes.

"Did he try anything?" Roscoe asked.

"No, he just asked me to pose." Misty twirled a strand of permed hair around a finger. "He's kind of cute."

"So why tell me?"

She picked up her lingerie bag and headed for the dressing room. "Just thought you should know."

"So now I know," Roscoe said.

He forgot about it until Champagne clocked in and told the same story. Her real name was Mary. All the strippers wanted to be rock singers or actors and figured they needed stage names. *Except Pris*, Roscoe thought, *the only one who could make something of herself uses her real name*. At two, Cassandra clocked in.

"What's with the cute guy across the street?" she asked.

Roscoe stood. If a guy came into the Hollywood, paid his cover charge, bought a few beers and tipped the girls, then it was all right if he hassled them, as long as it stayed friendly and no one got touched. But a nut hanging around outside could be dangerous. He cracked his knuckles, put on his sunglasses, and headed for the door.

"Watch the bar," he told Misty.

"Don't be long," Misty said, "I'm a dancer, not a bartender." Roscoe grunted as he stepped through the door. "And don't hurt him too bad!"

After fifteen minutes, Misty told herself Roscoe was just doing a thorough job. After an hour she reasoned that Roscoe had gone to lunch. After two hours she was angry. The afternoon crowd was coming in, and she was a dancer, *an artist*, damn it. Roscoe had no right to make her wait tables. She threw down her bar rag and marched across the street to the sidewalk beneath Duncan's window.

"Hey Roscoe," she called, "get your fat ass down here!"

"Don't move, Roscoe!" a male voice commanded.

Misty's hand flew to her mouth. Roscoe was not so big a bullet could not slow him down considerably. When Roscoe did not come to the window, Misty ran across the street and called 911. No one answered their knock, so the two policemen who answered her call drew their guns, pushed Duncan's door open, and cautiously stepped inside.

Roscoe sat in a torn leather chair, tattoos running like jackals across his naked chest. He stroked an orange cat on his lap with one hand and held an empty beer in the other. Duncan stood across the room before a canvas propped on an easel, his Stetson atop his head, a brush in one hand and a pallet in the other, furiously painting. Roscoe saw the police first.

"Hey, mothers," he said, "you got a warrant?"

The police holstered their guns, apologized, and left. Misty burst into the room.

"You scared me half to death, you goddamn ape!"

"Duncan," Roscoe said, "this is Misty."

Duncan smiled and nodded. "It's a pleasure, ma'am."

"We kind of already met," Misty said. She took the cat from Roscoe's lap. "What's his name?"

"He doesn't have one yet."

"A cat needs a name."

"Well," Duncan said, "I've just been calling him Cat."

"That's silly."

"Take a break, Roscoe," he said. "I'll get you a fresh beer."

The room smelled of paint and Lysol. Books and a stereo were stacked by a wall near a box of clothes. A brush sat on a paint can in the corner. A sleeping bag was laid out on the couch. Misty noticed there was no bed. She touched a wall. Her finger came back white and tacky. She went to Duncan's easel. The Roscoe in the unfinished painting looked cuddly. She frowned. Normally, something in Roscoe's eyes made you suspect that, given the choice, he would prefer to rip your lips off than kiss them, though she could not remember Roscoe ever trying to do either to anyone. Yet the eyes staring out of the painting were virtually gentle. Duncan returned with three beers. Misty reached for one but Roscoe waved her back.

"No thanks bro," he said as he put on his shirt. "We got to get back."

"Hey!" Misty said, "speak for yourself."

"I'll speak for us both. You got work to do."

"Thanks for explaining," Duncan said. "I won't bother the girls anymore."

"Screw 'em," Roscoe said, "they can take care of themselves."

"Nice meeting you, Misty."

"Nice meeting *you.*"

She followed Roscoe across the street. She stopped at the door and looked up at Duncan's window. The orange cat sat on the sill licking a paw. Duncan moved the easel and canvas close to the window and pushed his hat back. A fiery waterfall of hair streamed around his shoulders as he flicked his brush like a sword against the canvas.

Something happened there, Misty thought.

26

She was not sure what, but she no longer felt right calling herself an artist. She danced, an artist *created*. She mentally commanded Duncan to look down and favor her with his smile. But he did not.

Her real name was Joanne Kowalski. She had dropped out of an Ohio high school half way through her senior year and had hitch-hiked to Los Angeles, where she bought a fake ID and took a job as what the ad in the newspaper called a Dance Hostess. It was not easy stripping at first, but five years had hardened her to where she could bend over and stick her firm, g-stringed derriere in a stranger's face without a second thought. She had seen a lot in her twenty-two years, much of it bad, and God help her, she was not the swiftest deer in the concrete forest. But through it all she still believed in Prince Charming, and she half-suspected Duncan Delaney was his first cousin.

Misty wished Pris were there. Pris hung out with artists. Pris could advise her on how they felt and what they thought. But Pris was not scheduled to work that night. So Misty sighed and went back inside the Hollywood Bar and Grill and told Champagne and Cassandra about the peculiar painter across the street.

Duncan finished the painting at midnight.

A shaft of light divided Roscoe into sun and shadow, tattoos quiet across his muscles like the sleeping cat on his lap. All was harsh and dark except for a light in Roscoe's eyes that was not innocence. Instead there was wonder there, and a juvenile thrill Roscoe had thought lost years before.

Duncan sat on his window sill. Cat jumped into his lap beneath his hand. Long hairs and businessmen, union men and those without proper documentation, went in and out of the Hollywood. Each time the portal opened rock music drifted onto the street like a guitar call to arms. He turned off the lights, stripped, and crawled into the sleeping bag. A streetlight outside his window bathed him in its creme soda glow. He pulled his Stetson over his eyes and settled into a restless sleep.

Duncan dreamed he sat at a picnic table beside his father in a courtroom on the open prairie. Benjamin sat on the bench holding a gavel and wearing a robe black as his eyes. Fiona sat in a witness stand to his right. Woody wore a bailiff's uniform and carried a cattle prod in a holster. Tiffy stood before a jury box filled with Fiona's bridge club.

"What happened next, Mrs. Delaney?" Tiffy inquired.

"I remember smelling kerosene as the jet dumped its fuel. We heard a sound like a cork popping out of a champagne bottle, only louder, and then the jet trailed smoke."

Fiona touched a lace handkerchief to her eyes. Duncan, in a rare flash of perception, saw where she was heading.

"Your honor!" he yelled. "Benjamin! I object!"

Benjamin peered down from his seat near the clouds, mist swirling about him. "On what grounds?"

"This is irrelevant and pointless. My dad did what he had to do. He should have been given a medal but instead my mother has put his memory on trial every day since the day he died."

"Hey," Benjamin said, "that's good!"

Tiffy said, "the relevance, your honor, is that he didn't have to do anything. And the point is that what he did accomplished nothing except his death."

"Well," Benjamin wobbled, "since you put it that way. Overruled. Go on, Fiona."

"Thank you, your honor," Fiona said.

Duncan suspected it was a dream. Benjamin and Fiona were being too cordial. Plus, most courts were located indoors.

"When the jet came down Sean jumped onto his horse and rode away. That's the last I saw of him. Now I see the same thing happening with Duncan. This stupid desire to do what's right. Right for who? Not for me!"

Tiffy speared Duncan with her eyes. "I couldn't agree more."

"Hey," Duncan demanded, "who's on trial here anyway?"

"Exactly!" said Tiffy, and both Benjamin and the jury of old women fixed stony eyes on Duncan.

I'm losing my baby! cried Fiona.

"Quiet, woman," Sean Delaney said. "You're embarrassing the boy."

"Mr. Delaney, if you don't mind, I'll admonish the witness." Benjamin turned to Fiona. "Control yourself, Mrs. Delaney, or I'll be forced to have Woody discipline you."

Woody had been half-asleep through the proceedings, but he perked up some and produced a nasty looking bull whip.

Duncan turned to Sean. "I'd like to wake up now if you don't mind."

"Not at all." Sean Delaney clapped his hands.

Duncan woke to gunshots and screams. He tried to get up, but he was tangled in his sleeping bag. He fell hard to the floor. The gun fired again.

Glass shattered, tires squealed, an engine roared. Duncan crawled to his window and looked out.

A young Hispanic man lay on the sidewalk in front of the hardware store, glass strewn about his body and a dark stain spreading across the sidewalk around his head like a wet, black halo. He wore a white t-shirt, blue jeans, and a blue bandanna around his bleeding skull. A young girl with long black hair kneeled wailing beside him. A woman peered out of the Hollywood Bar and Grill and screamed. Soon spears of red light whizzed through Duncan's windows and across his walls and sirens and police radios filled the street. Girls from the Hollywood, clad in lace and high leather boots, pushed up against yellow police tape and watched paramedics work over the silent man. One paramedic stepped away and the other leaned back. A man and his wife walked beneath Duncan's window as a man in a coroner's jacket took a body bag out of his truck.

"Just another drive by," Duncan heard the man say and then he and his wife were gone.

Duncan pulled on his pants, put on his Stetson, and took a beer from the refrigerator. He set his easel beside the window and laid his paints and brushes across the desk. Cat paced between Duncan's legs as he watched the coroner load the dead man into a van and take him away. By the time the last police car had gone, Duncan had sketched a rough outline of the scene below. The street he painted with his eyes, but the dead man and the girl he painted from a snapshot in his mind. But his brain was not a camera and the picture evolving on canvas lacked the detail with which Duncan normally painted. The result was simple and dark and brutal. The young Mexican lay dead on the cement, his blood black, his face turned away, one leg bent backwards at the knee.

But the evolving painting was not about death, it was about grief, and the focus was the kneeling girl, her face in shadows but the anguish obvious in the curve of her back and her hands on her dead lover.

And all around them, dots of broken glass like diamonds cast unwanted into the gutter.

29

Four

All that remained of the rodeo clown was a mild stench.

It did not interfere with his sleep, but it vexed Benjamin during his waking hours, and made his meals unpalatable. He took shallow breaths until a deputy came after breakfast and led him to an interview room with a plexiglass partition and salmon colored walls. Benjamin did not suspect that he was about to endure the first of two tests of honor in what would be a day of minor tribulations. All he wondered was who had come calling. He settled in a metal chair facing the glass and surmised it must be Duncan. He was first sad that his friend had ceded his dream so easily, then pleasantly relieved when Woody entered the room opposite the glass. A laugh perished in his throat when Fiona followed him in.

"Well, slap my ass and call me Sally," Benjamin said. "Fiona, if you weren't the last person I expected to see here."

"Ben, for once in your life," Woody said, "just shut up and listen."

"What the hell." Benjamin sat back and folded his arms.

"The way it was explained to me," Fiona began, "is that, based on your previous criminal history, you can expect a significant period of incarceration in the state penitentiary for your most recent transgression."

Benjamin said nothing. This was his understanding too. Ten years was considered the best bet in the pool organized by Billy Masterson. Benjamin had put five dollars on two years and then only because three and four were already taken. One year and probation were left without takers. The winner stood to make fifty dollars.

"If you wish, I will post your bail and obtain a lawyer for you."

"I got a lawyer."

"What you have is a drunken public defender who couldn't get you out of here for the last four days. I'm offering a real lawyer and the money to make your case interesting." Fiona took a deep breath. "All I ask in return is my son's address."

"He just left a note saying he went to California," Woody explained.

The thought of a retained attorney tempted Benjamin. Public defenders had failed to gain acquittals for him four of five times, two of which he had actually been innocent. All he had to do was supply Fiona with Angela Moncini's phone number.

"What would you do, Woody?"

"Hell, Ben, you know what I'd do. I'd tell her. He's her son and she's worried sick. Duncan would understand."

"Still banging her, eh Woody?"

"Damn you!" Fiona yelled through the holes in the glass. "You can rot here on your way to hell if you want! But if anything happens to my boy I will bribe or buy your freedom so l can personally rip your heart out and stuff it back down your throat!"

A deputy came in. Her expression did not change when he whispered in her ear, though her complexion advanced into the pale end of the spectrum. The deputy left.

"You have my offer," Fiona said. "Take it or leave it."

"Fiona," Benjamin spoke so softly that she had to lean forward to hear, their faces segregated by four cumulative inches of atmosphere and one of glass, "you can take your offer and blow it out your sweet Irish ass."

Fiona leaped at the partition and struck it with her small fists. The glass vibrated with her wrath. Woody pulled her away.

"Ben, you always were a special kind of stupid," Woody commented as he dragged Fiona screaming from the interview room.

"That woman could screw up a wet dream," Benjamin muttered.

He sat back. Someone was always preventing Fiona from assaulting him. He did not doubt she could damage him before he finally put her down. He frowned. That would not benefit his friendship with Duncan. He resolved to be more cordial in future encounters, not for Fiona's benefit, but for Duncan's. Billy Masterson came in and led him from the room down a hall and to the left.

"Hey," Benjamin said, "my cell's back that other way."

"Jesus, Ben, I know that. It's my jail after all. We're letting you go."

Benjamin's public defender, a gray haired man named Conley whose breath whistled through his nose with a perpetual whiskey smell, waited in the lobby. Lightning struck Benjamin's brain. He turned to Masterson.

"You looked at the tape!"

"Actually," Conley said, "it was me who looked. They just assumed they knew what was on it."

"What took you so long?"

"Well," Conley admitted, "I guess I assumed the same thing they did."

"We're really sorry, Ben," Billy said.

Benjamin laughed, realizing what the deputy had whispered to Fiona. It must have rankled when she realized any leverage she possessed was lost. But she played it through and almost roped him. Billy gave Benjamin back his wallet, two hundred and forty-eight dollars in bills and seventy-three cents in change, a Canadian nickel, cigarette papers and a tobacco tin, two ribbed condoms, the keys to his truck, his belt, his shoelaces, and his hat.

"Let us know if you want to prefer charges against Leroy Kern," Masterson said.

"Let me think about that one."

Benjamin tied his shoelaces and put on his belt. Masterson gave him the fifty dollars from the pool.

"Your guess was closest," he explained.

"Thanks, Billy. You boys treated me okay this time."

"I've talked to the judge," Conley said. "He agreed to apply time served against your previous sentence and suspended the remainder. Your weekends are forthwith free."

"Thanks, Mr. Conley."

"You come see us again soon," Masterson said.

"Not me. I've mended my ways."

Conley laughed. "Sure, Ben. See you at church next Sunday."

Tiffy's white convertible Volkswagen Rabbit was parked in front of the Cheyenne Club when Benjamin drove up. Mr. Bradshaw had given her the car upon the successful completion of her cosmetology course work at the community college. She never aspired to or attained a position in the industry. She just had a thirst for knowledge. An *I Brake for Cowboys* decal adorned her rear bumper. Benjamin parked behind the Rabbit, wondering if she had the same logo tattooed on her ass.

It was early and the club was not crowded. Benjamin sat at the bar, took off his hat, and ordered a beer. He drank it without pause. He had been dry near a week and the beer quenched a burning within. He ordered another and looked to the dance floor. Tiffy danced there with a young cowboy. They both wore hats. Benjamin pondered why half the population of Wyoming found it imperative to wear their hats indoors.

Savages, he thought.

Tiffy wore a short denim skirt, white leather boots, and a white long sleeved blouse with a bolo tie. A flimsy bra beneath the blouse barely restrained her breasts. Benjamin pictured her naked. He felt no guilt. Countless men and boys and a proportionate number of women had envisioned Tiffy naked in the course of her young life. Benjamin did not see why he should be the first to forsake that pleasure. The young man she danced with was apparently of the same perspective, as he furtively glanced to ascertain which way her chest swayed. Tiffy left him on the dance floor when the music stopped. She sat at the bar beside Benjamin.

"How did you get out?"

"Hasn't been a jail built yet that can hold Benjamin Lonetree."

"Escaped, did you?"

"Three men died in the purchase of my liberty."

"Uh huh. Buy me a beer?"

Benjamin called for another round. Tiffy uncrossed and crossed her legs again. Her skirt's brevity impressed the hell out of him.

"I suppose you'll tell Duncan you saw me here."

"That was not my intent."

"Well, it doesn't matter. I'd tell him myself if I knew where he was. I'd tell him it don't mean nothing."

"What do you care? You dumped and forsook him."

"Is that what he said?" Tiffy touched his arm. "This is all a terrible mistake. I miss him so."

Benjamin glanced at the young cowboy who in turn eyed him with ill disguised envy. "I could tell."

"Oh, don't mind him." She moved closer. "We were just dancing." Benjamin smelled her jasmine perfume. "You know where Duncan is, don't you?"

Benjamin had stopped by the post office on the way to the Cheyenne Club. Amongst the bills and the advertisements in his box was a card from Duncan with his new address. Benjamin had put the card in his pocket and the remaining mail in the trash.

"I know."

"You'll tell me, won't you?" She touched his knee. "I'd be so grateful."

Benjamin sighed. He set his beer down. It would be rude to ignore an invitation that plain. He kissed her. She expanded her mouth to receive him and he indulged her with his tongue. After a moment she pushed him away and smirked.

"Well, now, Benjamin! Whatever did you do that for?"

"To see if I could."

"You always could have. You just never noticed."

Tiffy grasped his ears and kissed him again. She guided his hand to her breast. Benjamin had often laid in bed and mused what he would do to or with or for her if the opportunity ever tendered itself. But now, when she was (technically at least) broken up with Duncan and was as such fair game, he startled himself by resisting.

"You can touch me if you want," she whispered.

"Which is exactly why I'm not going to."

"It's all right. I wouldn't tell Duncan."

"I would."

Tiffy cuffed him once, hard. Benjamin slapped her back. She appeared surprised, then stimulated. She seized him and tried to kiss him again.

"Let's get out of here," she said.

"I've got a better idea." He pushed her away. "Why don't I get out of here and you find someone else to lead around by the pecker."

He paid for the beers and left. Tiffy followed him to the Purgatory Truck. Her previously smoldering eyes had cooled to glaciers. She handed him an envelope.

"Will you give this to Duncan?"

"Sure."

"If you tell him anything, I'll just deny it." She turned and walked away. "Candy ass pansy Indian fairy," she said as she retreated.

"White bow-legged cowgirl slut," Benjamin said as he got in his truck.

Tiffy stopped. "I am not bow-legged!" she yelled. Then she went back inside.

Leroy Kern stood behind the counter at the Lazy Rancher, absently rubbing the goose egg on his forehead. He had been seeing double since the incident and could only today successfully fuse his images. Earlier that morning, Billy Masterson had stopped by and explained the situation. It riled Leroy Kern that Benjamin could, in theory and if he so desired, prefer charges against him. He protested, but Billy held up his hand and said, *self defense don't include protecting yourself from being stared at.*

Leroy Kern looked up when he heard the Purgatory Truck. He reached under the counter. He panicked when he remembered Billy had confiscated his gun as evidence. Benjamin shut off the truck and went inside. He took a six pack of beer out of the cooler and placed it in a hand basket beside a plastic wrapped tuna salad sandwich, a bag of chocolate chip cookies, and a half pint of potato salad. He took a quart of thirty weight off a shelf and put it in the basket beside the six pack. He put the basket on the counter.

"Howdy, Leroy," Benjamin said.

"Hey, Ben."

Leroy Kern, pale and sweating, removed and totaled the items in Benjamin's basket. His goose egg was a painful purple, and both eyes were bruised. He looked like a fat, bald raccoon.

"No hard feelings?" he asked.

"Just because you tried to murder me? Of course not."

Leroy Kern relaxed. "That'll be twenty-one seventy-five."

"You take care of that, Leroy?

Benjamin picked up his goods and headed for the door. He stopped at the candy rack. He took a Milky Way bar and held it up. Leroy Kern stood there with his mouth open and his eyes dull.

"I believe you owe me one of these."

He pocketed the candy bar and stepped outside. He placed his appropriated goods on the passenger seat and got in. As he backed up, he looked through the glass and watched with grim satisfaction as Leroy Kern finally closed his mouth, took out his wallet, and put a twenty and three ones into the cash register.

A thin, ebony haired receptionist was sitting behind a chrome and glass desk when Duncan walked into Angela Moncini's office that Monday, her crossed legs covered in black mesh. Her name was Marie, and she was pretty as a mannequin, though substantially more lifelike. She surveyed him with an entomologist's indifference. Duncan leaned the two paintings wrapped in butcher paper against a wall and took off his hat.

"I'd like to see Angela Moncini if I could."

"Is she expecting you?"

"Well, yes and no."

"Which is it?"

"Both, I guess."

"Your name?"

"Duncan Delaney."

"I'll see if she's in." She stood and went through a door.

Duncan looked about. Framed newspaper and magazine clippings on the walls detailed the varying successes of Angela Moncini's clients and the importance of their work to Western civilization. Looking at the clippings, Duncan felt like a pretentious dung beetle from Wyoming competing with big city cockroaches. He picked up his paintings and turned to go, but a placid, euphonious female voice arrested him.

"You must be Duncan."

He turned. Angela Moncini's onyx hair was cut to her shoulders and her eyes were gray and soft above tan valleys cut deep beneath the ridges of her cheekbones. She wore a black skirt and stockings and a white silk blouse through which Duncan deciphered the intricate pattern of her bra. Duncan understood what Benjamin must have felt when first he gazed upon her.

"Yes, ma'am. I must be."

"Can I have Marie get you a drink?"

"Yes, please. Beer if you have it."

"I'll make a note to get some. Would you settle for champagne?"

"That would be fine." He really wanted a beer.

"So you're Duncan Delaney," Angela repeated.

"Yes ma'am." He took out his wallet. "I have identification."

Angela laughed. He put his wallet back, feeling stupid. She took his hand and led him through a door.

"I want to show you something," she said.

Her office was on the fifteenth floor of a high rise and its window offered a wide vista past concrete and steel stalagmites to the sea. The room itself was like a well-furnished gallery. Two leather chairs sat before an ebony desk with a third chair behind it. An elaborate oriental rug lay atop the mahogany floor. Recessed lights adorned the ceiling. But what seized Duncan's imagination were the paintings. He could identify a few of the canvases on the walls, and some signatures, but he stalled at a painting of a young blond woman on horseback riding a herd across a wide grassy plain to market. The girl wore blue jeans, a denim shirt, and a white cowboy hat. She was more than beautiful and the view would be idyllic if boring save that the herd she drove was comprised of naked, hairy men on all fours. Duncan scrutinized the signature. *Sheila* something. He could not make out the last name. He moved on until he came to a painting that routed an icy thrill up his back and down his arms. Benjamin's family, framed in rosewood and illuminated by recessed lighting, hung like an icon on her wall. Marie materialized with champagne. Duncan gulped a glass down.

"Did I paint that?" he asked.

"It's brilliant," Angela said.

He was not prepared to go that far. Still, six hundred dollars no longer seemed ludicrous.

"Holy Jesus," he said. "What a difference a frame makes."

Angela laughed. Duncan thought he said something stupid again but there was no malice in her eyes.

"I could sell it for twice what I paid. But I won't. I keep the first paintings of all my artists. Now let's see what I *can* sell."

Marie brought in his paintings. He tore the butcher paper off and set them against the desk. He stepped back and began to sweat. Angela shifted a foot and put one hand to her chin. Duncan fanned his face with his Stetson, ready to crawl back to Cheyenne. Angela looked up and smiled. Anxiety washed from his body like dye from a new pair of blue jeans.

"Duncan," she said, "you're going to be a big hit in this town."

Duncan was still feeling the champagne when he sauntered past the white, nineteen sixty-five Cadillac convertible parked below his window. Its top was down, and it had immaculate red leather seats and a high polish to its paint. Had he known what it was, and what it would one day do, he would have fetched the baseball bat he had bought that morning and reduced the car as best he could to scrap. Much later, as he watched the killer General Motors product crushed and pulverized at a scrap yard and many times after, he would think back to that day and wonder if he would have done anything different. But he would always conclude the only thing worth changing was the way it all turned out.

He climbed the stairs and ducked under the pipe in the hallway. Inside his studio he hung his Stetson on his easel. He picked up and waltzed Cat across the floor. Cat purred a question and Duncan chuckled an answer. He collapsed laughing on the couch. Cat jumped to the open window.

"Lighten up, Cat! If you can't stand the painter, get out of the studio!"

The Cadillac started outside. Its stereo blared *Only Women Bleed*. Cat glanced at Duncan and down at the sidewalk. Then he leaped out to the street. Duncan jumped up and ran to the window.

"Hey!" he yelled, "I was . . ."

Cat had landed in the Cadillac next to a young woman whose beauty shattered him and sent the shards crashing about her feet. She was maybe three years older than Duncan and oddly familiar. Her hair was as blond as his was red but much longer. Her Caribbean blue eyes smiled above full, laughing lips that had never felt the needle's collagen sting. Her skin was smooth and her teeth even and white. She wore a black leather jacket over a tight black dress. Black stockings sheathed long, athletic legs, ending in black pumps with sharp heels. Her breasts curved wonderfully within the low neck of her dress. She was as beautiful as any model or actress in print or on screen.

". . . joking," he finished.

"Hell of a way to treat a cat," she said in a voice suggesting gravel.

"He jumped!"

"Relax, I wasn't serious. I have a way of attracting strays."

She caressed Cat and held him to her chest. Duncan would have donated any of his redundant organs to change places. She leaned over and dropped Cat to the sidewalk. Cat jumped back into the car. She laughed.

"Maybe you ought to come get him . . ."

"Duncan," he said, "my name's Duncan."

"Hi, Duncan. I'm Pris."

"I'm an artist," he blurted, ruing the words even as he spoke, thinking them pretentious and hollow. "Painter, I mean."

"Really. Are you any good?"

"I'm okay. Maybe you could pose for me sometime."

"Then again maybe not." She dropped Cat onto the sidewalk and shifted the Cadillac into drive. "See you around, Duncan Delaney."

"Wait!" Duncan yelled.

He ran from his studio, wondering how she knew his last name. By the time he recalled the pipe in the hallway his head had already contacted cold metal with a sharp *thwang* at approximately fifteen miles per hour. A galaxy of lights that would have been stars had his life been a cartoon filled his eyes. He missed a step and tumbled down the stairs to the alley. The bum under the stairs drank from a bottle obscured in a paper bag and watched Duncan fall.

"Nice technique," the bum said, "and a good dismount."

Duncan looked up the street. The girl and the Cadillac were gone. He dusted himself off, picked up Cat, and climbed the stairs.

"Hey, buddy," called the bum. "Spare some change?"

"Not today," Duncan replied, "but thanks for asking."

Benjamin finally decided he was being followed at a gas station outside Bountiful. He had first noticed the forest green Taurus in Wyoming, but was not immediately wary as both car and color were common. The Taurus disappeared for prolonged periods when Benjamin implemented evasive tactics, like the high speed drift and subsequent u-turn across four lanes of traffic outside Steamboat Springs. The Taurus did not dare that maneuver. But after every such gambit and within fifty miles there would be the Taurus or another like it. Benjamin had been followed many times, mostly by police, and by eighteen he had developed a healthy paranoia and could spot a plainclothes police car with near ninety-seven percent accuracy. This green Taurus plainly did not contain police, for he had seen soda cans and burger boxes regularly sail out the passenger's window, and all the cops he knew were fastidious when it came to littering.

Benjamin got out of his truck. He stretched and yawned and scratched his armpit. He gave the attendant twenty dollars and filled his tank. The Taurus braked at an island on the remote side of the lot. A tall man with dark hair and dark glasses got out and slid a credit card into the pump. A second man reclined in the passenger seat, a newspaper over his face. Benjamin replaced the pump, got in his truck, and pulled onto the highway.

He stopped at a diner in Salina. The Taurus pulled into the lot and parked well away from the Purgatory Truck. Benjamin went inside. He settled in a booth and perused a menu. A tall, dark-haired man came in and sat at the counter and ordered coffee. If it was the same man, he had changed his shirt and put on a John Deere hat. Benjamin was schooled in the minor tricks of effective surveillance, and changing clothes was one. The man at the counter looked like a chicken farmer.

Benjamin ordered a t-bone steak with mashed potatoes, gravy, biscuits, and a vanilla milkshake. He stood and went to the men's room. He entered a stall and latched the door. He took off and placed his boots before the toilet. He climbed out the window above the stall. He ran barefoot to the Taurus and looked in the back. Empty beer cans littered the floor and half a six pack sat on the rear seat. Benjamin walked to the front and looked at the man sleeping there.

"Well, how about that," Benjamin said.

It was Leroy Kern, numb to the world, snoring and reeking of beer and sweat. Benjamin's original plan was to flatten the tires and pull the plug wires. As he observed Leroy Kern snort and whistle, he devised another. He retrieved the beers through the open window and poured one onto the driver's seat. The next he poured onto Leroy Kern's lap. He stirred but did not wake. The last Benjamin drank. He climbed back through the window, put his boots on, and returned to his booth.

He spent the next twenty minutes eating. The tall man toyed with a piece of pecan pie and nursed a coffee while Benjamin finished his potatoes and steak. He mopped up the gravy with a biscuit and stuffed it whole in his mouth. He ordered and devoured a slice of hot apple pie with ice cream and cinnamon sauce. He took his time with his milkshake and then ordered another and lingered over that. The tall man called for another cup of coffee. Benjamin ordered a coffee to go, threw the lid in the trash, paid his bill, and went to a pay phone by the door. As the tall man paid for his coffee and pie, Benjamin dialed three numbers and spoke rapidly into the phone. He hung up and left. The tall man followed. Benjamin walked to the Taurus and set his coffee on the roof. The tall man hung uncertainly back. Benjamin reached through the window, grabbed Leroy Kern, and bounced his head off the dashboard. He heard a small crack.

"Ow!" said Leroy Kern, finally awake.

"Hey!" said the tall man.

His name was Howard Lomo, and he had been a cop in Laramie until he was fired for ripping up speeding tickets in exchange for sexual favors in the back seat of his squad car. In fairness to Lomo, his sergeant's wife regularly exceeded her limits whenever she saw him and eagerly participated in a game in which she buried her head in Lomo's lap while he asked easy questions to which she nodded yes or no. But Lomo unwisely pulled her over in front of her house and the sergeant, returning home for lunch, discovered his wife's head in Howard Lomo's lap, and that was very much that. Otherwise he was a fair to decent officer and was not about to let a low life punk slap around his new partner, useless or not.

As Lomo ran up, Benjamin took his coffee from the Taurus's roof and threw it in his face. Benjamin had learned long before that one axiom of a successful cold cock and follow through was that the hands go to the pain. Lomo screamed and covered his eyes. Benjamin placed his boot hard to the testicles. Lomo grabbed his groin and crumpled. Benjamin unzipped and urinated onto the driver's seat. When he finished, he knelt beside Lomo and took a wallet out of his pocket. Fiona's number was on a small paper between a Visa and an NRA membership card. Benjamin threw the wallet on the floor by the gas pedal. He helped Lomo back into the car. He wadded the paper with Fiona's number and shoved it in Lomo's mouth.

"Try to keep up. Fiona won't be happy if you lose me."

Lomo spit the paper out. "You filthy red-skin bastard!"

Benjamin punched him in the face. Lomo groaned and slumped over the wheel. Benjamin got in his truck and pulled onto the highway. Lomo shook his head, then pulled out and followed so close their bumpers kissed. A police car passed by, made a U-turn of squealing tires and smoke, fell into line behind the green Taurus, and turned on its red lights. Lomo pulled over.

Benjamin parked and watched the police draw their guns and order Kern and Lomo out of the Taurus. Leroy Kern fell drunk to the ground, but Lomo hopped up and down, gesticulating wildly. A second police car appeared. The officers swarmed Lomo and hurled him to the pavement. One got him in a carotid choke hold and applied pressure. Lomo stopped moving. Benjamin turned around and stopped as two officers carried the now hog-tied Lomo to their car.

"Everything ok, officers?"

"Just a drunk driver," said one.

"He's got a gun in here," said another, "and it smells like he pissed himself."

"You're doing a fine job," Benjamin said, "and as a citizen I want you to know I appreciate you getting these filthy drunks off the road."

"Thank you, sir. Always nice to get positive feedback."

As Benjamin left, one officer commented, "That's the kind of thing that makes this job worthwhile."

Then he kicked Howard Lomo in the ribs, closed the car door, and drove Lomo and Leroy Kern off to jail.

Five

"Duncan," a voice sang in his sleeping ear, "wake up and play with us."

Duncan opened an eye. Two shadowy figures loomed above him. He screamed. The shadows leaped backwards. Duncan groped for the baseball bat under the couch. He had bought the bat in lieu of the door lock Assan had promised but failed to install. A shadow turned on a light.

"Remember us?" Cassandra and Champagne giggled in unison.

Champagne held a blender and Cassandra a brown paper bag. Duncan fell back on the couch and dropped the bat. Champagne sat beside him and stroked his naked shoulder.

"Why don't you have a bed?" she asked.

Duncan blushed. He could not help it. He fought the erection he was acquiring, but could not stop that either. *Damn that autonomic nervous system,* he thought. He had studied biology in high school and was dimly aware of some of the ways the body betrayed itself.

Cassandra and Champagne both wore faded jeans with many rips and holes in the denim. Cassandra was small and slim with brown wavy hair, eyes like Mediterranean olives, dark lips, and small taut breasts. She wore a white tank top through which Duncan traced the outline of her nipples. Champagne was taller and heavier in the legs, buttocks, and chest, with blond hair and a milkmaid's good looks. She wore a *Lillith Fair* t-shirt over freely swaying breasts. Duncan struggled into his jeans inside his sleeping bag. The effort quieted his tumescent organ. He slipped out of the bag and put on a shirt. Champagne took the blender and the paper bag into the kitchen. Duncan heard bottles clink and grinding ice.

"What can I do for you ladies?"

"You asked us to come up," Cassandra said.

Champagne appeared with three glasses on a tray. "To pose for you."

He sipped the Margarita she gave him. It was cold and tart and salty. Champagne and Cassandra sat on the couch and smiled.

"Ready anytime you are," Cassandra said.

Duncan looked at the clock. It was two thirty in the morning. He sighed and put a canvas on his easel. He picked up a brush and his palette and began to paint.

"Do either of you know a girl who drives a white Cadillac?"

Champagne said, "That's Pris. She dances with us at the Hollywood."

Cassandra said, "Forget about her. She's a dyke."

"You should be concerned with us," Champagne said. "We like men."

Duncan changed the subject. "Do you like dancing at the Hollywood?"

Champagne shrugged. "It's okay if you can put up with the assholes."

Cassandra took a wad of bills from her pocket. "Plus the tips are great."

"People tip you for dancing?"

"No, dummy." Champagne pulled her shirt off and waved her breasts at him. "They tip us for these!"

"Hey, put that back on!" Duncan said.

Cassandra giggled and took her shirt off too.

"Oh god," Duncan said with overdue clarity, "you're strippers."

"What the hell did you think we were," Cassandra asked, "stock brokers?"

"Roscoe said you were dancers."

"We're both," Champagne said.

Duncan gulped his Margarita and painted in embarrassed silence while Champagne made another pitcher. Cassandra flipped through his compact discs, finally putting *Beggar's Banquet* on the stereo.

"Jesus," she said, "don't you have any music from this century?"

Cassandra and Champagne threw crumpled dollar bills at him as he painted. Despite the two beautiful, topless women drinking and laughing on his couch, Duncan's thoughts returned to Pris. The idea of her dancing naked on stage before a room of drunk, horny men disappointed his heart. He thought about Tiffy. She didn't take her clothes off for a living, but she used her sex just the same.

Or was he just being bitter?

Much later, when the alcohol had dulled his brain to the point where thinking was difficult if not dangerous, he was dimly aware of two naked, laughing women tackling him and ripping his shirt off. He remembered Champagne holding a brush.

He woke the next morning on the floor beside his easel with Cat lying on his face. He spluttered and spit fur and Cat went away. Cassandra and Champagne and the dollar bills were gone. They were strippers, but they were not stupid. He crawled past his easel, wishing he was cold and covered with dirt. The painting was half finished and the remarkable thing was that he could not remember having painted it. It would one day be regarded as a pure example of his studio period. A southern Senator would falsely cite it as the sort of decadence funded by the NEA. But he did not consider that. He was only thinking of the incredible pain in his skull.

He crawled to the bathroom, hanging on to the hardwood to keep from plunging off the floor. He vomited in the toilet. He climbed to the mirror. A painted red arrow adorned his chest, pointing towards China. He looked down and groaned. His testicles were painted a bright, baby blue. He rolled into the tub and turned on the water. His throbbing skull matched his pounding heart. He wondered what else had happened. *Probably nothing,* he concluded. Past experience with Tiffy had proven that excessive alcohol and sex were, for him, incompatible. Tiffy always stopped him after a six-pack, though she would continue drinking until she caught his head between her legs in a scissors grip. Which was fine until the one time, after she had joined a gym and begun working out on a Nautilus machine, when she nearly dislocated his jaw at her moment of truth.

He scrubbed the paint from his chest and scrotum, dried himself, dressed, drank a quart of orange juice and took three aspirins. He ate three Neapolitan ice cream sandwiches in an effort to settle his stomach. He filled Cat's bowls with cat food and water.

Then he went to work on the painting.

"I been watching your bike," the bum under the stairs said as Duncan unchained the rusty Schwinn he had paid ten dollars for at a garage sale that afternoon. "Never know when someone might steal such a fine machine."

Duncan gave him a quarter.

"God bless you, Mr. Getty," said the bum.

"My name's not Getty."

"I'll say it's not."

Duncan rode away wondering who Getty was. He did not make the association with J. Paul as he had not expected sarcasm from a vagrant. Four miles later he locked the bike to a post outside a gallery on Melrose Avenue where Angela had arranged for his inclusion in an exhibition of promising Los Angeles artists. An Aryan named Sven attended the door. His wispy blond hair fell to his shoulders. He dressed in black from his linen shirt to his leather storm trooper boots. Duncan was six-two and weighed one sixty-five on a good day. This Nordic giant had six inches and ninety pounds on him and looked like an angry Thor.

"Your invitation," he growled.

Duncan searched his pockets. "I have forgotten it," he said. "But I'm one of the artists."

"Of course you are. Now leave quickly before I rupture your spleen."

Not sure where his spleen was but nonetheless not wanting it ruptured, Duncan left. He circled the block, hopped a fence, and entered through the kitchen. Cooks spoke heated Spanish at him and brandished sharp kitchen knives.

"Como esta usted?" Duncan kept his back to the walls and his eyes on the knives. *"Donde es cerveza?"*

A cook gave him a beer and guided him through a door into the main gallery where patrons dressed in silk and spandex and double-breasted wool congregated amid framed paintings and bronze statues. Duncan wore jeans and a gray tweed jacket over a paint-smeared t-shirt. His hair was tangled and whipped from his ride to the gallery. Some guests wore cowboy boots of the Italian variety favored by Tiffy. Duncan wore tennis shoes because his boots kept slipping off the bicycle pedals. He roamed through a crowd bent on ignoring him until he came to a painting that stopped him cold.

It was of a naked man strapped in an electric chair. Desperate, hollow eyes stared out of a shaved head. His muscles were tense, his teeth gritted, his eyes wide and legs spread to reveal a small, erect penis, the head of which sported a metal cap wired into the chair. A blond woman in a guard uniform stood in the shadows behind the chair, her hand on an electric switch, her face beatific in its indifference. It was not the subject that interested him though. It was the guard. It was the cowgirl in the painting in Angela's office and now, he realized, it was the girl in the Cadillac.

Achilles Last Stand, the card under the painting read, *by Sheila Rascowitz.*

"Isn't it horrible?"

Duncan turned. Pris stood by him regarding the painting, her eyes electric with disgust. She wore a short yellow skirt, a white silk blouse, and a yellow leather jacket. She pushed a strand of hair from her forehead and smiled at Duncan.

"Hey," he said, "that's you, isn't it?"

"Sadly, yes." She frowned. "It just sold for five thousand dollars."

He studied the painting from an alternative viewpoint. "Go figure."

"I understand you had a good time last night."

"Umm . . ." Duncan's face burned, "I don't actually remember if I did or not."

"Champagne told me your virtue remained intact." Pris touched his arm. "Though I understand you woke with a serious case of blue balls."

"Can we talk about something else?"

"Of course. She also said you asked about me."

A muscular woman with a brown brush cut wedged herself between them. She wore jeans stuffed in black boots and a white t-shirt beneath a black leather vest. She was nearly as tall as Duncan and at least as heavy, thirty years old, with light brown eyes and three silver studs piercing her right ear. Chains crossed her boots and vest. She was attractive in a masculine way.

"Come on." She grabbed Pris's arm. "I want you to meet someone."

"Don't pull your butch routine on me, Sheila." Pris shook loose. "You pay my rent but you don't own me. So buzz off. I'm talking to someone."

Sheila Rascowitz glared at Duncan. He smiled uncertainly. She shouldered him aside and joined a woman dressed like a member of the Hell's Angels ladies' auxiliary. The other woman's name was Samantha MacDonald, and she was an outwardly feminine accountant by day and butch dyke on a Harley by night. She never hooked up romantically with Sheila because neither was willing to sit on the back seat of the other's bike. Sheila gestured and Samantha stared. Pris took Duncan's hand.

"I need a drink," she said.

They walked to a table where croissants and crackers lay beside paté and cheese. A white jacketed waiter supplied plastic glasses of Chardonnay, though at the time Duncan could only distinguish with limited success between Mexican and American beers.

"She makes me so mad sometimes," Pris said.

Sheila found the doorman and spoke in his ear. Sven studied the room.

"Let's get some air," Duncan said.

Outside a string quartet played Bach. Women wearing pearls wandered around a fountain, arm in arm with men brandishing checkbooks.

"My dad used to call daisies sunshine on sticks. You look like that." Pris looked confused. Duncan felt clumsy. "I meant it as a compliment."

Pris smiled. "Then I'll take it as one."

Duncan peered into the galley. Sheila and the Swede were nowhere in sight. "Would you like to see my paintings?"

"I'd love to."

They found his canvases in an alcove by the toilets. The cards beneath read *Roscoe* and *Drive By,* with his name below the titles.

"They should have hung them above the urinals," he said. "At least then someone might see them."

Pris squeezed his arm. "I think they're wonderful."

Duncan's annoyance evaporated. His heart sprouted wings and fluttered up his chest to lodge in his throat.

"I'd like to paint you," he chanced.

Pris shook her head. "I don't think so."

Duncan felt as if his heart had been pierced by twelve gauge bird shot, as if the giddy wind stirred by her proximity had been knocked from his punctured lungs by her denial, like his wings were ripped off and his carcass had fallen bloody to be trampled in the gutter.

"Could we at least have dinner sometime and talk about it?"

"No!" Pris yelled.

Duncan doubted the invitation merited so harsh a response, and he quailed at the severity of the rejection. When he was lifted into the air and thrown bodily into the men's room, he realized her exclamation was not meant for him. He hit the tiles with a squeak. He rose as Sven came at him, eyes angrily furrowed. Duncan hit him as hard as he could across the jaw with absolutely no effect.

"Uh oh," said Duncan.

The Teutonic giant lifted him like a sack of rice. "You are not welcome here."

Sven was preparing to throw Duncan head-first into a urinal when Pris kicked him square between the legs from behind. His eyes crossed and he dropped Duncan. Sven grabbed his genitals and sank gasping to the floor, his face white as mold on last week's bread. Sheila grabbed Pris from behind. Pris elbowed her in the gut. It degenerated from there. Angela, on her way to show Duncan's paintings to the gallery's owner, found the four tangled on the floor as Sven applied a choke hold on Duncan.

"Duncan!" Angela cried.

"You mean . . ." the gallery owner was a small, well-dressed man of sixty, with worried eyes and expensively coifed and dyed hair.

"Yes! That's Duncan Delaney!"

"Sven!" the owner cried. "What have you *done?"*

Sven relaxed the choke hold. "I thought he was an intruder."

"No," Angela said, "he's one of my artists."

Duncan stood and helped Pris up. Sheila slapped his proffered hand away. Sven tried to rise, but Pris's kick had caused minor structural damage to the genitals.

"You're fired," the owner said, adding the insult.

"He thought he was doing his job," Duncan said. "That's all." He helped Sven to a chair and brought him a glass of water.

"I'm so sorry, Mr. Delaney," Sven said. "I could cry."

"Angela," Sheila said, "you represent this, this . . . person?"

"That's right."

"Not anymore you don't."

"Sorry?"

"Either he goes or I do."

Angela smiled sadly. "I'll be sorry to lose you."

"You're keeping him over *me?*"

"If you change your mind, I'd love to have you back."

Sheila stared at Angela for a long moment, her face red and her eyes sharp. She turned and stomped away. Angela dusted Duncan off.

"You should care more about your appearance," she said sternly.

Inside she smiled. A crowd, attracted by the commotion, gathered by his paintings and eyed him thoughtfully. Duncan turned to see Pris reach the door.

"I've got to go."

"Watch out for Sheila," Angela said. "She's not all there."

He burst onto Melrose in time to see the Cadillac's taillights fly from him. He heard motorcycles. Thundering Harleys ringed him. Sheila Rascowitz stopped before him. Samantha MacDonald and two others circled like gluttonous wolves. If he was not so scared, four women on motorcycles dressed like fugitives from a Marlon Brando fan club would have been comical.

But, he realized, *these women are perfectly capable of beating the piss out of me.*

"I'll tell you once," Rascowitz yelled above the roar of the bikes, "stay away from her."

The sound of engines lingered long after the women vanished around a corner. Duncan returned to the fence where he had left his Schwinn. Only a cut chain remained.

I've had problems with women before, he thought as he walked back to his studio, *but never like this.*

Six

Benjamin was sitting alone at a black jack table when he spied Howard Lomo and Leroy Kern. He had arrived at the casino two hours before, and the four red chips he began with had spawned a multitudinous pile in an assortment of colors. The dealer was a Hispanic looking man several years older than Benjamin, with a gut under his vest and piercing black eyes beneath wire rimmed glasses. Benjamin considered relinquishing his seat before they spotted him, but he would forfeit his fifty-dollar bet, and he was more curious about how Kern and Lomo had regained his trail than he was alarmed by the fact that they had.

"*In*-surance," said the dealer.

The dealer showed an ace. Benjamin held two tens. He put a twenty-five dollar chip out. The dealer took it and flipped his hole card. A queen.

"Blackjack," said the dealer.

Leroy Kern poked Howard Lomo and pointed to Benjamin. Lomo wore dark glasses which roughly concealed the shiner around his right eye. Leroy Kern wore a dirty bandage over his nose and a brace around his neck. They settled on stools to his left and to his right.

"I feel a run of bad lack coming," Benjamin said, but he left his bet on the table.

"Good morning, gentlemen," said the dealer, "will you be playing?"

"We just want a word with our friend," Lomo said. "Ain't that right?"

"That's right," said Leroy Kern.

"I'm amazed you boys found me. Considering your general lack of competence and all."

"Shut up and play."

Lomo surveyed the casino. Benjamin was dealt a ten and a deuce. The dealer gave himself an ace up.

"In-*sur*-ance."

Benjamin nodded *no*. The dealer looked at his hole card and put it back face down. Benjamin waved off another card.

"He's alone," Lomo said.

"Are you nuts?" Kern asked. "Standing on a twelve against an ace?"

The dealer turned up his card. A four. He busted with a jack and a nine.

"You play your way," Benjamin said. "I'll play mine."

"We're not here to play, boy."

Something poked Benjamin. He looked down. Lomo held a blue steel thirty-eight special against Benjamin's ribs. This was his old throw down gun, with a hair trigger and the serial number filed off. He had left his forty caliber duty weapon back in his hotel room, as it was too large to conceal.

"Tell you what," Benjamin said, "why don't you and your moron buddy take fifty dollars each and play awhile. On me."

"You must think we're pretty stupid," Lomo said.

"Well, him at least."

"Come on." Leroy Kern said, ignoring the insult, "it ain't like it's our money."

"Well, all right." Howard Lomo put the gun in his waistband and closed his jacket. He appropriated a pile of chips. "But when the money's gone, so are we."

"I said fifty each," Benjamin said.

"I heard what you said. But I chose to ignore it."

After ten hands Kern and Lomo were broke. Benjamin won eight of the ten and was now up seven hundred and eighty-five dollars.

"Jesus," Leroy Kern said, "how do you do that?"

"I got a system."

"Well, so do I." Howard Lomo snatched another pile of chips.

"Sir, management frowns upon players taking other player's chips."

Lomo read the dealer's name tag. "Stay out of this Keith Gomez." Something about the man plagued him. Lomo flashed a badge. "This is police business. I'm taking this boy out and don't want any interference."

Lomo had ordered the badge from a catalogue after his was ripped from his shirt by his former employer. It was a Soviet Intelligence officer's badge. Lomo had selected it because he liked the dagger dripping blood above the fractured heart. He had flashed and pocketed it so quickly that Gomez could not be faulted if he believed it legitimate.

Gomez said, "I'll notify security."

The glory of Lomo's old occupation reasserted itself in his chest. *Nothing as tasty as a good ass kissing,* he reflected. Gomez whispered to a pit boss. The boss looked to the table and picked up a phone.

"I could still press charges against you, Leroy," Benjamin said.

"Not if you're dead, you can't."

Benjamin turned to Lomo. "Fiona won't be happy if I vanish."

"I no longer work for Fiona," Lomo said, "and I believe she would be absolutely ecstatic if you disappeared."

Gomez returned. "Notifications have been made."

Lomo put a hundred dollars of Benjamin's money out. "Now deal."

Gomez stepped back from the table.

"I said deal."

Four sturdy men in plain clothes tackled Lomo. Three more grabbed Kern and threw him to the floor. Lomo kicked over the blackjack table as he fell. Benjamin sat untouched on his stool. An enormous man cranked Lomo's arm high behind his back with a loud pop reminiscent of a champagne bottle blowing its cork.

"Jesus God!" Lomo screamed.

He had first dislocated his shoulder playing football in college and ever since, Lomo would impress his drinking buddies by downing several shots of tequila and snapping it in and out with surprisingly little discomfort. But he was not drunk now, and through a painful haze he realized what bothered him about the dealer. It was the name tag. Not the name itself, but what was written beneath it.

"You goddamn filthy red-skin!" Lomo shrieked as the security men hauled him through the gathering crowd, "you set me up again!"

A slot machine paid a noisy jackpot aisles away and the crowd turned back to more serious pursuits. When a few gamblers thought to look back, Lomo and Kern were gone.

"I'm sorry, sir," the pit boss said to Benjamin, "I've seen dealers robbed, I've seen security guards robbed, I've seen the cashier held up, but I've never seen a player robbed at gunpoint." He spoke as if he just saw the Pope-mobile car-jacked by a baggy-panted, bald-headed Los Angeles gangster. "What the hell is this world coming to?"

"Outrageous," Benjamin agreed.

"How much in chips did you have before this, *ahem,* incident?"

"Two or three thousand."

The pit boss gave him a voucher for four thousand dollars and a free suite.

"I hope this won't affect your choice of casino," he said.

"Could have happened anywhere."

Well, Benjamin reflected after he had cashed the voucher, *not quite anywhere.*

He went to his suite and threw his bag on the couch. He opened the champagne waiting in an ice bucket and took the bottle into the bathroom. He turned on the Jacuzzi, stripped, and settled in for a long soak. An hour later he reluctantly got out of the water to answer a knock at his door. He dropped the bottle in the trash and put on the robe he found hanging on a hook. He opened the door. Keith Gomez stepped inside. Benjamin closed the door and hugged him. Then he gave Gomez one thousand dollars.

Gomez took off and threw his name tag on the bed. The words under the name said *Cheyenne Wyoming*.

"How's your mom?" Benjamin asked.

"Just fine. We got her a house in Henderson. You should go see her. She's always asking about you."

"Maybe I will," Benjamin said. "She's a hell of a lady."

Keith Gomez took a beer from the mini-bar. He sat on the bed and turned on the television. His father, a fifth generation Texan from El Paso, had met Benjamin's aunt while prospecting in Wyoming. They married a year later and settled in Cheyenne.

"Don't know why, but you always were her favorite nephew."

"Your sister still dealing at Circus Circus?"

"Nope." Gomez counted the money. "She's at the Mirage now."

"Maybe I'll stick around a few days and go visit."

"Sure." Gomez put the bills in his pocket. "She'd love to see you."

"Evening, Mr. Getty. Spare one of them beers?"

Duncan tore a can from the six-pack and tossed it to the bum under the stairs. He had since figured out whom Getty was, and he was not amused. At the top of the stairs he heard music. He ducked under the pipe and opened the door. *Only Women Bleed* played on his stereo. Pris lay on his couch, immaculate legs crossed, jacket off and shoulders smooth and bare. She held Cat on her stomach and stroked him in time to the music. Duncan's Stetson adorned her head. The hair spilling beneath the brim lit his heart like a two-hundred watt halogen floodlight.

"What took you so long?" she asked.

"Someone stole my bicycle. I had to walk."

She laughed, then stopped when she saw he was serious. "I was going to the Hollywood for a drink, but then I saw your cat in the window." She sat up. "Sorry about Sheila. I should have known she would do something stupid."

He sat beside her. "No one got hurt." He thought of Sven. "Much."

The music ceased. Pris rose and bent over his stereo. He remembered to breathe. *Only Women Bleed* started again.

"This is my theme song. Has been since I was fifteen."

"Why's that?"

Her smile evaporated and her eyes assumed a distant aspect reminiscent of Fiona standing over Sean Delaney's grave, looking through miles of misty memories at what her life might have been. Pris was as dismal a sight as the time he witnessed a calf's neck broken at the rodeo when he was ten. Cowboys put the dead animal on a sled, and as they dragged it away, someone behind Duncan said, *hamburger for dinner tonight, I guess.* Duncan had burst into tears to the crowd's general amusement.

"Maybe I'll tell you about it sometime."

She closed her eyes, leaned back, and stretched. Duncan bit his tongue. He felt like a voyeur watching her. Cat crawled back into her lap.

Duncan stood. "Can I get you something to drink?"

"Juice if you have it."

He put the beer in the refrigerator and picked up a carton of orange juice. It was frozen solid. He turned the temperature down. Two sodas sat on a shelf near a cup of cherry yogurt. Pris stood in the doorway.

"How about a soda?" he asked.

"That's fine."

He pulled the tab on a can. It exploded and drenched his shirt and jeans with icy foam. Pris laughed and Duncan grinned stupidly.

"Had a little accident?" she asked.

"I better change."

"You better."

Duncan stripped in the bathroom. He glimpsed his naked body in the mirror and cringed at his skin's luminosity. He realized he had brought no clothes in with him. He wrapped a towel around his waist and stuck his head out the door.

"Don't look," he said.

Pris closed her eyes. Duncan trotted to the box where he kept his clothes and pulled out boxers, a t-shirt, and jeans. When he turned to run back to the bathroom, Pris was regarding him.

"You've got a nice body, Duncan," she said.

"Thanks. You should see the rest of me."

She tossed his hat to the floor and retrieved her tape. She picked up her purse and jacket and headed for the door. Her eyes were cold and her smile was replaced by a frosty scowl.

"I'll pass," she said as she went by.

"What did I say?"

She tarried at the door. "I'm not interested in the size of your dick."

"That's not what I meant!"

"No? What did you mean?"

She had him. He could not say he meant he wanted to get naked with her, though that was he had in mind when he said it. She watched him with sapphire eyes, twice as cold and just as blue. He felt like he was back in sixth grade with Sister Mary Elizabeth questioning him regarding Mary's virtue. Duncan was raised on a ranch and personally doubted the concept of a virgin birth. But young as he was, he was old enough to know the truth would not in that instance set him free. That was the year Fiona had decided a parochial education might wean Duncan from Benjamin's opprobrious influence. His Catholic schooling lasted one week until Mother Margaret Mary (all the nuns' names contained a permutation of *Mary*), an imposingly fat nun with short black hair and a thin black mustache which she refused to dye or pluck, charged Duncan with throwing jelly beans during the Thursday hot dog sale. She held him after school until Fiona arrived to protest that Duncan did not even like jelly beans, as they stuck to his bridgework. Mother Margaret Mary was adamant. The rainbow projectiles she had witnessed emanated from the vicinity of Duncan's table, and the other children were known by her to be from reputable families, not the son of an idiot who essentially committed suicide with his reckless and irresponsible heroics. Mother Margaret Mary was unaware that Benjamin, playing hooky from Duncan's old school and stationed beneath the window with a slingshot and a bag of Jelly Bellys, was trying to bag himself a penguin. Unwisely, the good Mother voiced her opinion of Sean Delaney's final moments to Fiona. Father Fay, inquiring into the commotion in the principal's office, again was required to pull Fiona away from the object of her wrath just as Fiona landed a knee to Mother Margaret Mary's solar plexus. After regaining her breath, the nun slowly stood, and as Fiona struggled in Father Fay's clutches, planted a cheap right cross to Fiona's jaw. Duncan sent the nun profanely shrieking to the floor with a hard kick in the shin. He forthwith returned to education at the public expense.

But now Pris's question, like Sister Mary Elizabeth's concerning the Virgin Mary, awaited an answer. The recess bell had saved him then. He foresaw no like deliverance now. He ventured a variation of the truth.

"I was just flirting. I didn't mean to offend you."

But she left anyway. Duncan went to his window. Pris crossed the street and climbed into her Cadillac.

"Wait!" he called.

She extended a finger to him in a universal gesture of contempt and drove away. Duncan threw the t-shirt and pants back into the box. He pulled his Stetson down to his ears.

"I am a moron," he said.

Actually, Duncan's penis was on the large side of average. This he knew because Tiffy had once broken out a tape measure and compared his numbers with a dog-eared chart cut out of Cosmopolitan Magazine. The results had pleased her. Duncan now suspected (based on the notations and general wear on the chart) that her elation was derived from a wealth of previous comparisons. The results had merely relieved Duncan. Even if he was bigger than his fellow man, he did not believe he merited additional points for style or endurance. He had experienced sex with one female his entire life and though she had tutored him well, his knowledge was provincial. But as the Cadillac faded around a corner, the size of his manhood was Duncan's most distant concern.

He set a canvas on his easel. He pictured her when he walked in, the angle of his Stetson on her head and the shadow the brim cast across her eyes. He thought of the canary dress, of her legs and her shoulders and of her hand on Cat in her lap. He remembered her smile. When it was all projected from his mind onto the canvas, he painted.

Later that night, Sheila Rascowitz burst into Duncan's studio, her jaw tight as a sprung trap and her eyes as wild as the rat caught within. The towel lay on the floor by his feet where it had dropped unnoticed hours before. Duncan was naked from the hat down.

"Where is she?"

Duncan picked up and wrapped the towel around his waist. Sheila's lips stretched back to reveal fine sharp incisors.

"Where is who?"

"Don't who me! I can smell she's been here!"

Sheila lunged. Duncan darted aside. She came away with his towel, leaving him dangling.

"I know why you want her!" Sheila growled. She pursued him around the couch. "I see it between your legs!"

Duncan dove for his baseball bat. Sheila arrived first. She hefted the bat above her head and swung a home run at Duncan's skull. He ducked. The bat whistled through the air above his Stetson. Cat vaulted onto Sheila's shoulders and buried his teeth in her neck. She shrieked, dropped the bat, and threw Cat on the couch. The hand she touched to her neck came back wet and red. Duncan snatched Cat and fled to the bathroom.

"Arrggghhhh!" Sheila howled in deranged fury.

Duncan bolted himself in the bathroom. Sheila flung the bat aside and slammed her shoulder repeatedly against the door. Duncan set his back against the creaking wood, his kidneys perceiving each thundering blow. The assault stopped. He heard wood snap, glass shatter, and fabric rip. He heard her stomp a mad flamenco dance in army boots. A door slammed. He listened to silence a long while before he emerged from his tile and porcelain sanctuary. His easel lay in fractured pieces. Splintered brushes and crushed paint tubes littered the studio. A rainbow kaleidoscope of storm trooper boot prints danced across the floor. Duncan stepped carefully around the paint. He liked the way it looked. His canvas lay slashed on the floor, useless as old chamois at an automated car wash. He looked out the window. Duncan picked Cat up and held him to his cheek.

"Thanks, buddy," he said. "We're even now."

He set Cat down and wedged a chair against the door. He capped the tubes of paint he could save and trashed the ones he could not. He threw his broken brushes in the garbage and placed the remains of his easel beside the door. He shut off the light and went to bed.

When he was eight, Duncan's father had taken him to a river shrouded by pines and mountains, where trout jumped rainbow arcs across icy cascades and smooth green rocks. The dream took Duncan there. He held a fishing pole, the line loose across the water. A trout hit and his line went tight.

"Give her some slack," Sean Delaney urged.

It felt good to have his old man beside him. Old was not accurate. Sean was twenty-nine in the dream, an age when death was a remote promise not worth pondering.

"You're playing her too hard," Sean said. "You let her out and you reel her back. You play with her. You make her want to play with you. You never let her know what you're thinking because you can bet your sweet ass she won't let you know. When you've given her enough slack, you make her take the hook. Then you reel her in."

"Something tells me we're not talking about fishing," said Duncan in an uncharacteristically intuitive flash.

"What do you think we're talking about, boy?"

Duncan fought the trout and the trout fought back, its beauty dazzling with each jump. It seemed a shame to catch. Sean touched his shoulder.

"You're afraid to catch her because you think you can't hold on to her."

The line went limp. When he reeled it in all that remained of the trout was a small piece of flesh on the hook.

"She threw your hook, son," Sean said.

"Duhh!" Duncan said. Sean smacked the back of his head. "Ouch!"

"Don't get smart. I may be dead but I'm still your father."

"Whatever." Duncan got up.

Sean pulled him down. "Giving up are you?"

"I see what you're doing. The fish is a metaphor for Pris, right?"

"You tell me."

"It's obvious." Duncan took a beer from the cooler Sean had carried to the river's edge. "And I don't think she'd appreciate it. She's not a fish."

"Of course not." He took Duncan's beer. "You drink too much."

"I'm twenty-one, Dad."

"Not in this dream you're not." Sean Delaney emptied the can into the water. He walked from the river towards the mountains. "You're right about one thing though. The fish is a metaphor. But not about Pris."

Duncan followed. "I don't understand."

"My god, you're dense sometimes." Sean Delaney knelt and pulled his child to him. "The metaphor is about *you.*" He kissed Duncan's forehead and smiled sadly. "How do you expect to catch anything if you don't keep casting your line?"

Seven

When Roscoe came up the next day, Duncan was eating a bowl of Cheerios and reading a note delivered by a messenger that morning. *Sold Roscoe,* the note said. *Proceeds (less commission) enclosed.*

"I sold the painting of you for two thousand," Duncan said.

"Hell, I'm in the wrong business. Can I borrow some paint?"

"It's not that easy."

"How hard can it be? Art doesn't have to look like anything. Some is just a bunch of colors smeared around."

Duncan could not refute the point. He gave him two splintered brushes, ten mashed paint tubes, an old pallet, and a canvas. He reassembled his broken easel with wire and duct tape. Roscoe set the canvas on the easel and smeared paint on the pallet.

"Mind if I hang out and paint?"

Duncan got his hat. "Just close the door when you leave."

Duncan cashed the check and bought six hundred dollars of canvasses, oils, brushes, and a new easel at an art supply store. He stopped at a café on Melrose and drank a cappuccino. The woman at the next table had ordered one so he thought he would try it. He forced the bitter brew down and inspected the bill left on his table by a gaunt waiter with a bleached crewcut and four silver earrings.

"There's been a mistake. I just had a cappuccino."

The waiter regarded the bill. "No, that's right. Eight fifty."

Duncan was thankful he had forsaken the walnut brownie he eyed upon entering the café. He left ten dollars on the table and took a taxi home. He hauled his things upstairs and stopped in his doorway. Three bikers posed around a Harley that was parked behind his couch. Across the room, Roscoe bit his tongue and ran a brush against his canvas with the grace of a farmer painting a barn. The bikers stared at Duncan with faces cold as gravestones.

"Hi," Duncan said.

"Duncan!" Roscoe set the brush down. "Come meet my friends."

Marco was tall and imperturbable, with a brown pony tail, soft blue eyes of two discrete shades, and a scar ranging from nose to jaw. Peewee was big and smiling with tan eyes, curly blond hair, a dense mustache, and a bloody dagger tattooed on his forearm above a Harley Davidson logo. Wilson was lean and reflective with grim brown eyes, hair black as Benjamin's and cheeks as high, narrow cruel lips, and a keen hawk's nose. They wore oily Levi's, boots, and sleeveless denim jackets the back of which were embroidered with helmeted demon skulls above the words *Satan's Guardians*. A bleached blond in a red tube top and cut off jeans exited the bathroom and settled on Peewee's lap. Amber was Peewee's not so private harlot. All were in their thirties, though weathered and wrinkled and eroded by life.

"How did you get the bike up here?" Duncan asked.

"It wasn't easy," Wilson said.

Peewee laughed. Marco frowned. Duncan wondered if they were making fun of him. He did not pursue it. Roscoe pulled him to the easel.

"What do you think?"

Duncan had earned extra credit in high school teaching finger painting to first graders. Roscoe's painting was a notch below that.

"Interesting," he said.

Peewee came around and looked. "My dog paints better than that," he said. "Ain't that right, Amber?"

"I don't know." Amber scrutinized the canvas. "I never seen your dog paint."

"What the hell do you know?" A vein pulsed on Roscoe's forehead. The back of his neck flared red.

"Anyone like a beer?" Duncan asked.

"We drank them all," Wilson said.

Duncan reached for his hat. "There's more downstairs."

"Wait a goddamn minute. You making fun of my painting, Peewee?"

"Painting? I thought you puked on the canvas."

Roscoe seized Peewee and hoisted him over his head with inordinate strength. His eyes were wide and mad and froth edged his mouth.

"Goddamn it, Roscoe," Peewee yelped, "put me down!"

Roscoe veered to the windows. Wilson extracted a knife and stationed himself between Roscoe and the street below. Marco took out a bicycle chain and stood close by. Duncan shut his eyes and ached for the Circle D.

"Roscoe," Wilson said, his voice calm and deep as the Hollywood Reservoir, "I love you man, but Peewee's right. You can't paint worth shit. And if you don't put him down, I'll have to cut you."

Roscoe turned on Duncan. "What do you say? Is he right?"

Duncan gulped. "I'm afraid so."

Roscoe howled and threw Peewee onto the couch, upending it and Peewee and dumping him on the floor before the Harley.

"Oommpph!" said Peewee.

Wilson sheathed his knife in his boot. Marco wrapped the chain around his waist. Duncan let out a breath he had not realized he was holding. Peewee stood and up-righted the couch.

"He could have put it better," Roscoe said. "I got feelings."

"I know you do," Wilson said.

Peewee dusted himself off. "Sorry, man."

"Ah, don't worry about it." Roscoe hugged Peewee. "Maybe I can't paint. But I can tear down a Harley like a son of a bitch. Right, Marco?"

Marco nodded.

"Let's get out of here," Wilson said.

"Wait." Duncan placed a canvas on his new easel. "I'll paint you."

"He's good," Roscoe said.

Wilson slowly sank onto the couch, his wintry, stern eyes seeming to say *he'd better be*. Roscoe fetched two six packs from the Hollywood and passed the bottles out. Duncan painted, his brush a blur against the canvas. Hours later, as the sun set, he put down his pallet.

"That's all tonight. I can finish it without you."

Peewee rose and looked at the canvas. "Hey, that's good!"

"I told you," Roscoe said, "didn't I tell you?"

In the painting Roscoe sat on the Harley. Marco and Wilson sat at opposite ends of the couch, Amber's feet across Marco's knees and her head in Wilson's lap, her eyes hard and her lips twisted in a tart's vacuous smirk. Peewee sat on the floor in front of the couch, a dull normal grin on his cherub's face, his arms clasped above his knees. Marco gazed out of the painting with psychopath eyes, callous and void. And Wilson looked like what he was, a pirate, a gunfighter, something novel each generation, but always the one giving the orders, and now an outlaw biker with codes cruel and essential as nature. Looking at the painting, Wilson wondered what had become of the child who once played catch with a father whose sole aspiration was that his son grow up to play ball in the big leagues. His childhood was contented but his soul had never been appeased. At fifteen he hopped a freight train on a dare and for ten new Harley's and a ranch in Idaho he could not say why he kept going. Twenty years separated then from now. The final report he had of his father was contained in the obituary his sister sent when Wilson was behind bars for trouncing the manager at a McDonald's who had given him a cold bag of french fries. The painting touched him like the obituary had, and he did not know why.

"It's okay," he said.

"Mind if they leave the bike here a few days?" Roscoe asked.

"Sure."

"One thing." Wilson smeared the license plate in the painting. "Change that before you show it to anyone."

From his window Duncan observed the Guardians mount their Harleys and ride off. He watched Roscoe enter the Hollywood. He searched the street for a white Cadillac. All he saw were three Hondas, two Toyotas, a Dodge Dakota, and a Subaru wagon. He turned from the window, opened a beer, and changed the license in the painting.

Hours later, Duncan's phone rang.

"Hello."

"Duncan?"

"Pris?" His heart grew legs and kicked his ribs. His heart had been doing things like that ever since he met her. "How did you get my number?"

"The phone company has this thing. It's called information."

"Oh."

"I'm sorry. I don't mean to be bitchy."

"That's all right."

"I called to apologize. I know you weren't trying anything. I'm just so tired of hearing that crap. The creeps who come into the Hollywood think because they throw money at me they can say whatever they want. All I can do is smile when what I really want is to rip their hearts out with a claw hammer."

"Ummm . . ."

"I don't mean that."

"I know," Duncan said. "Can I ask you a question?"

"Sure."

"Will you have dinner with me tonight?"

"Can't. I'm working. But you could come in for a drink."

Duncan did not want to be equated with the other creeps or have cardiac surgery performed upon him with a carpentry tool. His desire to see her naked was tempered by an equal desire that when this vision occurred that he also be naked and that they be alone.

"I better not," he said. "I have a lot of work to do."

"That's probably best. Somebody stole Sheila's Harley. She's in a mood to kick ass." *Only Women Bleed* began in the background. "I have to go," she said. "But I get off at one. Maybe I could come up. We could talk."

"Sure!"

"Just talk. I'm serious, Duncan."

"I understand."

"All right. Maybe I'll see you tonight."

Duncan hung up and stared at the bike. He was not vain, but he believed he owned too nice a face for jail and possessed an inadequate desire to participate in shower room acrobatics.

Mr. Delaney, exactly how did this stolen motorcycle get up here?

Beats the hell out of me, sir.

The police would flay him with rubber hoses and jab him with electric cattle prods until he ratted on the Guardians whose tattooed Aryan jail house brothers would hunt him down and fillet him with sharpened bed springs like so much vermin. He covered the Harley with a sheet in a vain attempt to make it look like something other than a motorcycle.

He put on his hat, walked to a liquor store, and bought two bottles of champagne for fifty dollars. He bought a picnic basket of cheese, meat, bread, and crackers at an all-night deli. He bought grapes and a cantaloupe at a market. He bought a bag of ice, a plastic bucket, and two candles from Assan. He returned home and put all but the candles, the basket, and the bucket in the refrigerator. He swept the floor and laid a tablecloth in front of the couch. He wedged candles in shot glasses and put them on the cloth. He sliced the cantaloupe and set the pieces on a plate with the grapes and put the plate in the refrigerator. He stripped, showered, brushed his teeth, and combed his hair. He tried six shirts and three pairs of jeans before he hit a combination that suited him. He looked at his watch.

Ten thirty. Two and one half hours to go.

He tried to paint but he could not focus. He shut off the lights and picked up Cat. He sat in the window and watched people come and go from the Hollywood. At midnight he put the ice and a bottle of champagne in the bucket. He returned to the window. At twelve twenty he opened the picnic basket and laid out the cheese, meat, and bread. He returned to the window. At twelve forty he put the plate of cantaloupe and grapes on the table cloth and lit the candles.

He returned to the window.

At one, Pris left the Hollywood with a long haired, leather wearing, anorexic rock star. She wore black tights, a black halter, and her biker's jacket. Her hair was tied in long yellow braids. She sat on the rock star's motorcycle and put her arms around his waist. They rode west down Sunset towards Beverly Hills. Duncan's heart flew east to the Chicago stockyards where it was ground into dog meat. When it was clear neither Pris nor his heart would return he put Cat down and blew out the candles.

Later that night, Duncan brought a bottle downstairs to where the bum slept fitfully in his rags, snoring and dreaming of gin. He was maybe fifty, with light green eyes flecked with gold. His hair was mostly gray with random strands of brown. Wrinkles like small scars edged his eyes and the corners of his mouth. He had ample wear on the rest of his chassis and a stench that could drive lice to suicide. Duncan nudged him with his foot until he woke and cocked a wrinkled red eye.

"Yes, Mr. Getty," he said, "what can you do for me?"

Duncan gave him the champagne. "Thought you might like this."

He looked at the bottle. "French too. What's the occasion?"

"Just a broken promise."

"Could be worse. Could be a broken heart."

"Same thing."

"Some might disagree."

"That cost twenty-five dollars." Duncan chose not to argue his love life with a wino. "Maybe you can trade it at a liquor store for something stronger."

"No, they'd think I stole it. They'd take it from me and I'd end up with nothing." He popped the cork and took a long drink. He wiped his lips with a dirty sleeve and smiled. "Besides. I used to like champagne."

Something in his tone moved Duncan. "Do you want to get out of the cold for a while? You can use my shower and I'll find you some clothes."

"Sure," the bum said, "why not?"

Duncan led him upstairs. "The bathroom's in there."

"Thanks, Mr. Getty."

"My name's not Getty. It's Duncan."

"Sure it is." He shook Duncan's hand. "I'm Edward."

Edward retreated to the bathroom and turned on the water. Duncan went to the kitchen and washed his hand. The water stopped in the bathroom and splashing began. Edward sang in a sweet, strong tenor as he bathed. It sounded like Italian opera, though Duncan could not have identified it as such if it were Caruso himself singing in the tub.

I used to like champagne.

What would Duncan say he once liked when entropy finally caught up with his quivering molecules? Would his regrets merit remembering and his joys be impossible to forget? Would he recall Tiffy behind the barn and the fullness of his chest and shorts when she lay back in the hay and raised her skirt to reveal the interior of her tan, naked thighs? Would he remember Fiona's smile and his hand in hers as they crossed busy Cheyenne streets? Would he remember his father beside a river or anywhere else other than in his dreams? And would he remember a girl with dandelion hair and eyes blue and stormy as any ocean?

"About them clothes?"

Edward stood in the bathroom door, naked but for a towel circling his waist. His skin was scrubbed pink and the air was sweeter than when he first graced Duncan's studio. Duncan gave him a pair of jeans, shorts, a wool shirt, cotton socks, and an old sweater.

"The pants might be long, but the shirt should fit."

"Thanks." Edward dropped the towel and dressed. "I'll just roll up the cuffs." He was thin and scarred and white like death. He smiled a skull's weary grin. "Left your tub a bit dirty."

"Don't worry about it." Duncan saw him eye the spread on the sheet by the couch. "You want to eat?"

"Don't mind if I do."

He sat on the floor and stuffed a cheese wedge in his mouth. He ate for five minutes. When he was done only the salami remained.

"Gives me gas," he explained.

Duncan said, "Listen, think you could do me a favor?"

"I wondered if you'd get to this. Ok. What do you want me to do?"

Duncan put a canvas on his easel. "Just sit there."

Edward sat on the couch. "That's it?"

"Sure." Duncan began sketching.

"That's a relief. I thought you wanted me to blow you or something. Don't look so shocked. I done worse. A man in my situation can't afford pride. Don't think I like it, though."

"I don't imagine you would."

Duncan was staggered that there were men desperate enough to pay a foul-smelling bum to fellate them. He did not object to the desire or preference, merely to the hygiene of the service provider, though he was bothered that Edward judged him such a person with such a craving who would desire such a service.

"Hey," Edward asked, "do you have any more hootch?"

Duncan gave him the other bottle of champagne. Edward drank and sang while Duncan painted. The champagne was soon gone and the singing mumbled. Edward nodded into sleep. Duncan shrouded him with a blanket. He scrubbed dirt from the tub and wiped water off the floor while Edward slept. He took Edward's old clothes downstairs and tossed them in the dumpster behind the mini-mart. He went inside and bought a beef burrito and warmed it in Assan's microwave. He wondered as he climbed his stairs what Edward was like at twenty-one, whom he had loved and was that love requited, and if he had ever known anyone like Pris.

When Duncan returned, his studio was empty and his blanket gone. He looked in the bathroom. No Edward. He looked in the closet and kitchen. Still no Edward. He got undressed and spread his sleeping bag across the couch. He took the money from his pocket and counted. Of the sixteen hundred he had received for *Roscoe,* barely seven hundred remained. He took the shoe box from under the couch and opened it.

Empty.

Duncan picked up the phone and dialed 911. His eyes fell on the Harley. He hung up. He laughed when he looked in the refrigerator. Not satisfied with the money, Edward had also stolen his last beer. Duncan drank a glass of orange juice and finished the burrito. He looked out the window. The Hollywood was dark, the blue neon sign black in the night. He placed a fresh canvas on the easel. He painted a woman in a red dress with yellow hair falling around her shoulders. He painted her leaning on the wall outside the Hollywood, her arms crossed, knee bent and the sole of her boot flat against the dirty red bricks. Her face he painted with ease. Her eyes and her smile were branded deep onto his neurons, disrupting his synapses until all he could think of was her smile. A Harley thundered by outside. Duncan wedged a chair against his door. He laughed when he returned to the easel and saw what he had done.

The Pris in the painting was smiling, her eyes bright and her arms crossed before her. But the middle finger of her exposed hand was once again extended to him in that traditionally contemptuous salute.

Eight

Duncan was sitting in his window reading a *People* magazine the next day when Pris came out of the Hollywood Bar and Grill. She crossed to her Cadillac which, by design or coincidence or by that random series of events men call fate, was parked below his studio. She wore a red tank top tucked into faded blue jeans, sandals, and sunglasses. Her hair was loose and wild.

"Improving your mind?" she asked.

He dropped the magazine. He had been sitting there since he first noticed her car hours before, and had rehearsed this conversation forty seven times in his brain, but *improving your mind* was not an opening he had prepared for.

"Just wasting time," he said.

"Sorry about last night. I would've come up but your lights were out."

"I was here."

"Maybe another time."

"Don't move."

He jumped up and stuffed a hundred dollars in his pocket. He took a whiskey bottle from its hiding place in the back of a cabinet behind a box of cherry tarts. He grabbed his hat and ran from the studio. He almost hit his head on the pipe again. Pris was in her car when he reached the street.

"How about now?" he asked.

She frowned. Then she leaned over and opened the door.

"Get in," she said.

She took him to a restaurant on the ocean side of Pacific Coast Highway north of Malibu. All the way there Duncan kept her talking and laughing so she would not think to change her mind. When they arrived, Pris was relaxed and happy and Duncan was nervous. Bolo Giulliano, Café Bella's owner, met them at the door. He hugged Pris and kissed her and sat them at a table overlooking the beach and the sun falling orange into the Pacific.

They shared a bottle of Chianti over dinner. Bolo imported it from his family's Sicilian vineyards and only served it to his favorite customers. After dinner they sipped coffee spiked with Duncan's bottle of Irish whiskey. It was one of two bottles Sean Delaney bought the day Duncan was born. Sean had drunk the first as Duncan screamed in his jackhammer arms. He promised the wailing child that they would share the second on Duncan's twenty first birthday. Sean had not made it, but Duncan did not believe his father would object if he shared it with Pris instead. Duncan felt good despite the uncertainty pervading his intestines whenever he looked in her eyes. Bolo joined them for dessert and shared a cup of Irish coffee.

"Him I like," Bolo said.

"He's okay," Pris laughed.

"When you first came in," Bolo said, "I thought, *she's with one of those degenerate rock stars again.*"

"Shut up, Bolo," Pris said pleasantly.

"Despite needing a haircut, you I like."

"Shut up, Bolo. You're embarrassing him."

"I can't tell him I like him?"

"Thank you, Bolo. I like you too."

"She's like a daughter to me. You treat her right."

"Shut the fuck up, Bolo."

"Such a mouth on her."

"Don't worry," Duncan said. "My intentions are honorable."

Pris frowned but Bolo smiled and clapped Duncan's back. He kissed Pris and left. When the bill came Duncan was pleased to see Bolo had not charged them for the wine or the dessert. They shared a final cup of Irish coffee and when they got up to leave, both were pleasantly inebriated.

"Let's walk," she said.

They took off their shoes and strolled beside a phosphorescent ocean, the sea rinsing sand between their toes. Pris did not resist when Duncan took her hand. It was soft and warm and her grip was strong.

"Tell me about your family," she said.

"It's just me and my mom. She's rich and beautiful and relatively young. She likes getting her own way. Got a temper, too. You're a lot like her."

"Thanks. I think."

"Don't get me wrong. I love her. More than she thinks I do. After my dad died, she was the world to me."

"Do you have a girlfriend in Wyoming?"

"I did. But we had a difference of opinion about my coming out here."

"What's she like?"

"You know," he said, "I'm not so sure anymore."

Duncan skipped a flat rock out to sea. He had just made up his mind to kiss her when she said, "What was your father like?"

"He was short and wide and strong and always laughing. He was Irish, real Irish, you know, born in Ireland," he felt the alcohol, "his accent was so thick he sometimes had to repeat himself three or four times to be understood. Everybody loved him."

"How did he die?"

Duncan resumed walking. "There's an air force base in Cheyenne. When I was nine, one of the jets crashed on our ranch. Dad jumped on his horse and rode out to see what he could do. I followed. When we got there, the jet was still in one piece. Mostly, anyway. I think part of the tail broke off. Anyway, Dad got off his horse and ran up to see if the pilot was okay. He made me stay back. He climbed up a wing, put his hands on the cockpit, and pulled himself up."

She was pale under the moon, her eyes vast and caring. A blond tress fell against her forehead and she pushed it back.

"That's when the jet exploded," he said.

"Oh, Duncan . . ."

"Thing is, the pilot had ejected. He landed two miles away in a pasture. Not a scratch on him though he twisted an ankle running from a bull."

"Oh, Duncan . . ."

"I used to lie in bed wondering if my dad knew the cockpit was empty. He probably had just enough time to say, *oh shit.*"

She was crying. Duncan felt like an ass. He had not intended that. He took her and held her, the ocean washing unnoticed around their feet.

"I'm so sorry," she cried.

"It's not your fault," he said. "It's nobody's fault."

"My father died when I was young too," she sobbed.

He put his head on her shoulder and smelled the floral scent of her hair. He brushed his lips against the smooth skin on her neck, barely touching her. She stiffened and pushed him away. The tears were gone and her eyes were bright and angry.

Here we go again, Duncan thought.

"You're not so different after all, are you? Why do you bother? Don't you realize I'll never let you fuck me?"

"I don't want to *fuck* you."

"Right. You want to make love to me." Duncan was dumbstruck at the intensity of her wrath. "Don't make me gag."

"I didn't realize I was so repulsive to you."

The blue anger in her eyes thawed slowly. She stroked his cheek.

"No," she said, "I think you're beautiful."

She turned and ran. Duncan tried to catch her, but she was fast, and more important, she was in shape from long hours dancing. After a hard minute running, Duncan dropped panting to his knees. She ran like a gazelle away from him, the moon shining in her hair, her pony tail flopping side to side in time with her long, athletic strides.

Great, Duncan thought as he watched her flee, *I've fallen for a lunatic.*

When Duncan returned to Café Bella, Pris and the Cadillac were gone. He sat at the bar and ordered a beer. Bolo sat beside him. He was a small, round man with bright, wet eyes and thin gray hair combed over the top of a balding skull.

"Where's Pris?"

"Beats the hell out of me."

"She ditched you, eh? Don't worry. She likes you. I can tell."

"I sure can't."

"I've known her longer. Since she was fifteen. And let me tell you, she doesn't usually bring men here. And I've never seen her look at anyone the way she looks at you."

Bolo started coughing. The coughs grew louder and more violent and for a minute Duncan thought he would cough up a bronchial tube. The bartender set a glass of water on the bar. Bolo drank it quickly.

"Are you okay?" Duncan asked.

Bolo nodded yes, but the coughing had taken something out of him. Duncan unpleasantly perceived Bolo's skin and gentle eyes were all that separated him from life as a corpse.

"Be patient with her," Bolo said. "She's had a hard life. But you listen to me. If you want her, you must be strong, gentle, understanding and patient. Especially patient."

Duncan could handle gentle, but he doubted he possessed the capacity for that much strength or understanding or patience. He nodded anyway.

"Good." Bolo stood. "I'll drive you home."

Duncan followed him to the door. "Has she stranded anyone before?"

Bolo laughed. "You're the first to make it through dessert. When I saw you leave together I thought you had a chance. How did you screw it up?"

"I tried to kiss her."

"So you're a bastard too." He gripped Duncan's shoulder. "But I still like you. You know how you can tell? No? I'll tell you." He whispered in Duncan's ear. "I've never given any of the other bastards a ride home."

Bolo dropped Duncan off in front of the mini-mart. The alcohol had cleared from his brain, but the depression caused by his near miss with Pris combined with a lack of sleep over the last few days to grab his eyelids and pull down hard. He stumbled upstairs and fell onto his couch.

He heard someone urinating in his bathroom.

He jumped up and fell to the floor. He grabbed for the bat under the couch, panicked when he could not find it, relaxed when his hand touched cold, hard wood. He stood outside the bathroom, bat held tight and poised to knock the head off the poor unfortunate emptying his bladder behind the battered bathroom door. The sound of urine joining water stopped.

"Get the hell out here," he said.

The toilet flushed. Duncan raised the bat and waited for the door to open. He heard the sounds of brushing teeth.

"I'm not kidding," he said, "come out or I'm coming in after you."

The urinator rinsed and spat. Duncan imagined the fiend behind the door flossing his teeth. That stopped him. What if the urinator was, in reality, a urinatrix? What if it was *Sheila Rascowitz?* The shower went on.

That's it, Duncan thought.

He flung the door open and stepped inside. Something moved to his right, but before he could swing, unseen hands turned him and shoved him into the tub. He dropped the bat and fell beneath the shower. The urinator picked up the bat and turned off the water. He was short and lean with high cheeks, dark eyes, and long black hair falling across wiry shoulders. The smile he sported and the hand he reached out were two of the nicest human features Duncan could hope to see. Duncan allowed himself to be pulled out of the tub. He hugged the naked man with all his feeble might, his clothes dripping unnoticed onto the cracked tile floor.

"Benjamin," Duncan said, "am I ever glad to see you."

Misty required nine days to accrue sufficient nerve to return to Duncan's studio. It was noon on a crystalline Saturday. She had been up preparing since six. She wore a lace teddy under a silk blouse, tight jeans, and hundred dollar Italian leather sandals. Her hair fell light and dense around her face. Her glossy violet nails duplicated her lipstick. She had never

70

received more second looks as she did that morning driving into town from her apartment in Venice in her BMW convertible with the top down.

She imagined she looked like crap.

In truth she was a winsome young woman who, if graced by God with a few more grams of brain cells, might have succeeded in numerous professions not requiring a college degree outside the adult entertainment or food service industries. She was hard working and loyal and not afraid to go for what she desired. Right now, lurking below the first centimeter of cortex, was the desire to seduce Duncan. But as she stood below his studio listening to his stereo she was nervous enough to vomit. She bought a Snickers and a diet Coke from Assan. She slumped against the wall by the pay phone and ate the bar and quaffed the soda. She belched twice softly. She inhaled deeply until she became dizzy.

"All right, Misty," she said, "he's just a guy."

She did not believe it though, intellectually (so to speak), she understood it was true. He was an artist. He created. He did not pump gas or strum variations of the same three chords or program computers or add numbers like the dozens of losers who filled the Hollywood Bar and Grill each day. He had vision, and Misty wanted to be part of what he saw. She stalled as long as she could, but finally her excuses were depleted, and she strode past a ratty old truck, took the stairs two at a time, ducked under the pipe in the hallway, and rapped on the door with a fist of fine tan knuckles. A young, lean, dark-haired man answered her knock. He was naked save for red candy striped boxers and a necklace of mountain lion teeth. His eyes set off the smoke alarm in the bedroom of her mind.

"Come on in," he said. Misty smelled bacon and butter. "You hungry?"

"I just ate."

"You must be Pris. Duncan told me about you."

Her heart sank to where her arch supports would be if she had worn running shoes instead of sandals.

"My name is *Misty,*" she said.

"Whoops." He flipped bacon with a fork. "I'm Benjamin." Hot grease splattered his chest. "Jesus that smarts," he said, and then, "Duncan just left for the Laundromat."

"You ought to put on a shirt."

"Sure. That's what they're expecting me to do."

Misty wondered who *they* were, but inferred he was fooling just as she opened her mouth to ask. Despite her cranial weakness, Misty pegged Benjamin as a wise guy who had already exceeded life's allotment of trouble. She closed her mouth and lay her carnal thoughts aside. She required innocence in a man, not just raw animal appeal. Duncan better fit the job description from what she had seen.

"What's he doing at the Laundromat?" she asked. Benjamin looked at her. She nodded. "Oh, right. Laundry."

He slapped the bacon on a plate beside a mound of scrambled eggs. He put four slices of buttered toast heaped with grape jam over the eggs. He sat on the couch and ate with his fingers. Misty sat beside him.

"Are you Mexican?"

"Arapaho."

"Oh, wow," Misty said, "you're from Italy?"

Benjamin laughed so hard he spit out his food. He kept laughing while he wiped masticated meat and poultry from the floor with a paper towel.

"Native American," he finally said.

"You mean like an Indian?"

"You're not the brightest candle, are you?" Her blank look answered him. "Never mind." He put his plate in the sink. "I have to perform my morning ablutions." He saw her embarrassed look. "That means ritual washing."

Misty relaxed. "Oh."

She studied Duncan's paintings while Benjamin showered. Edward's portrait moved her to pity and the one of the Guardians scared her. The painting of Champagne and Cassandra made her jealous. The collected canvases made her horny as hell. She lifted the sheet from the Harley. She knew Sheila's bike had been stolen but she missed the connection. She spotted a fourth canvas covered by a cloth behind the Harley. She lifted the cloth and looked. She was sobbing on the couch when Benjamin emerged from the bathroom, her head in her hands and her elbows on her knees. He knelt and pushed the hair from her face. Her eyes were red and her make up streaked.

"You okay?" Benjamin asked.

"Sure," she said, "just wonderful."

Then she jumped up and ran from the studio.

Duncan sat on a washing machine, his clothes spinning infinitely beneath him. He wore his Stetson and a tank top. His legs poked white and mostly hairless through a pair of shorts. He was reading a Dear Duncan letter.

Dear Duncan, it began, *Danny has asked me to be his bride. I said I would answer in one week. That's time enough for you to come to your senses and get home where you belong. If I don't hear from you by Sunday, the next time you see me you better call me Mrs. Carpenter.*

P.S. I don't think you should hang around Benjamin anymore. He was fresh with me and refused to give your mother or me your address.

Love, Tiffy.

Benjamin had told him of Tiffy's aborted attempt at seduction. He was surprised but not shocked. Nor was he upset for several reasons. First, he and Tiffy were broken up. That made Tiffy fair game, even for Benjamin. Second, he had since fallen for a crazy woman, so the affections of what Benjamin termed *that whore former girlfriend of yours* no longer mattered. And third, he was proud that Benjamin possessed the moral conviction and fortitude to resist Tiffy's bountiful charms in deference to a friend. Duncan pocketed the letter and put his clothes in a dryer. He thought about Tiffy and he thought about Pris. He thought about Benjamin and he thought about Sheila. He thought about Fiona and Sean and imagined how his father would answer Tiffy's ultimatum. He remembered the dream.

Tiffy doesn't love you, Sean Delaney had told him and, *you will love again.*

He reflected on his life's peculiar course as he loaded his warm, clean clothes into a basket. He stepped onto the street, speculating on what it was like in Cheyenne and where Tiffy was and who she was with and it took him a minute of walking and thinking before he realized he no longer cared.

Duncan breathed deep a nostalgic odor fresh from his childhood as he climbed his stairs. It was the sweet, smothering smell of violets, not overpowering in the orthodox sense but insidious in its infiltration of the sinuses. He opened the door and dropped his laundry basket.

"Jesus God!" he yelped.

Fiona and Woody stood by the window looking down to the street. Duncan put his hand to his beating chest. A fragrance reminiscent of Fiona was one thing but the woman in person was another. In a practical sense, even if he had made the connection he still would have ascended the stairs and opened the door. He just would have been better prepared. His mother wore a staid green business suit, light green stockings, and black pumps. Woody stood awkwardly by in a western shirt with a bolo tie, brown nylon pants, and brown penny loafers over white socks. Benjamin lay on the couch, naked save his boxers, leafing through a *Playboy* purchased from Assan in the interim between Misty's departure and Fiona's arrival.

"Duncan," Benjamin sang, "your mommy wants you."

73

"You scared the hell out of me," Duncan said.

"It's nice to see you too," Fiona said.

"You know that's not what I meant." He hugged her. "Hey, Mom. Hey, Woody. What brings you out here?"

"I'd guess an airplane," Benjamin offered.

Fiona ignored him. "It's time to come home."

Duncan released her and picked up his basket. He knelt and sorted his laundry into his clothes box.

"This is home now."

"Now, Duncan," Woody said, "maybe we should talk about this."

"How can you live in this, this . . ." Fiona encompassed the room with a sweep of her hand. "Words fail me."

"It's not so bad," Benjamin said, "once you get used to the roaches, the drug dealers, the discarded needles, the squalid toilet, and the fetid, stinking, haggard whores who ply their trade on the boulevard."

Fiona glanced about the room. She went for the baseball bat, but Duncan got there first. He set it out of her reach in the hall.

"You're not helping any, Benjamin," Woody said.

"Still bang . . ." Benjamin remembered his jailhouse resolution. "Never mind." He put his pants on. "I'm off for beer. You want one Woody?"

"Sure, I'll have a beer."

"No, you won't," Fiona said, "you're driving the rental."

Woody hung his head. "On second thought maybe I shouldn't."

Benjamin theorized that Fiona had impounded Woody's testicles long ago and held them hostage in a jar of murky liquid in the back of the refrigerator at the Circle D. Duncan claimed the jar held old olives. Benjamin did not buy it. He could not discern other grounds for Woody's craven conduct. Sure, Fiona sporadically warmed the testicles in the microwave to allow Woody their use, but that was not the same as operating one's gonads one's self.

"And what about Tiffy?" Fiona demanded after Benjamin left. "You'll lose her if you stay here."

"She's already lost, mom. She made that clear enough."

"I am through arguing." She searched in her purse. "If you won't listen to reason maybe you'll pay attention to this."

Fiona found her checkbook. She opened it and wrote. Benjamin returned with the beers. He popped two and handed one to Duncan.

Woody licked his lips but said nothing. Fiona ripped out a check and handed it to Duncan. Benjamin looked over his shoulder and whistled.

"That's three thousand dollars. It's yours if you come home."

"This isn't about money, mom."

"All right." Fiona wrote another. "Five thousand. No job required. You can rent an apartment in Cheyenne and paint there if you like."

"Tell you what." Benjamin took a wad of hundreds from his pocket and threw it on the floor at Fiona's feet. "I'll give him six thousand to stay."

"Holy Jesus," Woody said. "Where did you get that kind of money?"

"Stole it from a church collection box no doubt," Fiona said, "or maybe telemarketing." She wrote a third check. "Seven thousand."

"I may be a lot of things but I'm no damn telemarketer." Benjamin took a wad of bills from his other pocket and threw it down. "Eight thousand."

Fiona scribbled a fourth check and held it to heaven like a bible in the hands of an evangelist at a snake handlers' prayer meeting. *"Ten thousand dollars!"*

Benjamin shrugged. "Out of my league."

Duncan took the check. It would buy a hell of a lot of paint. But in the end it made no difference. He offered the check back.

"Thank you, mom. But no."

Fiona's spine became an iron rod in opposition to Duncan's defiance. She had never struck her son but she now experienced the urge. The last time she had felt this way towards a relative was two years before Sean Delaney's death, when he voyaged to Ireland for his father's funeral. Patrick Delaney was an alcoholic womanizer and petty thief known for smash and grab burglaries until a thrown brick bounced off a jeweler's plexiglass window and hit him in the forehead. He awoke bloody in the gutter with the brick under his chin and an alarm ringing in his ears. After that he could not throw a brick without breaking out in a shivering sweat. He tried picking pockets, but his hands were clumsy. He eventually gave up thievery and made a living as a beggar, charming tourists into tossing as much as a fiver into his outstretched cap.

Patrick had left Sean's mother when Sean was twelve. A month before his death, he had appeared on Mary Delaney's doorstep with a liver as big as a goat's and a cancer eating from colon to throat. Mary took him in and cared for him. She was Catholic, never divorced, and only God knew why she still loved her errant husband. Fiona blew up when she heard the tale. She would have journeyed to Ireland herself to kill the bastard for his sins. But Patrick Delaney was five days' cold, murder was moot, and an overseas trip for a rogue's funeral was just so much squandered money. Fiona did not realize until Sean was gone that he went for his mother's sake, not his father's, and because it was the right thing to do. And now she saw Sean in Duncan, and it subdued and moved her virtually to tears.

"Keep it," she said. "But at least move into a place fit for humans."

The door slammed open. Pris stormed in. She wore jeans, tennis shoes, and a yellow collared blouse. Her hair was tied in a long pony tail. She wore no make up. She tore the cloth off the painting and stared at the canvas.

"Pris . . ."

She brushed between Fiona and Woody and obtained a butcher knife from a drawer in the kitchen. They watched in fear and fascination as she slashed the painting to tatters. If not for her vengeful eyes and the knife in her hand she would have looked like a college girl instead of a homicidal maniac. She threw the knife to the floor between Duncan's feet. It stuck in the wood, twanging like a cheap tuning fork.

"I decide who paints me. Not you. And if I ever do decide to let you paint me I expect to be paid for it. Understand?"

"Yes ma'am. I'm sorry."

Pris turned to Fiona and Woody. "Please forgive the interruption."

Then she was gone. Fiona and Woody looked at each other in bewilderment.

"What the hell was that?" Fiona asked.

"That," Duncan said, "is one reason I'm reluctant to go home."

"Well," Benjamin said, "she left the door open for you to paint her in the future."

Duncan smiled. "She did, didn't she?"

"Who is she?" Fiona asked.

"Her name is Pris. She works across the street."

"Pris what?"

That took Duncan by surprise. "You know, I never thought to ask."

"What was she so mad about?" Woody asked.

"Hard to say." Duncan yanked the butcher knife from the floor and put it away. "I guess the painting didn't appeal to her."

Fiona watched Pris enter the Hollywood. "What does she do?"

Benjamin's face assumed the aspect of a man who, at the onset of an attack of Tourette's syndrome, had just realized he forgot his medication. Duncan sat on the couch, picked up the check, and shook his head.

"Go ahead," he said.

"She's a fucking stripper!" Benjamin blurted in deranged glee. "Your boy's in love with a goddamn exotic dancer! How do you like them apples, Fiona?"

Fiona took the check from Duncan's hands and tore it into small pieces. She dropped the bits on the floor at his feet and walked out.

"I'll talk to her," Woody said. "A stripper, huh?"

"I'm afraid so."

Woody turned to go. "We're at the Beverly Hills Hotel if you need us."

"Hey, Woody!" Duncan called. Woody stopped. "How did you find me, anyway?"

He shrugged towards Benjamin. "Fiona had him followed."

"Wait just a minute. I lost those morons in Vegas. I know I did. Hell, I can spot a car tailing me from fifty miles."

"Who said anything about a car? Fiona hired a Cessna, too. One mile up and two miles off."

"Air support!" Benjamin slapped his forehead, surprised at the expense to which Fiona would go to find her baby. So that was how Lomo and Kern located him time and again. "Damn if I didn't underestimate the bitch."

Woody laughed. "You never had a chance."

Fiona waited at the curb beneath Duncan's studio, staring across the street at the Hollywood Bar and Grill. Woody joined her.

"Ever been to one of those places?" she asked.

"Once or twice."

"What's it like?"

"I don't know. Dark mostly. Dark and loud."

Fiona stepped across the gutter into the street.

"Where you going?"

"To talk with that girl."

"Duncan won't like that!" Woody yelled as she crossed the street. She opened the door and went inside. "Oh lord," he groaned.

He crossed after her. Inside the bar, an imminently naked girl swayed half heartedly on an oval stage to a blaring rock song. The girl smiled at him. Woody blushed and looked away. He spotted Fiona handing a check to Pris at a table in the back. Pris folded the check and put it in her shirt pocket. She stood and went back stage.

"That went well," Fiona said when Woody sat beside her. A waitress set a beer before her. "Thank you, dear."

The music stopped. The girl picked up the bills scattered at her feet and retreated behind a curtain. Woody looked around. Fiona was the only female in the room not clad in lingerie and thigh boots.

"Let's go," he said.

"What?" Fiona looked distracted. "After I finish my beer."

The music commenced anew. Misty emerged from the curtain, strutting to a salsa beat. She wore a vinyl skirt, a white blouse, and high black leather boots. The shirt was the first to go. Fiona watched, her breathing rapid and shallow. She rubbed Woody's thigh.

"Fiona!" he hissed.

"Hush! No one can see us."

Woody shuddered. He imagined Duncan walking in. Fiona mistook his reaction and squeezed his leg. Woody surrendered in the darkness as Misty, now down to bra and G-string and young enough to be his daughter, hung upside down from a steel pole. *Lord,* he prayed, as Fiona worked her way up his inseam, knowing as he prayed that he was in the devil's workshop and that divine intervention would not be forthcoming, *save me from this woman and her twisted ways.*

"So," Benjamin said, "what did Tiffy's letter say?"

"Didn't you read it?"

"Sure. But I was willing to pretend I didn't."

"Well, that makes me feel better."

"Two bikers came by and took your Harley."

"It wasn't mine."

"I figured. Otherwise, I'd have stopped them." Duncan did not doubt Benjamin would have tried. "Oh," he went on, "you had a female visitor."

"I was here."

"Not your psychotic girlfriend."

"She's not my girlfriend."

"But you don't dispute the psychotic part."

Duncan looked at the shredded canvas. "That would be difficult."

"Misty."

"What about her?"

"I told you. She came by."

"What did she want?"

"You I think."

"More's the pity."

Benjamin picked up his money from the floor and pocketed it.

"Where'd you get that anyway?"

"I won it. Perfectly legal."

"Uh huh. Stopped by to see your cousins, did you?"

"Yup."

Duncan changed into fresh, warm jeans and a long sleeved shirt. He gathered his paintings and put on his hat.

"Drive me to Angela's?"

"Oh, no. I'm not ready to go there yet."

"Fine. If you're so yellow you can't face her I'll take the bus."

"Who are you calling yellow, white man?"

"If the color fits . . ."

"Fine. But you can't make me go inside."

"I don't care what you do. I just need a ride."

Duncan stowed his paintings in the back of the Purgatory Truck. He covered them with a cloth and tucked the edges around the frames. Benjamin got in the truck. He wore new jeans, new boots, a shirt with factory creases, and a hefty dose of cologne.

"You got prettied up just for me?" Duncan laughed as he slid in beside him. "Is it wrong to love another man?"

"I don't know what you're talking about, you damn potato eater."

"Sure, bring my cultural heritage into it, you bigot." Duncan was enjoying Benjamin's anxiety. "Hell, it's Saturday. She probably won't be there. Besides, I'm sure she forgot about you. You aren't that memorable."

"You seen my pliers?"

"What do you want them for?"

"To pull out your teeth," Benjamin growled as he pulled into traffic.

Duncan pulled his hat down over his eyes. "Haven't seen them."

Sven was behind the reception desk when Duncan and Benjamin arrived. Marie had landed a part dancing in a rock video and, having lost his gallery job, Sven was happy to sit in. He wore white linen pants, brown sandals, and a white silk shirt buttoned to his neck. He was tan, tall, muscular, and blond. He looked the perfect human male.

"How's the scrotum?" Benjamin asked. Duncan had told him about the ruckus at the gallery.

"Better, thank you." Sven stood. "I will tell Angela you are here."

"You asshole!"

Sven stepped menacingly back towards Benjamin. "Excuse me?"

"Not you," Benjamin said. "Him. He told me she wouldn't be here."

"I said she probably wouldn't be."

Duncan grabbed Benjamin as he turned to flee. Benjamin contemplated snapping Duncan's wrist, but before his brain could send the requisite impulses across axon to dendrite, Angela strolled through the door and his neurons ceased heeding his commands. She wore a dark-blue dress cut above the knee, a pearl necklace hanging to her sternum in the vee of her blouse, and precision make-up that enhanced her exotic splendor. Despite believing all history culminated in the moment, Benjamin felt out of his depth. On a western road beneath a wide sky with only the wind to come between them he could handle her, but here? Duncan had not seen Benjamin so nervous since the sixth grade, when he discovered him behind the oil rig showing Stephanie Haskell his organic tomahawk.

"Coward," Duncan whispered.

"Let go before I damage you. I feel the need for flight."

"Angela," Duncan said as he released him, "you remember Benjamin."

"Of course. How are you Benjamin?"

Benjamin breathed deep and stood straight. "I am as a man standing in awe before a goddess," he said in a deep clear voice.

Angela rolled her eyes. "With a rattler penis as I recall."

"More like a boa constrictor after seeing you again."

"Do you always come on this strong?"

"Only in the face of overwhelming beauty."

"You don't seem overwhelmed."

"I'm so nervous I could shit."

Angela laughed. Duncan leaned his paintings against Sven's desk.

"I'll just leave these here. You can tell me what you think later."

"Would you like a beer, Duncan?" Angela had purchased a case after their first meeting.

"No thank you."

"Benjamin?"

"I could sorely use one."

"Sven, two bottles and two glasses in my office, please."

She was three inches taller than Benjamin despite his boots. But, as Benjamin was fond of saying whenever his stature was questioned, *height don't mean nothing when you're lying down,* which was equally applicable, though in differing senses, when either a man or a woman was doing the questioning. Sven took two bottles from a refrigerator. Duncan was a card-carrying heterosexual but he could not help but notice Sven's great physical beauty. He was a male version of Pris on a modified steroid diet. Duncan

80

envisioned Sven on his couch across from Roscoe, two men from disparate planetary ends, creatures of light and darkness.

"Hey, Sven," Duncan said, "would you pose for me sometime?"

"I would be delighted."

Duncan reflected on his life's peculiar course as he waited downstairs for the bus. He had sold a painting and his prospects were good for more sales. His best friend had joined him. And despite the inevitable conflicts, he was glad Fiona had found him. Though he resented it, he knew her meddling was motivated by love. And if necessary, he would pay Pris to pose, as often as it took, until his money ran out. He smiled. The world seemed right. A bus stopped with pneumatic flatulence and a diesel smell. Duncan got on and sat beside an old woman who stunk faintly of urine. She wore a dirty shawl and a stained dress and battered athletic shoes. She bobbed her head like a water witch in tune to an internal rhythm. Every so often she threw her head back. Her shoulders shook and her jaw worked but no laughter erupted from her lips.

Well, Duncan thought as he changed seats, *most of the world anyway.*

Nine

Duncan's door was open when he returned home. Despite having become inured to surprise visits by a menagerie of characters, he approached the door cautiously. He hoped Pris awaited within, but feared that it was Sheila who lay in ambush. He peeked inside. Two men in suits, their backs to him, sorted through papers on the desk beside the typewriter.

"Can I help you?" Duncan asked.

They turned. Both had mustaches, military haircuts, and bodies sculpted by long hours in the gym. Duncan smelled *Old Spice*. The taller of the two pushed back his coat to reveal an LAPD badge and a gun on his belt.

"I'm Detective Randolph. He's Detective Phillips. Who are you?"

"Duncan Delaney."

"Can't be," Phillips said.

"Why not?"

"Because Duncan Delaney is dead," Randolph said.

Duncan sat in the back of the unmarked car Randolph and Phillips drove down a nameless street.

"Am I under arrest?"

"Do you want to be?" Phillips asked.

"Well," Duncan asked, "do I need a lawyer?"

"Did you do anything wrong?" Randolph asked.

"Can't I get a straight answer from you guys?"

Phillips laughed. "Apparently not. Just relax and enjoy the ride."

"If I'm not under arrest, why did you tell me I had to come with you?"

"You got it wrong," Randolph said, "we *asked* if you wanted to come."

That was not the way Duncan remembered it, but he did not challenge the deceit. Instead, he said, "I've changed my mind."

"Too late." Randolph stopped behind a big white building. Two patrol cars and three ambulances were parked near the entrance. "We're here."

Duncan trailed them inside the building, down an elevator to a cold basement, and along a protracted corridor paved with tiles. He followed Randolph through the doors at the end of the hall. Fluorescent lamps lit a clean, barren room. It smelled of formaldehyde and was colder than the hall. Steel doors, three feet wide and two feet high, covered the walls. Each had a handle and a frame the size of a business card. Some held tags, others did not. Phillips led him to a steel door on the far side of the room.

Delaney, Duncan, the tag there read.

Randolph turned the handle and pulled out a long table. A covered body lay there. Two skinny feet poked out from under the sheet. A red tag hung from the right big toe.

"If you're Delaney," Phillips pulled the sheet back, "then who is this?"

The body was thin and scarred and white like death. The skull's weary smile had fled along with the body's brittle soul. All that remained was skin tight over bone and a hollow space in the open eyes. An expanding vertigo touched Duncan's brain and he had to look away lest he fall.

"His name was Edward," he finally said.

"Edward who?"

"I don't know. He was homeless. He lived beneath my stairs."

"A bum you mean," said Phillips. "What else can you tell us?"

"Not much. I only really spoke with him once. He posed for me."

"You mean like photographs?"

"No. For a painting. I'm an artist."

"Sure you are. What else?"

"He had a good singing voice." Duncan shrugged. "And he used to like champagne."

"Apparently he still did," Phillips said. "A maid at the Roosevelt Hotel found him naked in bed with a pair of panty hose stuffed in his mouth and an empty bottle of Dom Perignon on the floor beside him."

"It should have taken more than one bottle to kill him."

Randolph took a sealed plastic bag out of his pocket. Inside was a wad of bills, a slip of paper, and a cracked and empty bottle with a child-safe lid.

"Phenobarbital. He couldn't get the lid off so he smashed it with the television remote control. He washed the pills down with champagne. He put a do not disturb sign on the door. He lay down, fell asleep, and choked to death on the panty hose. There was a receipt for telephone service with your name and address in his pocket. Any idea how it got there?"

"I gave him clean clothes. It must have been in the pocket."

The money in the bag was his, of course, but he could not claim it. They would ask why he did not report the theft. *Because I was minding a purloined Harley for Satan's Guardians and I didn't think you would understand.* He recalled a time in kindergarten when he confused *bring your favorite book day* with *bring your favorite toy day.* He brought a plastic sub with a working propeller and three red trident nuclear missiles that fired but did not explode. He was embarrassed by his mistake, so he hid the toy in the school yard. A second grader found it and turned it in. The principal went classroom to classroom asking whose it was. Duncan misinterpreted his interest and, fearing retribution, remained silent. Whitey Carpenter, the bastard, claimed the submarine as his own. Now, like then, he kept his interest to himself.

"All right, sport," Randolph said, "you can go."

"How about a ride home?"

"No can do. Because of you we have to rewrite our report."

Phillips covered Edward's face and closed the locker. He scratched *Delaney, Duncan* off the tag and wrote *Doe, Edward.*

"Bus stop out front," he said.

Out on the street Duncan searched his pockets and came up with seventy-five cents and a stick of sugarless gum. He waved on an approaching bus. Edward's singing echoed in his mind as he walked. He could not get the song out of his head. When he at last gave up he realized that, despite the thievery, he regretted not asking the name of the song, and he regretted that he would never hear Edward sing it again.

Something was missing.

Duncan looked in his closet and in the bathroom. He looked in the kitchen and under the sink. He looked in the box that served as his dresser. He scratched his head and went into the kitchen. A typewritten note was taped to the six-pack on a shelf near the front of the refrigerator.

Stay away from her, the note said above a bloody smear, *or the cat dies.*

Duncan dialed 911. "Someone stole my cat," he told the operator.

"Sir," the operator said, "this line is for emergencies. Come to the station and an officer will take a report."

Duncan hung up. By tomorrow Cat could be worm fodder putrefying in a superficial grave. Worse, what if Sheila dismembered the poor feline and dissolved the bloody pieces in a tub of hydrochloric acid? Duncan came to one of those gallant yet foolish decisions that the Delaneys were historically prone to make. Cat had saved him from Sheila. He would save Cat from her. He dialed Angela's number.

"Duncan here," he said when Sven answered, "is Benjamin there?"

"He and Ms. Moncini just left. Can I help you, Mr. Delaney?"

"No. Yes. Where does Sheila Rascowitz live?"

Duncan wrote down the address Sven gave him and hung up. He dialed the Hollywood Bar and Grill. Misty answered.

"This is Duncan. Is Roscoe there?"

"Hi, Duncan. No, he doesn't work until nine."

"Damn!" Duncan thought fast. "Misty, would you do me a favor?"

"Anything." She meant it. She literally drooled as she spoke. She wiped her saliva from the phone with a bar rag.

"I need a ride."

"I'll be right there."

He ran to the curb as Misty pulled up in her car. He got in and gave her the address. She slammed her foot to the floor. The car took off like a bronco out of the chute. She wore a loose shirt over a black lace teddy, a tartan skirt, garter belt, black mesh stockings, and black leather pumps. She looked like a Catholic high school girl gone wrong. Misty had hoped he would notice her apparel but was disappointed by what she incorrectly assumed was his indifference. She let him off at the bottom of a long, winding street in the Hollywood hills.

"You go on, Misty. You don't want to get involved in this."

"Be careful!" she called as he hiked up the hill.

Sheila's house overlooked city lights stretching forever across the basin into the night. The front door opened. Duncan dove into the bushes to the side of the house. Sheila and Samantha came out. Parallel scratch marks ran down Sheila's cheek. Duncan surmised the origin of the blood on the note. They started their Harleys and rode down the hill. Duncan crept up and peered in a window. A plaid couch stood against one wall. A red leather lounger, a long rip in the seat, stood beside a particle board coffee table. Two wicker chairs sat opposite the table. Sheila could paint but she was no interior decorator. Duncan tried the front door. Locked.

He sneaked around the house. A wine bottle and two glasses sat on a bench beside a Jacuzzi. A chain link fence surrounded an overgrown yard. Spare motorcycle parts lay amongst the dirt and the weeds. He tried the glass patio door. Locked. He looked in a bedroom window. Light spilled through a half-open door to illuminate a wire cage in the corner by a bed. The window slid open two inches, then stopped when a wooden dowel blocked its progress. Duncan heard a soft feline wail. It was the most forlorn sound in existence. The wail flicked a dusty switch in his brain. Most of his life he had let adversity slide from him like rain off a shingle. The few times violence had been called for, however, he had accounted for himself moderately well. Like in fifth grade, when Willy Raskin asked him why his stupid father let himself get killed when any idiot could see by the missing cockpit that the pilot had ejected. Duncan could not have answered if he wanted to, because a rage was on him. His fist flew on its own into Willy's nose, smashing the bone there and two of Duncan's knuckles. Willy had been held back a year, and was considerably bigger, but Duncan laid him out like astro-turf, and for once Benjamin had to pull Duncan off an enemy instead of the reverse. It might have gone bad back at the Circle D except, while sitting in the school office with Fiona, the principal had insensitively commented, *Mr. Delaney's action hadn't exactly been the brightest thing, had it?* Fiona brained him with a bronze paper weight and pinned him to the ground with her hands around his throat. She later apologized, as she was running out of schools and principals. The same rage was in Duncan as he stood outside Sheila's window. He lifted a rusty carburetor from the dirt and hurled it through the glass door. He stepped through, oblivious to the broken glass dangling in the frame. He opened the cage. Cat jumped to his arms, claws digging into him in a hold reminiscent of his predatory past. Duncan heard the Harleys pull into the driveway. The engines stopped. He ran out through the broken patio door, around the house, and to the street. A raging scream loud enough to activate car alarms and turn on porch lights echoed between the hills. Duncan clutched Cat and ran. The Harleys roared to life. He looked behind him. Headlights white and bright and pulsating bore down on him. He turned, ready for one last desperate dodge. Sheila saw him and screamed.

I am a dead man, Duncan thought.

A white Cadillac convertible roared past, missing him by inches. The car swerved sideways to a stop thirty feet in front of him. Sheila and Samantha laid their Harleys down to avoid crashing into the car, skidding by either side in a display of sparks like fireworks. Sheila's eyes were wide with rage and her teeth showed fierce through grimacing lips. She made Three Stooges noises as she bounced past him into a yard of poison sumac. Samantha landed in a patch of ice plant. A blond woman with cupric eyes leaned across the Cadillac's seat and opened a door.

"Get in you moron," said Pris.

"I'm lucky you came along," Duncan said.

"Lucky hell. Misty told me where you were."

Her hair streamed gold behind and around her face as she drove west on Sunset. Cat purred in Duncan's lap. Pris stopped at the curb beneath his studio. She shut off the engine and glared.

"That was stupid. I could have gotten Cat back. She would have killed you."

The notion that he could not defend himself against a female, even one who outweighed him by thirty pounds and could out bench him by fifty, was an affront to his testosterone producing capabilities. He sighed and got out.

"I'm not through yelling at you."

"You can yell at me upstairs."

She followed him to his studio. Aspirations shot down despair and he dared hope again. Benjamin and Roscoe were waiting inside. Duncan put Cat down and sagged onto the couch.

"We were just getting ready to rescue you," Benjamin said.

"I guess you two met. Benjamin, this is Pris."

"Howdy. I caught your act this morning."

"I wasn't working this morning."

"Here, I mean."

"How come she didn't kill you?" Roscoe asked.

"Sheila or Pris?" Duncan asked.

Benjamin laughed. Pris smiled despite herself. Roscoe looked confused.

"Sheila," he finally said.

"Why does everyone think I can't take care of myself?" Roscoe and Benjamin and Pris traded knowing looks. "I'm serious!"

"Rascowitz is nuts," Roscoe said. "You're lucky to be alive."

Pris picked up Cat and sat on the couch beside Duncan.

"The night is young," she said.

"Come on, Roscoe," Benjamin said. "I want to see what this bitch looks like. Don't worry," he said when Duncan frowned, "nothing's going to happen."

"What's he going to do?" Pris asked after they left.

"Something pointless and stupid."

"You're bleeding."

Duncan pulled his cuff back. A gash ran halfway from his wrist to his biceps. He had not felt the cut until he looked at it, then it throbbed and burned. Pris led him to the bathroom and unbuttoned his shirt. He took it off and held out his arm. Duncan watched her, awed by one small perfect part of God's creation. He noticed two white, rough lines against her tan wrists. The scars ran two inches from the bottom of each palm toward her elbows. A potent wave of empathy washed through his soul. She poured Mercurochrome onto his wound and the pain drove the evolving question from his brain. She dried his arm and wrapped it with gauze and tape.

"Thank you," he said, "for everything."

Her hair fell across her forehead into her clear blue eyes. A sigh whispered past her lips. She pushed the hair away and headed for the door.

"Give it up," she said. "I'm not falling for you."

"What did I say this time?"

She stopped. "You wouldn't understand."

"Try me."

"What could you give me? You don't even have a car. How would you take me out, on a bicycle? Grow up, Duncan. I'm high maintenance. All you could offer is love and long ago I learned love doesn't matter. It should, but it doesn't. Sooner or later someone gets hurt."

He struggled into a shirt and followed her downstairs. "Maybe you shouldn't go home," he said when they reached the street. "If Sheila . . ."

"Sheila's one of the few people in the world who would never hurt me. And besides. I don't live with Sheila."

"But at the gallery you said . . ."

"I said she paid my rent."

She got in her car and started it. Duncan jumped in front of the Cadillac. Pris rolled her eyes.

"Get out of the way."

"I want more than money. I think you do too."

"Easy to say when you've always had it. Get out of the way."

"Not until you answer one question."

She shifted back into park and sighed. "One question."

Duncan knelt by her door. "If all you care about is money then why haven't you married it? You're beautiful and charming when you're not being psychotic." His frustration pushed him past the point of tact. "You could have any man you wanted."

She took a folded paper from her purse and put it in his pocket. She stroked his hair and almost smiled.

"Because I've never wanted a man before you."

She floored the Cadillac and roared into the night, her tail lights flying away like the afterburners of his heart. He took the paper out of his pocket. It was a check drawn on Fiona's bank in Cheyenne made out to Priscilla Nolan for twenty thousand dollars. He put the check back in his pocket.

Well, he thought as he climbed his stairs, *at least now I know her last name.*

Benjamin stood outside Sheila Rascowitz's window and watched her sleep on the couch. Samantha lay across the room beside an empty quart beer bottle, face down in the dusty shag carpet. Benjamin turned away from the window. Roscoe knelt in the driveway examining one of two Harleys.

"This bad boy is brand new," Roscoe said when Benjamin joined him. "And she's laid it down already."

Benjamin obtained bolt cutters from the Purgatory Truck. He kept them ever near, having learned by age ten the value of easy access. He cut the chain between the two motorcycles and wheeled Sheila's bike to the street. Roscoe did the same with Samantha's. They muscled the Harleys into the back of the Purgatory truck.

"How do we get to the beach?" Benjamin asked.

"What do you want to go to there for?"

Benjamin shrugged. "Never been."

Roscoe directed him to an empty parking lot at Zuma Beach. Benjamin stood on the asphalt and listened to the Pacific smite the continent. Together they wrestled the motorcycles from the truck. Benjamin hot-wired Sheila's and kicked it over. Roscoe did the same with Samantha's.

"Where to?"

Benjamin rode onto the beach. "To the sea," he yelled.

Benjamin fish tailed in the sand, the Harley's throbbing engine competing with the ocean's clamor. He stopped in firm, wet sand thirty yards from the surf. Roscoe stopped beside him. The distant look in Benjamin's eyes made Roscoe stare out to sea. But he could see nothing save frothing water and a half moon in the clouds.

"What the hell are you doing?" Roscoe yelled over the engines.

Benjamin grinned a demon grin and screamed an Arapaho war cry. It was loud and cruel over the engines and surf. He twisted the throttle and popped the clutch. He hit the Pacific at thirty miles an hour. The water stopped the motorcycle, but inertia insisted the rider continue. He flipped over the handlebars in a pinwheel of hair and arms and legs and sailed forty feet before he belly flopped and disappeared beneath the waves.

Roscoe did not know whether to laugh or call a lifeguard. Benjamin bobbed up and whipped his wet hair behind his back.

"What a rush!" he yelled. "Come on in, Roscoe. The water's fine!"

"What the hell," Roscoe said.

He twisted the throttle. He hit a big wave and went over the handlebars as Benjamin had. On the second flip he landed flat on his belly. He knocked the wind out of himself and floundered badly. Benjamin had to drag him to the beach, where he spent five minutes retching up seawater. All the while Benjamin stood over him, dripping and laughing madly, and if the little bastard had not just saved his life Roscoe would have ripped his lungs out.

Duncan stood at bat in his Cheyenne Dodgers uniform, squinting at the boy on the mound. Dewey Humboldt's fast ball was fabled in Wyoming little league. Only Benjamin was more dreaded, but since his early retirement, Dewey reigned supreme. Rumor was that Deputy Steve Humboldt, Dewey's father, had clocked his fast ball at eighty-six miles per hour using a Laramie County traffic radar gun. Duncan had never hit off Dewey. He imagined the ball smacking his helmet and knocking him brain dead to the dirt. He near wished it would. Fiona had pushed him into sports when he expressed an interest in art, even though she knew he was not what you would call an athlete. Hands sweating, he watched ten-year-old Dewey pitch. Duncan closed his eyes and swung.

"Strike one!" yelled the umpire.

Duncan wondered what chewing tobacco was like. He heard Dewey chewed and his dad allowed it. That was intimidating in itself. Add an eighty-six mile per hour fast ball and Satan himself was no more feared. Dewey spit brown fluid in the dirt and pitched. Duncan swung.

"Strike two!" the umpire yelled.

Fiona leapt to her feet in the stands, yelling what he hoped was encouragement. Her mouth moved but no words emerged. *That's odd,* Duncan thought. Sean Delaney sat three rows behind her. He smiled and waved. Duncan waved back. Tiffy sat in the next row back. She was naked again. Young Benjamin sat in her lap. Duncan turned back to the mound, vaguely disturbed. He crouched and held the bat high behind his shoulder.

I'll show them, he thought.

Dewey pitched. Duncan swung. He heard a deafening crack and thought, *hey, I did it!* But his feet refused to move and the ground rose up to meet him and the next thing he knew he was sucking dirt. He pulled his head up far enough to see Benjamin run from the stands to lay Dewey flat with a malicious right cross. Officer Humboldt grabbed Benjamin. Benjamin kneed him in the groin and father joined son on the turf. Benjamin raised his fist to the sky and yelled his battle cry. That's when the outfield dog piled him. Duncan tried to rise, but his limbs were as ponderous as his eyelids. The last thing he saw before the world faded into darkness was Fiona assisting Dewey to his feet. She coldly regarded Duncan lying battered on the earth, and all he could think of as he drifted into the grip of a concussion, was that he had let her down again.

Duncan woke at noon and found Benjamin laying naked on the kitchen floor, the wet clothes beside him smelling of seaweed. He covered him with a blanket and threw the clothes in the sink. He took a quart of juice from the refrigerator and drank until his sinuses hurt. He showered and brushed his teeth. He wiped the steam from the mirror and looked at himself. He chanced a smile and his reflection smiled back.

Because I've never wanted a man before.

He dressed and went back into the kitchen. He stepped over Benjamin and started frying bacon and eggs.

"Make mine over easy," Benjamin mumbled.

"Make your own damn eggs," Duncan said.

But he buttered some toast, put it and the bacon and the eggs on a plate and set the plate on the floor next to Benjamin's head. Benjamin rolled his face onto the plate and began eating without benefit of hands or utensils while Duncan cooked another portion for himself.

"We took care of that bitch for you," Benjamin muttered into his eggs.

"You didn't hurt her, did you?"

"Hell no! What do you think I am? Hurt a woman."

"Well," Duncan said, "well, good."

"We hurt her pocketbook."

"I don't want to know about it."

Duncan put a fresh canvas on his easel. He set his plate aside and picked up his pallet. He stared at the canvas for a minute. He put his pallet down and sat on the couch. Benjamin rolled off his plate, got up, and wiped his face with a paper towel. He went into the bathroom and turned on the shower. Duncan stared at the canvas, wondering what it meant that she did not live with Sheila. Maybe Champagne and Cassandra were wrong. He hoped so, as much as he feared they were right. If Pris was a lesbian, fine, he could not change that. A preference was a preference. God could alter it but seldom did. But the way she looked at him, the words she said and how she said them, convinced him that she was at least sixty percent heterosexual. Duncan would have settled for fifty-one percent.

Because I've never wanted a man before you.

He did not know whether to be ecstatic or depressed. She took all hope away, ripped it up, and handed the torn pieces back. He wished he could make sense of the jigsaw puzzle that remained. He got a beer and sat back on the couch. Cat crawled into his lap and rubbed his head against Duncan's chest. Duncan kissed his head.

"It's your fault," he said, knowing it was not true even as he spoke, "if it wasn't for you I never would have met her."

Benjamin came out of the shower. He dressed and brushed his hair. He grabbed a six-pack from the refrigerator and picked up his keys.

"Come on," he said, "let's get out of here."

Duncan stood and put on his hat. "Where are we going?"

"How should I know?"

Duncan followed him out the door. "You're driving though, right?"

"Of course."

"Good," Duncan said, "I'd hate to get lost."

At dusk Benjamin parked on a bluff overlooking the valley. They had spent the day following a map of stars' homes bought from a street corner girl in Beverly Hills. They saw seventeen houses and thirty parked cars but not a single star, though Benjamin claimed he spied a reporter for *Entertainment Tonight*. Now Los Angeles spread below them like a circuit board, with lights like electrons pulsing down the streets and around the hills to the mountains beyond. Thunder heads drifted in over the valley from the north but the night was otherwise warm. They sat on the tailgate and drank beer.

"I've been having strange dreams," Duncan said.

"*You've* been having strange dreams. Last night I dreamed I was back on the reservation standing on a grassy hill with a shaven head and an Igloo brand cooler. Two virgins in wet suits smeared mayonnaise on my scalp. They took bread from the cooler and sprinkled crumbs on the mayonnaise. Crows fell from the clouds and perched on my shoulders, pecking at the bread crumbs. When the crumbs were gone, the crows kept pecking and soon bloodied my head. I ran but the crows flew beside me. I put my arms out and the crows grabbed my sleeves in their claws and lifted me into the sky. We flew across Wyoming until my shirt ripped and fell away and I dropped into a swimming pool. When I came up for air, there was Fiona, naked on a rubber raft beneath a wildly humping Woody. Not wanting to be rude, I submerged and sat on the bottom. I breathed water and watched fish swim by." Benjamin turned to Duncan. "What could it mean?"

"Haven't a clue," Duncan admitted.

"Me neither. Are your dreams anything like that?"

"Not even close."

Lightning struck far off in the valley. A minute later thunder rolled past. Duncan said, "how did your date go?"

"It wasn't a date."

"Struck out, did you?"

"Yes and no. She wanted to go to bed with me. I refused. I told her I wasn't that kind of guy."

"But you are that kind of guy."

"She doesn't have to know that." He took binoculars out of the glove compartment. He sat back in the bed with Duncan and raised the glasses.

"Let me guess," Duncan said, "Angela lives down there."

"Yellow Spanish Colonial with the pool."

"And stalking her is a good idea because . . ."

"I'm not stalking. I'm gathering intelligence. We're going out tonight. I want to see what she's wearing."

"More like you want to see her put it on."

"That too."

They watched the rain cross the valley from the mountains. Lightning sparked, thunder burst. A Mercedes parked beside the Purgatory Truck. A thin woman with expensive hair and a rottweiler got out and stood beside them. Together they watched the sky poke its fiery tongue from its mouth to lick the ground. A bolt struck a mile off. Thunder rattled Duncan's bones. When the rain came, Benjamin put the glasses down and lay back in the bed. He closed his eyes and opened his mouth and let the rain beat down upon him. Lightning struck again.

"It's all so beautiful," the woman with the rottweiler said.

The dog lifted its leg and urinated on the Purgatory Truck.

"Most of it, anyway," Duncan agreed.

Ten

The water was warmer, the sun brighter, and the day nicer than any one of the three had a legitimate right to be. *Still,* Fiona thought as she pulled herself out of the hotel pool, *it certainly is a nice change from Cheyenne.* She slipped her sandals on and dried herself with a thick towel, conscious of the reverent stares of seven males and three females of various ages and economic status who lounged by the pool. She wore a white bikini recently purchased at a boutique on Rodeo Drive, and three days by the pool had transformed her skin from a pasty cream to an earthy tan that accented her luminous blue eyes. Her body was already trim from riding, but hours a day in the pool and in the hotel gym had made her downright tight. She frowned. It would be an ideal vacation if not for her troubles with Duncan.

She donned tan Bermuda shorts and a white cotton tank top over her damp bikini. She relinquished her towel to a towel boy and signed the tag for the banana daiquiri she had sipped by the pool. She thought about Woody as she strolled back to her bungalow. The sex of the last few days was as close to perfect as any she had experienced since Sean Delaney's death. She sighed. Now there was a man with stamina. Woody could not compare in vigor, technique, or inventiveness, but what the man lacked in talent was more than compensated by the recent mood. She reached her room and went inside. She showered then stood naked before the mirror. Her breasts were not big, but that had saved her from sagging, and though she seldom did, she could venture out braless with no fear of embarrassing herself. There was no sag in her backside either, she proudly noted. She put on a floral patterned silk skirt, a lace bra, a light yellow silk blouse, and tan leather sandals. She regarded herself again. She took off the blouse and bra and put the blouse back on. She wondered if Woody would notice. She looked at her watch. One o'clock. She was late for lunch.

As she walked down a garden path to the main building, she speculated on what she would do if Duncan found out about her and Woody. Despite Benjamin's repeated assertions, she had no clue that Duncan actually believed that she had relentlessly humped Woody since Duncan was old enough to know what humping was. He did not care and never had. If fornicating made Fiona happy, then it was all right by him. Duncan liked and respected Woody, though he wished the man would show more spine.

"Mrs. Delaney," the maitre'de said when Fiona entered the restaurant, "Mr. McCune asked that your lunch be sent to the pool."

That was like Woody. *Downright obsequious,* she thought. But as bothersome as that could be, it was also one of his principal attractions. She invariably knew what to expect from Woody and that held its own comfort. It was like having a friend, a lover, and a butler all for a working man's wage. She felt a little guilty. She cared for Woody, and if not for the memory of her departed husband and Duncan's imagined disapproval, she could have considered making their relationship permanent. That was not the right word. *Legal* was more like it.

She spotted Woody at a table by the deep end. What appeared from a distance to be a woman sat beside him with her back to Fiona. The woman wore faded jeans and a t-shirt and had long black hair. Woody wore shorts and sandals and a tank top that said *I Love LA!!!* Woody's arms were tan to mid-biceps, as was his face and neck, but the rest of his skin and the legs protruding from the shorts were an angry red despite repeated applications of sun block. He spoke earnestly to his companion, gesticulating as he talked. Woody's friend appeared to be eating Fiona's lunch. Woody saw her coming. She could not hear, but Fiona imagined the two syllables he uttered were *uh* and *oh.* Woody grabbed the fork from his companion's hand and the knife from her plate and threw them along with his own cutlery into the pool. Fiona wondered why he did that, until Woody's friend stood and turned and then she forgot all about the silverware at the bottom of the pool.

"Hey, Fiona," Benjamin said, "what's new in bitch world?"

Fiona looked about. A radio and a tube of sun screen sat on the table to the left and a towel and a paperback novel sat on the table to the right. Fiona seized the spoon from Woody's cream of mushroom soup and lunged. Woody caught her.

Benjamin laughed. "What were you going to do, spoon my eyes out?"

"For starters," Fiona said. "What are you doing here?"

"Duncan asked me to come." Benjamin sat back down and finished eating Fiona's lunch with his fingers. "He wanted me to deliver a message. He would have come himself but right now he's a trifle upset with you."

That calmed her. She dropped the spoon. Woody kicked it into the pool and let her go.

"Do you want to hear the message?" Benjamin asked.

"Anything my son has to say to me he can say in person."

"Ok." Benjamin wiped his hands with a napkin. "Thanks for lunch."

"Hold on there," Fiona said, "I'm not paying for your food."

"I told him he could eat it," Woody said. "I didn't think you were coming."

"Nevertheless. Either he pays or it's coming out of your salary."

Woody picked up the check and gulped. The lunch Benjamin had consumed represented close to a day's salary.

"I got it, Woody," Benjamin said.

He opened his wallet and took out a check. It was drawn on Fiona's bank in Cheyenne and was made out to Priscilla Nolan for twenty thousand dollars. He tossed it on the table.

"That ought to cover it," he said.

Fiona opened her mouth, closed it. She looked at Woody then at Benjamin. She picked up and crumpled the check. Then she turned and walked quickly away.

"Jesus, Ben," Woody said, "why do you always do that?"

"She deserved it."

"For once I guess she did."

Benjamin ordered two beers. "That was a low thing."

"I tried to talk her out of it. But what could I do? This is between her and Duncan."

Benjamin and Woody took long pulls off the beers, ignoring the chilled glasses the waiter had left behind.

"So what's this big problem you said you were having?"

"It's sensitive," Woody said. "You'd just laugh."

"No, I wouldn't!" Benjamin reconsidered. "Not much anyway."

Woody leaned close and in a soft voice he said, "it's about sex."

"Damn it, Woody, for the last time no! Sure, you're an attractive man, but I'm just not interested in you that way."

Woody sat back. "I knew you'd do this."

"I'm sorry. Go on."

"It's like this. Fiona went to that place to talk to Duncan's girlfriend."

"And to buy her off."

"I guess. Then she wanted to stay. I was embarrassed as hell. I dragged her out when Duncan's girl came on stage. So she's quiet all the way to the hotel. Breathing low and fast. I thought she was mad. But we get to the room I'll be damned if she didn't throw me down on the bed and rip my clothes off!"

"You making this up to get a rise out of me, Woody?"

"Hell no! I wish to God I was. She ruined my favorite shirt. You know the white one with the embroidery around the cuffs and the shoulders? And then she hikes her skirt up, rips off her panties and rides me like a prize Brahma bull. And I'm thinking, *okay, this is nice.* But damn if she didn't want to do it again half an hour later. I did the best I could because, you know, it was pretty exciting. She wanted to go a third time and it was all I could do to pretend I was asleep."

"Doesn't sound like much of a problem."

"You wouldn't think so. But the next day she drags me to another bawdy house and the same thing happens. And she wants to go again tonight! I'm all for trying out different things. Hell, I didn't even object the time she dressed up like Cleopatra and made me dress like Julius Caesar - don't you tell Duncan - but I'm not a young man. I don't know how much more I can take." Woody fanned his face with his hat. "What the hell should I do?"

Benjamin stood. For once he felt a real empathy with Woody. He threw ten dollars on the table for the beers and picked up his hat.

"Just do your best, Woody," he said. "That's all anyone can do. And if she makes you pay for lunch, let me know. I'll pay you back."

For once, and despite her swelling rage, Fiona regretted her attempted attack on Benjamin. Not that she ever *thought* about attacking, it was all reflex. But as she stared at the crumpled check in her hand, she felt like an ass. Woody came in and sat beside her.

"I should have listened to you," she said. "I shouldn't have tried to buy that woman off. It was the wrong strategy all together. I see that now."

"I don't like to say it, but I said as much."

"I know you did." Fiona picked up the phone and dialed. While the phone rang, she asked, "what were you two talking about anyway?"

Before Woody could respond her call was answered and she said, "Hello, William, Fiona here. I know. It's terrible. I'm in Los Angeles right now trying to set it right. Uh huh. That's why I'm calling. Yes, I'll wait."

"We were just talking," Woody said.

"What?" Fiona had already forgotten her question. She held up a hand for silence. "Yes, it's Fiona. I've encountered a small problem. Pack your bags and come on out. I'll make the arrangements." She looked at Woody and put a hand over the phone. "You get ready," she said. He anticipated her words and he shuddered as she spoke. "We're going out tonight. I found another club in the sports section of the Times."

Duncan did not feel like painting that evening.

He turned off the lights and sat with Cat in his window, the night breeze cool against his face. He scratched Cat's ears and watched men go in and out of the Hollywood. He sipped a beer and observed traffic flow by beneath him. Exhaust mingled with the smell of his paints as a bus roared by. Misty parked her BMW beneath his window and got out. She took her lingerie bag out of the back seat and slung it across her shoulder.

"Hi, Duncan."

"Hey, Misty."

"Want to invite me in for a beer later? I get off at two. You could paint me. You haven't painted me yet."

"I don't feel much like painting," he said.

Misty looked like she might cry. "Why don't you like me?"

"I like you fine. Why do you say that?"

"Champagne and Cassandra talk about you painting them all the time. I feel left out. They act like they're better than me."

"There's lots of girls I haven't painted." Duncan wished the bottle he held was whiskey instead of beer. "I'll paint you, Misty. Just not tonight."

"Great." She started to go, but then stopped and turned back. "I could still come up after I get off. We could just, you know, talk."

Misty was taller than Pris, with hair as blond, bigger breasts, and with legs that could crush the breath from his lungs. But the blond was out of a bottle and the breasts were enhanced and if they discussed who Duncan painted they would no doubt confer on with whom he slept. *And I must stay pure for Pris,* he thought. He laughed bitterly.

"Does that mean yes?"

"It means not tonight. I want to be alone tonight."

Misty looked down. "The girls wonder why you don't hit on them."

"I'm just being professional."

"Bull." Misty looked up. "When are you going to give up? She doesn't even like men. You could have any other girl at the Hollywood." Misty not so subconsciously emphasized the *any.* "Why do you waste your time?"

"I don't know what you're talking about."

"You're a lousy liar."

Duncan's face burned. He looked down the neck of his beer bottle.

"Ok." Misty laughed. "I'll see you later. When you paint me."

She crossed the street and went inside. *Maybe she wouldn't tell,* Duncan thought, *and I could go for a tune-up.* He leaned back against the sill and closed his eyes. *God, why do you torment me with strippers?* Two motorcycles parked across the street. Skinny men with long hair and tattoos dismounted and went into the Hollywood.

"I got to get out of here," Duncan said to no one.

He put his hat on and went downstairs. He went for a long walk nowhere. When he returned the Cadillac was still absent. He went into the mini-mart.

"Good evening, Duncan my friend. Hey you!" Assan yelled to a pimply child of fifteen who stood by the magazine rack. The boy's greasy brown hair was stuffed into a backwards baseball cap. "Yes, you! If you want to read it, buy it first! I am not a library."

The kid dropped the magazine on the floor and brushed past Duncan.

"Fuck you, towel-head," he said as he left.

Duncan put the magazine back. "Don't sweat it, Assan. He's just a kid."

"I would like to shoot him with my twelve gauge police model semiautomatic Benelli shotgun. It has a pistol grip." Assan reached under the counter. "Would you like to see it?"

"No," Duncan said. "You just keep your gun concealed."

"As you wish. But it is quite an equalizer. I am very proud of it."

Duncan put a quart of nonfat milk and a pint of butter caramel crunch ice cream in his basket. He took a frozen chicken enchilada dinner out of the freezer and scrutinized the directions. He put it and another in his basket. He grabbed a six-pack and brought it all up to the counter.

"Ah yes," Assan said, "health food."

Duncan paid and left. He stopped at his stairs, put the bag down and reached into his pockets for a stick of gum. Cat meowed from above. He looked up and smiled. Someone hit him hard in the back. Duncan cried out as his knees buckled. He tried to catch himself, but his hands were still in his pockets. His face hit the wall and then the sidewalk. Cat hissed from above. He was pulled by his hair to his knees. A fist slammed his mouth. His lip split and he tasted blood. He was hit hard in the kidney and he fell again. His assailant kicked his ribs and kicked him again. Duncan moaned and tried to get up. Cat screamed in rage and the blows stopped.

"Get it off me!" a high voice yelled.

Duncan blacked out. He woke to the sound of engines. He got to his knees. Two motorcycles pulled out of the lot beside his building and drove west down Sunset. He heard a woman's fading laughter. He touched his face and looked at the blood on his hand. He sagged to the ground and Cat nudged his cheek. Cat's claws were wet and red.

"I hope that's not your blood, buddy," Duncan said.

He passed out again.

Hours later, as Misty walked to her car, she saw Duncan slumped against the stairs, Cat pacing before him like a sentry. She ran across the street. Cat bared his teeth and hissed when she neared.

"Knock it off, Cat." She sat Duncan up and saw his face. "Oh, Jesus!"

One eye was swollen above the brow and his lip was badly split. Dried blood painted his face a dark red that looked black in the darkness.

"Hi," he said.

"What happened?"

"Hell if I know." Duncan tried to get up. "Think you could help me get inside?"

She pulled him up and half-carried him up the stairs. She put him on the couch and went back to gather his groceries. But the beer was gone and the ice cream melted and the frozen dinners looked unhealthy to her vegetarian eye so she just came back up. Duncan was staring at his face in the bathroom mirror when she returned.

"Was my hat down there?"

"I didn't see it."

"Damn."

"Forget about your stupid hat. You need a doctor."

"I'm okay."

She dabbed the blood off Duncan's face with a wet cloth. "That explains you lying unconscious in the gutter."

"It wasn't the gutter. It was the sidewalk."

"That makes a big difference, doesn't it?" Duncan winced as she wiped the blood from his lip. "Sorry."

"I wasn't unconscious. I was resting."

She rinsed the cloth. The water in the sink colored pink. She threw the cloth into the laundry basket.

"It's not as bad as it looked."

"I need a beer," Duncan said.

Misty opened the refrigerator. One bottle lay on a shelf above a dry head of lettuce. There were three eggs in the door. A mayonnaise jar sat beside a loaf of bread. She brought the beer to Duncan. He touched the bottle to his torn lip and drank half. He shut his eyes against the pain. He drank the other half and dropped the bottle in the trash.

"I'd like another," he said.

"That was your last."

Duncan limped to the closet, took out his coat, and struggled to put it on.

"What are you doing?"

"Going to the store."

"Oh, god." She picked up her purse. "I'll get your damn beer." She stopped at the door. "Stupid men. Why can't you be more like women?"

"Well, for one thing," Duncan said, "the penis would get in the way."

"Ha, ha." She slammed the door as she left.

Duncan looked in the mirror again. Blood painted crimson streaks in his hair. His eye was a splendid purple. His lip was black against the white of his chin.

"God, but you're colorful," he said to his reflection.

He set up his easel by the mirror and placed a canvas upon it. He set his paints and brushes on the sink. He sat on the toilet and urinated. When he got up the water in the bowl was brown. He drained the sink, flushed the toilet, and closed the lid. Cat curled up on the toilet seat. Duncan picked him up and kissed him. Cat purred and closed his eyes.

"Thanks, buddy. Looks like I owe you again."

Duncan set him back on the toilet seat and stared in the mirror. He began to paint. Misty found him that way when she returned with the beer. She gave him a bottle.

"You're nuts," she said.

Only the light from the bathroom illuminated the studio. She turned on the stereo and danced alone in the dark, watching Duncan work as she swayed. The compact disc stopped and she put on another. She took off her blouse and her jeans. Duncan did not notice. She took off her bra and panties and lay naked on the couch. Duncan kept painting. She sighed, opened her work bag, took out a white tube top and a white miniskirt, put them on, and pulled on black vinyl boots. She brushed her hair and looked at her face in her compact. She got two beers and joined him. She dropped his empty bottle in the trash. She picked up Cat and sat on the toilet. He rubbed his head against her ribs. Duncan gulped his beer and stared at her.

He looked at her legs, at her hips, at her bare stomach, at her breasts, and finally at her face and eyes and hair. Misty blushed and started to get up.

"Don't move."

"You make me feel naked looking at me like that," Misty said. "I know, that's a crazy thing for a stripper to say."

"You wanted me to paint you, didn't you?"

With a few strokes Duncan began painting her into the picture. Misty was amazed at how quickly he worked.

"Sure," she said, "but I wanted you to paint me alone."

"This is better. You'll be in my first ever self-portrait."

"How come you never painted yourself?"

"I've never been worth painting."

Misty looked at the canvas. The swollen eye, the bloody hair, and the split lip were all there, painted in deft, bloody strokes, lacking only detail to bring the portrait to life. And there she was, growing rapidly in black and white and yellow, coming to life too. He was right. The other girls could not match this. She sipped her beer and tried to look pretty for his brush. And all the time he painted, Cat lay sleeping in her lap, his purrs sounding to her ears like the thunder of a distant Harley.

Duncan finished at dawn. Misty put Cat down and stood behind him. It was all there, Duncan and the easel, the brush in his hand poised near the canvas while his eyes, one swollen red and the other clear blue, stared out of the mirror into nothing. He looked terrible, and yet, the way he looked out of the canvas was beautiful. And there Misty sat on the toilet, her makeup and clothes making her look hard and her eyes on Duncan making her look soft. She had never felt so naked on stage as she did looking at herself in Duncan's painting. She thought of her eighth grade graduation picture. Her hair was brown then, like her eyes, but the innocence she now saw in the canvas had vanished from her smile long before that photograph was taken, and now she wanted it back.

"What's wrong?" Duncan asked when she began to cry. "I thought you liked it."

"I've never liked anything so much."

"Why are you crying then?"

"You know, for someone who can see so clear to paint a picture like that you sure are blind."

"I'm not sure what you want me to say."

"Don't say anything."

She took his hand and led him to the couch. She pulled her boots off, took off her skirt and her top. She pulled his shirt over his head.

"Misty," Duncan said, "I can't."

She took his shoes off, undid his belt, then pulled off his pants. She pulled him down onto the couch and pulled the sleeping bag over them.

"I just want you to hold me. All right? Just hold me."

He put his arm around her. She pressed her head into his shoulder. He smelled roses in her hair and felt her breasts against his ribs. He found himself with an erection. He fought it, but he could feel Misty's leg across his hip, her pubic hair tickling his groin. He was flustered and he tried to move away. Misty would not release him.

"We don't have to make love if you don't want to," she whispered.

"I want to. I just can't."

"Poor Duncan," Misty said. "You're in love with someone who can't love you back. And she'll never know how lucky she is."

Lucky? Duncan did not know about that. He had not been anything special in Cheyenne. He really was not even a cowboy. Sure, he could ride and do odd jobs about the ranch, but he had never roped a steer and never fired a gun and did not care to, and the girls back home liked their steaks tender and their men tough, and Duncan cried at the rodeo when he was ten when a wrangler's rope jerked a calf's head into an unlikely position. Fiona, shamed by Duncan's tears, had dragged him by the ear from the grandstand to the general amusement of those around them. And she brought him to a psychiatrist when he told her he wanted to be an artist.

His chest ached, not so much from the beating, but from the desolation within. He pondered his emptiness until Misty's breathing softened and slowed. He lay his face near her hair and breathed deeply, her hair's rosy smell mixed with her skin's sweet and sour odor.

Mother, he thought, *if you could see your pansy son now.*

Duncan held Misty, his breathing synchronous with the pressure of her breast on his side, and holding her, fell asleep, and sleeping, dreamed of a mountain stream in Canada where he returned with his father in the penultimate month of Scan Delaney's life.

Eleven

"Maybe you ought to slow down," Danny Bradshaw said.

"Maybe you ought to stop being such a weenie."

Tiffy changed lanes and punched the gas. The new red Mustang Cobra convertible shot around a Lincoln driven by a woman with steel wool hair and telescopic glasses. Tiffy laughed and waved when the old woman honked and then the Lincoln was a half mile behind and mattered not at all. Danny had first rented a four-door Lumina, but when he pulled to the curb at the airport and popped the trunk, Tiffy refused to put her bags into the car much less her body. Danny had to visit five more rental counters before he finally found a vehicle satisfactory to Tiffy.

"After all," she had said, "we *are* in Los Angeles."

She swept through four lanes of freeway to the Sunset Boulevard exit. Danny gripped the door handle. The sign on the ramp said twenty-five miles per hour. He did not know their exact velocity, but he knew it was significantly greater. Attendants ran to the car when they pulled up to the Beverly Hills Hotel. A valet opened Danny's door and he fell out. He had forgotten to let go of the door. He lay panting on the driveway until the valet pried his white fingers from the handle. He watched Tiffy enter the lobby, marveling at the perspective his placement against the planet afforded of her legs and firm buttocks. It was an indication of Danny's pure love that, though he would rather she turn to him for comfort than to Duncan, ultimately he only sought her happiness, and if getting Duncan back accomplished that, he would be sad but satisfied. And forty years hence, when Tiffy cried over Duncan's casket like Fiona had over Sean's, Danny planned to be there with a handkerchief and a shoulder for her tears. Still picturing a gray haired yet magnificently built Tiffy leaning on his arm, he allowed the valets to help him to his feet and dust him off. He followed a bell hop pulling a cart with Tiffy's four suitcases and his duffel bag. Tiffy already had her key when he reached the front desk.

"I'm in bungalow 35," she said.

"What room am I in?"

"How would I know? Fiona made my reservations. I assumed you made your own."

Danny turned to the girl behind the desk. "I'd like a room."

"I'm sorry, we're booked up. May I suggest another hotel?"

"Well," Danny said, "I guess I'll stay in your room, Tiffy."

Tiffy frowned. "I don't think Fiona would understand my sharing the room she's paid for with a man who is not her son."

"Oh." That did sound bad. "Ok."

In the end Danny found a room at a motel just over Coldwater Canyon in Studio City, and it was not until Danny reached the valet stand that he realized Tiffy had the receipt for his rental. He took a taxi over the hill, checked into his motel, and spent the next four hours in his room waiting for Tiffy to return any one of his fifteen phone calls.

"Fiona," Tiffy said, "just look at you!"

Fiona spun in delight. "You like?"

Woody sat back in a chair across from the television. He put down the remote and smiled. Fiona did look tasty, better than ever, and he was proud to have her on his arm, so to speak. She rarely allowed him to hold her arm in public, and in private it was not usually her arm she was on.

"This California sun has done you a world of good."

A shadow established residence for voting purposes in Fiona's eyes. "I'd feel better if it wasn't for Duncan. He seems to blame you for the break up."

"All I did was register my disapproval with an unwise life choice."

"Duncan said you hit him," Woody said.

"You stay out of this," Fiona said.

"Cold-cocked him from what Benjamin said."

Tiffy rolled her eyes. "As if you'd believe that reprobate over me."

"Nevertheless," Fiona said, "he blames you. And he has found solace in the devil's own."

"You mean that stripper you told me about. Well, don't worry about her. I am not above competing for my man."

"You haven't seen her," Woody said.

Both turned on him. "What the hell does that mean?" they asked.

Woody shrugged. "I was just saying . . ."

"Go on," said Fiona.

"Nothing. I wasn't saying nothing." He went into the bedroom.

"I didn't think so." Fiona turned back to Tiffy. "You should get right over there before that woman sinks her talons any deeper into him. I'm afraid he'll do something stupid."

"Like what? Sleep with her?"

"Tiffy!"

"Oh, hell, Fiona. Let him get it out of his system. It'll make him appreciate me more."

"I'm not sure I want to discuss this with you."

"Then let's not. Besides. First I need to lay by the pool a few days and get a tan like yours. And I want to check out the competition."

"We can do that right now." Fiona seemed strangely animated at the prospect. "Woody and I will take you to where she works."

"Oh, lord," Woody groaned from the bedroom.

"What is wrong with that man?" Fiona asked. A knock on the door diverted her. "Who could that be?"

"Evening Mrs. Delaney," Danny said when Tiffy opened the door.

"Now Fiona," Tiffy said, "there's no need for you to go to a place like that. That's why I brought Danny. He's always made Duncan jealous."

"God knows why. He's no competition for my boy."

"I'm standing here," Danny said. "I can hear you."

"I don't know why you tolerate him sniffing after you like he was a hound dog and you were a bitch in heat."

"Jesus, Mrs. Delaney! I'm standing right here."

"No offense," Fiona said. "I'm sure you're a fine young man in your own right. But you're no Duncan."

"Well, from what I've seen and heard," Danny said, showing a small segment of spine, "I wouldn't want to be."

Tiffy said, "Danny, you watch your mouth and wait outside."

Danny left in a sulk. Tiffy closed the door.

"Don't worry, Fiona. He's harmless."

"I know that. I just don't know why you have to complicate things."

Tiffy hugged Fiona. "Don't worry. I know how to handle your boy."

Fiona held her at arm's length and looked into her enormous brown eyes. She was exquisite in her rural way. But Woody was right. That other woman was just as beautiful. Probably more so. Fiona smiled sadly.

"I used to think I could handle him too," she said.

Duncan woke late that afternoon. Misty had stocked his refrigerator with fruit and yogurt, twelve-grain bread and cheese, apple juice, lettuce, broccoli, and sprouts. He drank a jar of juice. It was cold and sweet and tasted as good as the beer he had intended to have. He made a salad for breakfast. He spent the day reading about the aliens among us in a *National Enquirer* and staring at his painting of Edward.

"Holy shit," Benjamin said when he returned, "what happened to you?"

"Got the crap beat out of me."

"I can see that. It was that Rascowitz bitch, wasn't it?"

"Maybe. I don't know."

"What do you want to do about it?"

"Nothing until I'm sure she did it. Maybe you could just hang around for a while until I feel a little better."

"Well," Benjamin looked uncomfortable, "thing is, Angela invited me to her condo in Santa Barbara for a few days."

"Well, go on. I'll just do crossword puzzles and feel sorry for myself."

Misty came to see him the next day. She held his chin and moved his head from side to side. His lip was scabbed but the swelling had ebbed in both his lip and in his wonderfully purple eye.

"You should've had your lip stitched. You'll have a nice scar."

"Thanks for the groceries."

"I thought you might not want to go out." She faltered at the door. "Do you want me to come up later?"

"No thanks. I just want to be alone for a while."

Duncan sat on the couch with Cat after she left. He listened to the radio and stared out his window at the darkening sky. At nine he went to the mini-mart to buy cat food. As he came out, he saw the Cadillac parked in front of the Hollywood. He sighed and climbed the stairs. He was surprised to find Pris waiting in the studio. She wore a short black dress, black silk stockings, black cowboy boots, and a black imitation cowboy hat with a wide, flat brim. She looked like a fashion conscious cowgirl in mourning. She came to him and touched his lip. Duncan winced.

"Still a bit tender," he said.

He filled a bowl with cat food and another with water and put both on the floor. He sat on the linoleum and leaned against a cabinet and watched Cat eat. Pris sat on the floor beside him and took his hand.

"Misty told me what happened."

Duncan panicked. "What did she say?"

"Only that someone had beaten you up. It was Sheila, wasn't it?"

"Beats me. I was hit from behind. All I heard were motorcycles. That and a woman laughing."

Pris stood. "I'll kill her."

Duncan grabbed her. "Don't do anything on account of me."

She softened slowly and tenderly kissed his battered lips.

Duncan smiled. "Ow," he said.

"Did I hurt you?"

"It was the smile that done it."

"Be careful, ok? Sheila doesn't understand you. Or me for that matter."

"I don't understand you either."

She stroked his cheek and smiled. "I'm late for work."

"Angela arranged for my paintings to be in a gallery opening next Sunday. Would you come with me?"

"What the hell," she said, "I'll pick you up at seven."

From his window he watched her wait at the curb for traffic to clear. He smiled so hard his lip cracked and bled. Her hat fell off unnoticed when she ran across the street. She went inside. He went downstairs and picked up her hat. He heard motorcycles. He turned and looked and dropped her hat on his steps. Sheila, Samantha, and two friends had parked in front of the Hollywood. They wore jeans and t-shirts and leather boots. Sheila wore a black leather vest crossed with chains. All had short hair, and if it was not for the curves of their breasts and the shape of their hips they could have been men. But that was not what Duncan stared at.

Instead of a helmet, Sheila wore his hat. She smiled when she saw him coming. Her friends stood behind her and watched him come. Duncan stopped a yard away.

"That's my hat," he said.

"I don't see your name on it."

"Nonetheless," Duncan said, "it's mine."

"I found it in the street." She turned her back and started toward the Hollywood. "Finders keepers."

"Aw, look," said Samantha, "I think he's going to cry."

"Damn it! I want my hat back!"

Sheila turned. Samantha circled behind him. Sheila smiled and wrapped a chain around her fist.

"Why don't you come get it?"

"All right," he said, "I will."

He heard more motorcycles behind him. *I am a dead man,* he thought. Sheila's smirk changed to a frown. When he looked behind, he saw it was not more lesbians come to participate in a sacrifice of male flesh. Wilson, Marco, and Peewee sat on the newly arrived Harleys, looking like death minus the scythes but with the requisite scars and tattoos, calm and dangerous and not at all to be trifled with. Duncan thought them beautiful. Samantha stepped quietly aside.

Wilson glanced at Sheila and then to Duncan. "Anything wrong?"

"Not a thing," Duncan said.

He took the Stetson from Sheila's head, brushed it off, and put it on. By the fury in her eyes Duncan believed she was contemplating taking on the Guardians. But then she sagged and she and her friends got on their motorcycles and rode away.

"Nice bikes," Peewee said, "friends of yours?"

"More like acquaintances," Duncan replied.

The Guardians gazed in wonder at the painting on Duncan's easel.

"Jesus," Peewee said. "Aren't we beautiful?"

"How much is that worth?" asked Wilson.

"Whatever you can get for it." Duncan took the canvas off the easel and gave it to him. "It's yours."

"Why?" Wilson asked.

"Why not?"

Duncan took off his hat and with a permanent marker he wrote *Delaney* in big black letters on the white satin liner.

"All right!" Peewee said. "Roscoe said the painting of him sold for two thousand. I bet we get three for this one."

"We're not selling it." Wilson took a plastic bag full of a fine white powder from his pocket and gave it to Duncan.

"What's this?"

"Something in return."

After the Guardians left, Duncan sat on the couch holding the baggie. He heard a siren in the distance grow stronger. He stood in the bathroom until the siren faded past his window. Then he flushed a small fortune in what he could not have known was China White Heroin down the toilet.

While Duncan watched white powder swirl down a porcelain portal, Tiffy and Danny were sitting in the Hollywood at a table near the bar. Tiffy had inadvertently selected amateur night for her reconnaissance, and the bar was packed. A five hundred dollar prize awaited the alleged nonprofessional judged best at removing her clothing to the music of her choice. Tiffy wore a shawl and dark glasses. She had seen Jackie O dressed like this in a photo in which Jackie was surrounded by four burly body guards. Tiffy did not have bodyguards but she had Danny which, she supposed, was better than nothing. She could get the body guards later, when she was . . .

When she was what?

"Go get me a beer," she said.

Danny went to the bar. Tiffy took off her sunglasses. The place was filled with an eclectic assortment of suits and jeans and various females with large hair and painted skin who could best be described as tramps, harlots, and possibly sluts. Tiffy experienced a strange sense of sisterhood. She shook her head and the feeling left. Danny set two beers on the table and sat. Tiffy drank half her bottle.

"Slow down!"

"Do you believe someone would pay any of these women five hundred dollars for stripping?"

"They don't look so bad."

"Oh come on!" Tiffy pointed at a tall red haired girl in a tight red velvet dress. "Take her. Nose job, liposuction, and fake tits. And there. Bleached hair, chin implant, and fake tits."

"I'll give you the tits," Danny said. "But how could you know the rest?"

"I did graduate third in my cosmetology class, didn't I? And that one. Thirty-five if she's a day. Lipo, chemical peel, nose job, bleached hair, and fake tits." Tiffy snorted. "Not a genuine beauty in the lot."

"Not like you." Danny blushed. "Your beauty is natural."

"How sweet!" Tiffy pinched his cheek. "But how would you know that?"

"Hell, I've watched you since I was five. Don't you think I'd know?"

"Hush now." The lights dimmed. Music began. "They're starting."

Over three songs Champagne went from a cheerleader's outfit with pom poms and bobby socks to a pair of white panties. The crowd, including Danny, appreciated her efforts. She spent two minutes picking up the currency littering the stage.

"I could do that," Tiffy muttered.

Misty was next. She wore a nurse's uniform and was down to a G-string and support hose in three songs, including a heartfelt segment involving a stethoscope staged to *Stairway to Heaven*. She spent several minutes retrieving several denominations of paper money from the stage.

"What's so special about her?" Tiffy asked.

"Hold on, Tiffy. Give the girl her due. You should appreciate someone who's good at their job."

"Maybe you ought to appreciate them a little less and me a little more."

Danny stopped clapping. "Sorry."

The room darkened and the crowd hushed. When the lights came back, Pris sat backwards on a chair facing the audience, her arms folded over the seat and her head in her arms. She wore a simple skirt and blouse, silk stockings and shoes with stiletto heels. She slowly raised her head as *Only Women Bleed* began to play. Tiffy felt an electric jolt.

"It's her!" she hissed.

The woman on stage exuded an intoxicating mixture of innocence and sexuality. Her eyes were sad and angry and challenging. Tiffy had never before been intimidated by another woman's beauty, but there it was. This had to be her. Pris stood as if grabbed and pulled to her feet. She fell backwards against the pole and leaned there breathing heavily and looking angrily at nothing before her. She ripped her shirt open. A button flew across the audience and hit Danny in the face.

"Hey," he said, rubbing his eye, "that hurt!"

"Quiet!" Tiffy commanded.

Pris moved about the stage with the music, as if fleeing an unseen assailant. She kicked out once and her right shoe flew into the audience.

"Ow!" someone said.

"Shhh!" several voices responded.

She kicked again. Her left shoe knocked a pitcher of beer unnoticed into a bald man's lap. She ripped her shirt off and threw it into the crowd. She unhooked her dress as she writhed in mock combat and the dress floated off the stage. She fell to the floor, unbuttoning her bra and throwing her arms to her sides as though pinned. She kicked and fought, naked except for her plain cotton panties. She started to pull those down. Men and women both held their collective breath. She flipped onto her hands and knees, her breasts moving back and forth, up and down. She rolled violently over and stood. She smashed the chair against the pole. She picked up a broken leg and stabbed the splintered end repeatedly into the stage. The men in the room clasped their hands over their hearts. The music stopped.

"Holy Jesus," Danny said.

"Amen," Tiffy whispered.

Pris slowly stood and looked out over the audience.

"I'd like my clothes back, please," she said, "line forms to the right."

A man opened his wallet and stuffed the shoe he held with twenties. The bald man did the same with the other shoe and a third wrapped a wad of tens in her shirt. They lined up along the stage with men holding nothing but money. Danny wrapped the button in a fifty-dollar bill and got in line behind a man holding a bra he had brought himself and stuffed with singles. Pris smiled at the bald man. He was the only one so graced. He sat down with a face so smug that the heavy metal pretenders in the back resolved to later beat him senseless. Pris clutched her clothes and went backstage. Danny returned and set two beers on the table. Tiffy stood.

"Where you going?"

"To enter that contest."

"I won't allow it!"

Tiffy took Danny's face in her hand and squeezed so hard his cheeks met between his teeth and painful tears came to his eyes.

"Don't ever tell me what I can or can't do."

"Ho kah," he mumbled. *"Har ee."*

Tiffy released him. He rubbed his jaw. She drank deep from her beer.

"All right," she said, "wish me luck."

"Good luck." Danny rubbed his cheek as she elbowed her way to the bar. He regarded the other contestants with pity. *Though you're not the one who needs it,* he thought.

"You drive," Tiffy said.

She got in the Cobra beside Danny. He turned over the engine and shifted into first. He stalled the engine three times.

"It's a powerful engine. You have to give it more gas."

Danny lurched into traffic. He drove like a zombie, unnerved and sickly fascinated by what he had beheld. Tiffy took a wad of money from her bra and counted. Danny was afraid and very much her slave.

"You've watched me ever since kindergarten but I bet you never saw anything like that."

"No," Danny said, "can't say I have."

Tiffy had taken the stage seventh out of ten contestants, and after she finished, the remaining three refused to go on. The first six were good, but when introduced for judgement, the audience booed until Tiffy took the stage to unanimous applause. Danny was unaware of her decisive victory until he came out of the bathroom where he was cleaning up after an unfortunate accident that had dampened his lap.

"Spilled my beer," he had told her.

"With the five hundred dollar prize I made nine seventy three in cash."
She stuffed the money into her bra. "I would have more only Duncan's
bitch cleaned out a couple of them."

"Too bad you couldn't take checks," Danny said.

"Who says I didn't? That's another three hundred or so. I'm not set up
for credit cards. Not yet, at least."

"I'll never forget tonight."

"Well, don't get too attached to the memory. A girl told me about
another contest at a club in the valley tomorrow night."

"You're going to do that again?"

"Why not? Easiest money I ever made."

"What happens if Mrs. Delaney finds out?"

Tiffy turned to him, her eyes hot. "The only way she could find out is
if you tell her, and if that happens, you'll never see me again, naked or
otherwise. Understand?"

"Yes, ma'am."

"All I'm doing is making some pocket change. So I don't want to hear
any more objections out of you."

"Yes, ma'am."

"Good." They pulled up to the valet at the hotel. They got out and Tiffy
took the claim check. "Now you get yourself a taxi and go on home."

Danny looked down and kicked gravel. "Well, I was hoping . . ."

"Danny, you've had enough fun for one night. Now go on home and
change your pants. And be back here tomorrow night at eight."

The valet called for a taxi. When it came, Danny got in and looked
longingly at her. A Hispanic valet who looked so much like Valentino that
the hotel matrons called him Rudolph stood beside her and watched the
taxi coast down the driveway.

"He wants you, no?"

"He wants me, yes."

Tiffy looked him over. She had never heard of Valentino but she was a
good judge of horseflesh. And the experience on stage had her hornier than
the time she gave the captain of the high school basketball team a special
congratulations after they won the state championship her junior year.

"What time do you get off?" she asked.

"Eleven thirty."

"Good." Tiffy wrote her room number on a slip of paper. "Be at my
room at eleven forty five. I plan on getting off myself by twelve."

Twelve

The next morning Duncan received a letter from Fiona's bank. It bore a yellow sticker with his new address and had been forwarded from Cheyenne. He read it slowly, then read the letter again. He picked up the phone and dialed the number listed beneath the bank's address.

"Mr. Ambrose, please," he said to the woman who answered.

Stuart Ambrose was his mother's banker and Sean's old friend, a big, white-haired man who played Santa Claus in the parade every Christmas until his wife of thirty years died a half decade before. After that, the stuffing escaped from his jolly belly, and his laugh resounded no more.

"Duncan! Where are you boy? Fiona's been worried as hell."

"I'm in Los Angeles, sir."

"Hell, son, we knew that. What are you doing there?"

"Well, right now I'm trying to find out about a letter I got today."

"A letter?" Ambrose was suddenly wary.

"A letter from you. The way I read this letter is that my father left me a trust fund worth fifty thousand dollars when he died. That sound right?"

"I don't have the figures handy."

"The way I read this letter, that same trust fund is now worth twenty-two thousand six hundred and ninety dollars." Duncan waited for a response. When none came he said, "you did write this letter didn't you?"

"Is my name on it?"

"Yes sir."

"Then I suppose I did." Ambrose sounded bitter.

"And the way I read this letter," Duncan went on, "this money should have been made available to me when I was eighteen."

"Fiona thought you couldn't manage the investing of it."

"Looks like she didn't do so well herself," Duncan said.

"She made a few bad choices. But she tried her best."

"That's a comfort. Now if you don't mind I'll just take my money out of your bank while there's still money left to get."

"I don't think I like your tone, son."

"And I don't like the fact that I'm out thirty thousand dollars."

"Maybe you should talk to your mother about this."

"You leave her out of this. Mr. Ambrose, I'll tell you what. She's done enough damage. You talk to her about this and I talk to my lawyer."

"You don't have a lawyer."

"No, but they're not hard to find." Ambrose sighed over the miles. "Mr. Ambrose," Duncan said, "I always liked you. I know my dad did too. But if you don't make my money available immediately there will be trouble."

"All right." Ambrose sounded defeated. "But your mother won't like it. She's my fourth biggest account." He gave Duncan the address of a branch in Los Angeles. "I'll let them know you're coming."

Duncan hung up. He put on his old leather jacket, pocketed the letter, put on his hat, and walked out the door. He waited at a bus stop on the boulevard for half an hour before a pick up truck with Colorado plates stopped to ask for directions. An ancient cowboy sat behind the wheel. The smoke from a cigarette hanging from the spit on his lip drifted between his squinting eyes. A gray-haired woman sat beside him. They both started to smile but changed their minds when they saw the damage done to his face.

"Good lord," the old cowboy said, "what happened to you?"

"I got beaten up by bikers."

"Hell's Angels?" the woman asked.

"Lesbians."

They both laughed and smiled and looked friendly as hell.

"Well, heck," said the cowboy. "Can you tell us how to get to the Hollywood Wax Museum?"

"That's near where I'm going." Duncan gave them directions.

"Thank you, son. Would you like a ride?"

Duncan got in the back of the truck with a mongrel dog. He played with the dog until the cowboy let him off at the bank. He went inside and walked to a desk near the back of the lobby. A stout, middle-aged woman with big blond hair looked up. He doffed his hat and introduced himself.

"Oh yes, Mr. Delaney," she said. "Mr. Ambrose called. Everything is arranged." She smiled brightly. "Cash or check?"

Duncan returned her smile. "A check would be just fine."

When Duncan came out of the bank the first thing he noticed was a Saturn dealership across the street. He sat at the bus stop in front of the bank and looked at the cars gleaming behind the showroom window. Unlike Benjamin, he did not care about cars. Public transportation was all right by him. But he remembered what Pris said: *You don't even have a car.* He let a bus go by and then another. He regarded the bank check.

I've done more walking recently than I've done in the three years previous, he thought as he stood and crossed the street. *And it won't hurt to look.*

Benjamin was in such a good mood on the way back from Santa Barbara that he decided to pay Sheila Rascowitz another visit. The notion that she could beat up his best friend and get away with it plagued his subconscious, and after he dropped Angela off at her house, the notion tap danced past the anterior of his brain and across his frontal lobe.

They had arrived in Santa Barbara early Wednesday afternoon, stopping first at a hotel near the beach where Benjamin drank a strawberry daiquiri at Angela's request and she drank tequila at his, and both ate spicy chicken wings and crab puffs. Benjamin had never had a crab puff before, and was put off by the name, but when the plate was empty he ordered another. When he dropped his napkin on the floor Angela sucked the chicken marinade off his fingers with an encouraging enthusiasm. Afterwards they walked on the beach and shopped on State Street and had a cocktail at a restaurant known locally for the vigor of its drinks. They dined at a Cajun restaurant and again Angela's appetite for things spicy amazed him. They ended up on the beach across from her condo. She threw him onto the wet sand beneath a fingernail moon and so skillfully performed an act of oral love upon him that when it was over he swore his head had shrunk three hat sizes. They spent the next day making love in her bedroom, stopping only to order pizza and beer. He was so cleaned out that if she wanted to cut off his hair at the expense of his strength he could not have stopped her.

He slowly drove by Sheila's house. A replacement Harley was parked in front. He stopped down the block and took a rope from behind the seat and tied one end to his trailer hitch. The other end he made into a noose. He took the license plates off the truck and placed them on the seat. Long ago he had fastened them with Velcro to expedite this task. He got into the Purgatory Truck and held the rope out his window.

He missed on the first pass. He did not have the range and he underestimated the effect of velocity and wind drag on a thrown lariat. The second pass the rope bounced off the seat. On the third the rope snagged and broke off a mirror and sent the bike teetering. A lesser man might have given up, fearing exposure and apprehension, but failure emboldened Benjamin. The rope caught the handle bars on the fourth pass and the noose tightened. The Harley leaped the curb like a frightened calf. It bounced behind the Purgatory Truck, sparks flying every time metal hit pavement. He made a U-turn. When he passed the house again, the lights were on. Sheila peered out the window. Her eyes fell on the Harley bouncing behind Benjamin's truck. The bike burst into flames as if ignited by her stare.

"Oh shit!" Benjamin said.

He sped up, irrationally attempting to outdistance the burning Harley. He made a long broad U-turn at the cul-de-sac at the end of the street. He gunned the truck and neared the house at forty miles an hour. Sheila stood screaming in the driveway. The flaming bike took a vicious bounce. The rope broke. Vectors of velocity and gravity juxtaposed and the Harley flew by so near that Sheila felt its heat of passage. It sailed through her living room window, landed on the sofa, and promptly exploded. Benjamin stomped on the gas and kept going.

All the fire department could do was make sure none of the neighbors' houses caught fire. Two fire fighters restrained the screaming victim. They wrongly believed she wanted to enter the burning house. Her voice was hoarse from constant shrieking.

"What the hell is she saying?" one firefighter asked.

"I don't know. Sounds like *felony juice bed pan.*"

The police finally handcuffed her and it was not until she was breathless from screaming, her voice reduced to a shadow, that an arson investigator deciphered her raging litany.

"Delaney," she whispered over and over, *"you are a dead man!"*

Benjamin pulled into the lot of an all night body shop. He undid what remained of the rope from the trailer hitch and threw it down a storm drain. A salesman approached.

"Give me the works," Benjamin said to him. "I'd like leather seats too."

The salesman took out an invoice and wrote. "What color?"

"Red." He did not care what color. It was the first that came to mind.

The salesman walked about the truck taking notes. He added figures on a calculator. He showed the final number to Benjamin, who whistled softly.

"What the hell. Go ahead." Benjamin yielded his keys. "But could you park it somewhere it can't be seen from the street?"

Duncan lay on the floor reading his Saturn owner's manual when Benjamin returned. He had driven out of the dealership hours before in a red wagon with air conditioning, a deluxe stereo system, and a check representing the remaining several thousand dollars of his trust fund.

"How's the face?" Benjamin asked.

"Better. How's the boa?"

"Tired."

"Got a work out, did it?"

"Spent a lot of time hunting in the jungle."

"Did it catch anything?"

"God, I hope not."

Duncan put the manual down. "Where's your truck?"

"You mean my red truck?"

"You don't have a red truck. It's gray. Kind of."

"You're mistaken. It's red."

"Whatever. I didn't hear it pull up. Where is it?"

"Still in Wyoming."

"What the hell are you talking about?"

"My red truck. It's still in Wyoming. I took the bus out here."

"Uh huh. Well, I guess you'll tell me when you're ready."

"By the way," Benjamin said, "if anyone asks, I've been here all day."

"Uh huh. Doing what?"

"Crossword puzzles." Benjamin had never done a crossword puzzle in his life. "Or reading. You know. Stuff. Just if anyone asks."

Duncan stood to answer a rap on the door. Two men in suits stood on the landing. They looked like Eastern European versions of Randolph and Phillips right down to the crew cuts and mustaches. They flashed badges.

"Mind if we come in?" asked the taller as he stepped through the door.

The other detective took out a radio. "Bring her up," he said.

A uniformed female officer brought Sheila Rascowitz into the studio, holding her firmly by the arm. Duncan thought that odd until he noticed that her hands were cuffed behind her back.

"That's him!" she hissed when she spotted Benjamin.

"Why is she whispering?" Duncan asked.

Neither detective answered. One looked at the self portrait on the easel. "You're pretty good." He looked at Duncan's face. "Who did that?"

Sheila smiled viciously.

"Don't know," Duncan said, "I didn't see him."

"Or her," Benjamin said.

The other detective approached Benjamin. "What's your name, boy?"

"Boy?" Benjamin stood and unzipped his pants, "you ever see a boy with a twelve-inch dick?"

"Ok, smart guy," the detective said, "what's your name, *sir?*"

"Benjamin Lonetree." He zipped his pants. "What's yours?"

"Detective Harkanian. That's Detective Romanowski. Where were you an hour ago?"

Benjamin smiled. "With Mrs. Harkanian."

Harkanian smiled back. "I'm not married."

"You got a mother, don't you?"

Harkanian started for Benjamin. Romanowski grabbed his arm.

"Not now, Hark." Romanowski turned to Benjamin. "You going to answer the question or not?"

"He was here," Duncan said, "doing crossword puzzles."

"You lying sack of shit!" hissed Rascowitz.

"Shut up!" Romanowski turned to Benjamin. "You got a truck?"

"Sure."

"I'd like to see it."

"It's not here."

"All right. Enough of this." Harkanian took Duncan into the hallway. "Where's your smart ass friend's truck?"

"Wyoming." Duncan gulped. "He took the bus out here."

"Gray truck?" Harkanian asked.

"No sir. Red. May I ask what this is about?"

"Ms. Rascowitz alleges that your buddy stole her motorcycle and burned down her house. That something your friend is capable of?"

When Duncan and Benjamin were thirteen, Benjamin got a model rocket. After ten flights, vertical launches no longer satisfied him, and he determined to see what horizontal distance he could achieve. So he set the launch pad at a forty-five degree angle and hit the start button. The rocket traveled further than anticipated, through Fiona's open barn door, where its burning engine ignited a pile of hay. Duncan was astounded at how fast a barn could be reduced to ashes and smoking timber.

"Not intentionally," he said.

Duncan and Harkanian went back inside. The detectives conferred.

"Ok," Romanowski said. "Take her down to the car."

"What," Sheila whispered, "aren't you going to arrest him?"

"Keep it up," Harkanian said as the female officer took her down, "we'll charge you with filing a false report."

Romanowski said, "she got a grudge against you?"

"I stole her girl friend."

"Uh huh. All right. Sorry to bother you." Romanowski left.

Harkanian stopped at the door. "Twelve-inch dick, huh?"

"That's right," Benjamin said.

"Lonetree," Harkanian said as he left, "if you got a twelve-inch dick you better spit it out, because it ain't yours."

Duncan sat in his window and watched the police take Sheila away in a marked patrol car. He shook his head.

"Though I appreciate the thought, you didn't have to burn her house down."

"I only planned on the bike." Benjamin shrugged. "It got out of hand."

Duncan opened a beer and sipped. The escalation of hostilities bothered him, but he could not say he was completely unpleased. He put the beer down and smiled sadly.

"It always does, doesn't it?"

Thirteen

At eight-thirty Duncan decided he had been stood up again.

It was no surprise but the lack of fulfillment distressed him. He had invested much of his self-esteem and part of his capital in what now seemed a futile dream, and the dividends were bitter. He had even allowed Misty to take him shopping. He agreed to the clothes she selected, but in truth he would have worn tights, a codpiece, and felt shoes with belled toes if Misty had told him Pris preferred the look. Luckily, she selected light wool pants, a matching coat, leather loafers, and a knit green t-shirt. Misty broke out her make-up after they had finished shopping and covered his bruises with pancake. He denied her the lipstick. Duncan looked in the mirror.

"Jesus," he said, having visited the Wax Museum as he waited for the dealer to prepare his Saturn, "I look like a mannequin."

"It's an improvement over what you looked like before."

On the way to the gallery he looked at his mouth in the mirror. The swelling was gone, but the blue remained. He regretted forsaking the lipstick. He parked a block away from the gallery. Once inside, he felt more relaxed than he had at the Melrose exhibit. He was dressed more appropriately and he was heartened by the sale of *Roscoe*. He roamed the gallery until he found a painting of a man with long red hair, naked from the waist down, hanging by the neck from a rope attached to a lamp fixture. An orange cat hung from a rafter beside him. A chair lay on the floor to the left of his dangling feet. A black cowboy hat lay beside the chair.

A Christmas Wish, the card under the painting said, *Sheila Rascowitz.*

Angela stood across the room speaking to a tall man in a herring bone suit. She wore a long black dress with a falling back. An onyx necklace hung above her breasts. She waved Duncan over and introduced him to Robert Armstrong, an art critic for the Times.

"I like your work," Armstrong said. "It's not technically proficient and lacks maturity but both will come in time."

"Thanks," Duncan said, "I think."

"I don't think he heard the first part," Angela said.

"What happened to your lip?"

"Another critic was less appreciative of my efforts."

Armstrong laughed. "Nice meeting you, Duncan. I will certainly consider you." He kissed Angela's cheek and left.

"Consider me for what?"

"It's a surprise." She took his arm. "Come with me."

They obtained champagne from a waiter, and Angela led him to his paintings. In one, Champagne and Cassandra, naked and laughing drunk, sat on his couch holding empty Margarita glasses. In the other Edward, clothed and sleeping drunk, sat on the couch. Duncan lifted his glass to Edward's image and sipped. He noted the cards below the paintings. He choked and spit champagne. *Edward,* one said, *$8,000. Margarita Time,* said the other, *$9,500.*

"Holy Jesus, Angela!" he said when he stopped coughing, "you don't expect anyone to pay that much, do you?"

"I've been offered six thousand for *Margarita Time* and seven for *Edward.*"

"And you didn't take it?"

"Who's the agent here? If you're short on cash, I'll advance you something. You don't have to pay me back until the paintings sell. Now if you'll excuse me, I have to pee."

Duncan wandered through the gallery feeling absurdly pleased with himself until he saw Pris standing across the room next to Rascowitz. Pris spoke to Sheila, who turned away.

Here we go again, Duncan thought as Pris approached.

"I'm mad at you," she said. "Because of you I have a roommate now."

"Wait a minute. I had nothing to do with the fire."

She looked him in the eye. He looked back. She relaxed. "You couldn't lie if your life depended on it, could you?"

"Sure I could. Just not very well." From across the room Sheila stared at him with poisonous eyes. "She's not going to hurt me, is she?"

"I told her if she laid a hand on you I would never see her again."

Duncan then did one of the few truly cruel deeds of his life. He cupped Pris's head in his hands and kissed her. She did not resist. A shattering of china and a cold, murderous scream bounced against walls and rattled windows. Pris gasped at the sound and pushed him away. Sheila stood next to *A Christmas Wish*, a felled waiter and a broken plate of appetizers at her feet. She turned and ran out of the gallery.

"You shouldn't have done that."

"I'm sorry."

"I should go after her. She needs me."

Duncan took her hand. "I need you more."

A busboy with a broom and a dustpan helped the waiter to his feet, then swept up the broken plate. Pris exhaled a long, sad sigh.

"Benjamin?"

Duncan nodded. "He didn't mean for her house to burn."

"She has a thousand dollar deductible. She shouldn't have to pay that."

He took a glass of champagne from a passing tray and gulped it down. A thousand dollars represented a good portion of his remaining capital.

"I'll pay it. I have it at home. But before I go, I'd like you to see my paintings."

"I already have."

"What did you think?"

"Sheila says your paintings are degrading to women. She says you celebrate degradation."

"What about her? What about the guy with the metal hat on his penis? What about the cattle drive of naked men? And what would Santa think about that, that . . ." he pointed at *A Christmas Wish*, "*thing* over there?"

"She says her paintings are from the heart. And yours are from the testicles."

"I don't really care what Sheila thinks of my paintings."

"Then why are you so defensive?"

"I'm not defensive." He felt annoyed despite her playful eyes. "I just want to know what you think."

She stroked his cheek. "I think they're beautiful. Just like you." She stood and pulled him up. "Come on. Let's go get your money."

Cat was so happy when he spied Pris driving up that he leaped from his vantage point in the window and landed in the seat beside her before her Cadillac had stopped. Duncan parked his Saturn in the mini-mart lot. Pris held Cat to her chest and followed Duncan upstairs. He opened the door and turned on the light. She put Cat down and sat on the couch. Duncan got her a coke and himself a beer.

"You drink too much," she said.

"I'm Irish," he said.

"Like that makes a difference."

He put the beer down and removed his shoe box from the closet. He counted out one thousand dollars. He sat by her and held out the money.

"I'm not that kind of girl," Pris said.

Duncan blushed. "It's the money for Sheila's deductible."

"I know that! I was joking." She put the money in her purse. "What do we do now?"

"You know what I want to do."

"All right. But I have to warn you. I won't be any good at it."

"Are you kidding? You're a natural."

She looked down and clasped his hands. "Tell me what you want."

"Just sit there. I'll do the rest."

She dropped his hands. "Excuse me?"

"Just sit there," he repeated.

He jumped up and grabbed his easel and positioned it across from the couch. He set a fresh canvas on it and picked up his palette and a brush.

"You're going to paint me?"

"What did you . . ." Duncan sagged. "Oh god. I am a moron."

"No, you're not."

She kissed him. Sheila Rascowitz, watching from her place on the roof of the hardware store across the street, screamed long and hard. The sound of her banshee wail made sewer rats shiver and stray dogs howl, but as a testimony to the quality of the kiss, neither Pris nor Duncan heard a thing.

Several times that night as Pris lay sleeping, Duncan set down his brush and palette and knelt beside her and studied her tranquil face. Her angry cocoon had split and the resultant butterfly had not a worry in the universe. Duncan stroked stray hair from her closed eyes and dried spittle from her chin with his cuff. Cat slept across her hips, her blouse open to reveal the arc of her breast. She might be dead she was so peaceful. He twice held his hand above her lips to feel her breath against his skin. He painted quickly, his concentration broken by stray thoughts of how his life was evolving. Watching her sleep, he empathized with Fiona and how she must have felt hovering over his crib and later his bed as he slept in his dark room. He silently forgave the bribery and her backfiring evil, as it ultimately had united them. He even absolved Sheila for the catnapping and the beating as all were inspired by the love they shared for Pris. When she awoke hours later most of the painting was complete. She yawned and stretched and

Duncan felt a swelling in his throat and shorts. She sat up and rubbed her eyes and stretched again.

"I'm hungry," she said.

Duncan put down his brush. "I could use a cup of coffee myself."

"Can I see it?"

"Not yet."

"Is it that bad?"

No, Duncan thought, *it's that good.*

"I want it to be a surprise."

Duncan led her downstairs. They reached the street and turned into the mini-mart lot. Assan stood beside Duncan's station wagon. He held a fire extinguisher and shook his head sadly.

"Oh lord," Duncan said.

Every window in the wagon was shattered. A two-by-four impaled the windshield. The upholstery was shredded and the seats smoldered black beneath extinguisher foam. *Fuck me, Fuck me* was spray painted in black on the driver's door. A siren became a fire truck but the fire was already out and when the police arrived all they could do was fill out a report. Pris took the thousand dollars from her purse and put it in his pocket.

"You need this more than Sheila does," she said.

"You can pick up the report at the station tomorrow." The policeman gave him a card with a report number on it. "Your insurance company will want to see it."

Duncan put the card in his pocket and smiled at Pris. She smiled uncertainly back.

"What say we take your car?" he asked.

Fourteen

"Tiffy, dear," Fiona said, "don't you think that bikini is a bit small?"

Tiffy put her book down beside her pool chair and lowered her sunglasses. She pointed to a young woman in a thong bikini at the far end of the pool.

"Not compared to that."

"Still, it is not exactly modest. And you're such a full figured girl."

Expressed as a ratio, Fiona's bikini covered more skin with less fabric and frankly Fiona wanted a little ogling herself. But with Tiffy beside her in that piece of string she had no chance of being the focus of pool society.

"People are looking at you," Fiona continued.

Exactly, Tiffy thought. She adjusted her bikini. "I'll put on my other after lunch."

"Another thing. You've been here a week. It's time you approached Duncan."

"I want to lose another five pounds first," she said.

She had actually gained five since her arrival, four of which was muscle grown during her daily work outs in the hotel gym and in the dance class she had signed up for. The final pound had found its way to her chest.

"I know you're worried you can't get him back . . ."

As if, Tiffy thought.

". . . but you must fight for the man you love. You go see him tonight."

Tiffy had a lucrative contest that night in Hollywood. The prize was one thousand dollars, and she did not want to pass up a sure thing.

"Oh, you're right," she said. "But I need a new dress and my hair done and the shoes I brought are all wrong. I couldn't possibly be ready tonight. I want to look my best when I see Duncan."

"Tomorrow then."

There was a contest the next night at a club in the valley, but that prize was only two fifty. If missing it preserved her bungalow for a few more nights, she would still come out ahead. And she did want to see Duncan. She wanted to show him what he had given up. She wanted to take him back from that tramp and, when she had him squirming beneath her one last time, she wanted to spit him out for the insolence of leaving her.

"It's settled." Tiffy smiled. "Tomorrow I'll go see our dear Duncan."

When Duncan returned from breakfast, Benjamin was practicing bottom-dealing cards with Assan. Keith Gomez had just made Pit Boss and had offered Benjamin a job as a dealer. Benjamin wanted to see if he would be any good at it. Assan shook his head.

"No good. I see the card slide off the bottom."

"Who's minding the store?" Duncan asked.

"My cousin Abdul. He arrived from Pakistan last week. He doesn't speak much English but he knows how to work the cash register."

Duncan scraped a can of cat food into a bowl. He set the bowl on the kitchen floor next to a water dish. Cat settled into eating. Duncan opened the refrigerator. He hesitated before taking out two beers. Pris was right, he drank too much. But after seeing his new car destroyed he felt the need for cold liquid comfort. He gave Benjamin a beer and Assan a coke.

"No! Your hands are too slow!"

Assan took the deck. He took the five of diamonds off the top and showed it to Benjamin. He placed it on the bottom and dealt two poker hands face down.

"All right, Mr. Benjamin. Which of us has the five of diamonds?"

"Neither. You dealt them all off the top."

Assan turned over the first card he had dealt. The five of diamonds.

"Hey," Benjamin said, "you cheated!"

"Where did you learn that?" Duncan asked.

"Yale. Tuition was quite expensive and my fellow students were anxious to part with their parents' money."

"This cheating is hard work," Benjamin said. "I thought it was supposed to make things easier." But he picked up the cards anyway.

"I have a favor to ask," Assan said to Duncan. "My mother's birthday is next month. I would like you to paint a portrait of me for her. I will pay you. One month's free rent."

"I'm a little busy now. Can't you find another artist?"

"No! I have seen your paintings. I want *you*. Six months free rent."

"It's not that . . ."

"You drive a hard bargain. One year free rent."

"Sold!" Benjamin said.

Assan smiled broadly. "When can we start?"

Duncan surrendered. "Tonight," he said. He lay back in the couch and closed his eyes. "Give me a few hours sleep and I'll paint you tonight."

In the dream, Sean Delaney sat in the Hollywood at a table near the bar, playing gin rummy with Bolo. A bottle of whiskey split the table between them. Bolo discarded a ten. Sean picked it up and laid down his cards.

"Gin," he said.

"Damn," said Bolo, "that's three in a row."

Duncan sat with them. "You two know each other?"

"We just met," said Sean. "Care for a whiskey?"

"Thanks. I will."

Duncan drank the glass Sean poured in one gulp. He looked up. Fiona danced on the stage wearing only a G-string and an arm across her nipples.

"Jesus!" Duncan averted his eyes. "Mom, get down from there!"

Bolo said, "Something wrong with being a stripper?"

"No. I mean yes. I mean . . . I don't know what I mean."

"Relax." Sean threw a wadded dollar bill on stage. "It's only a dream."

"And a fairly sick one at that," Bolo said.

Duncan poured another whiskey and downed it. When he dared look back, Fiona was gone. Now Tiffy hung upside down from the pole. Pendant breasts framed her chin. She waved and smiled an inverted smile. Duncan looked away. Bolo dealt another hand.

"Look who's up there now," Bolo said.

"I don't want to."

"Why not?" Sean asked.

"Why do you think?" Bolo asked. "He's afraid it might be Pris."

"Is that right?"

"I don't know. Maybe."

"Well, get over it," Sean said. "If you end up with her you'll spend the rest of your life dealing with the fact that she was a stripper."

"I don't care about that."

Sean picked up two cards from the discard pile. He laid his hand down. "Gin."

"Damn!" said Bolo.

"I thought you were a poker playing man," Duncan said.

"All the good poker players ended up in the other place."

"Wait a minute. Does this mean that Bolo is . . ."

"Dead?" Bolo shuffled and dealt. "Not yet. Soon though."

"Jesus. This is going to kill Pris."

Bolo and Sean looked at each other.

"No, it won't," Sean said.

"You have to help her through it," Bolo said. "Only you can."

Duncan looked to the stage. Sister Mary Elizabeth and Mother Margaret Mary swung around the pole, throwing off pieces of habit with each revolution. Duncan looked away when they got down to their girdles.

"Don't tell me you've not been to one of these places before," Sean said.

"I have not. And, frankly, I'm embarrassed to be here with my father."

"What's wrong with father and son enjoying a little rump together?" asked Bolo.

"Nothing," Duncan said, "if it's over the dinner table and it's beef." He stood. "I should go. I have work to do when I wake up."

Sean put his arm around Duncan and walked him to the door. "Do me a favor, son. Tell Fiona it's ok to remarry. Woody's a good man. They belong together whether she admits it or not."

"I'll tell her."

Sean hugged his son. Duncan held tight and looked over his father's shoulder. Benjamin was on stage, naked except for a loin cloth, grinding his hips in a suggestive and disturbingly erotic rhythm.

"This really is a sick dream," Bolo commented.

"Benjamin!" Duncan closed his eyes again. "Get down from there!"

"Why?"

Duncan opened his eyes. Benjamin sat in the window reading a comic book. Duncan shook his head.

"Never mind."

He went into the bathroom. He undressed and stood beneath the shower. He soaped himself and washed his hair. He closed his eyes and stood there until the water grew cold. He dried himself and wrapped the towel around his waist and opened the door. Assan awaited in a pin-striped, three-piece suit with a gold watch and chain in the vest and a bright yellow tie with blue dots. His hair was greased back. Duncan laughed.

"Is it the tie? The girl at the store assured me it worked with the suit."

"The tie works fine," Duncan said. "But not the suit. Go dress in your regular clothes. And get the grease out of your hair."

Assan left. Duncan put on a denim shirt and faded levis. He rolled up his sleeves and took a slice of pepperoni pizza out of the refrigerator. He ate that piece, and another, and washed the pizza down with a beer. Assan returned wearing blue polyester pants and a white button down shirt.

"Much better."

"Are you sure?"

"Trust me," Duncan said, "who's the artist here?"

"This certainly is the nicest place we've been," Fiona said.

The club was immaculate and immense. Mahogany rails circled three stages, and the girls swaying upon them were illuminated by a variety of concealed lights. The ratio of well-dressed men in coats and ties to women in dresses and business suits almost reflected the general population. A young black girl in red lingerie with a microscopic waist and an inversely proportional chest approached their table.

"Care for a table dance?" she asked.

"No thank you," Woody said, "my religion forbids it."

Fiona laughed and squeezed his hand. He did not tell her he had stolen the line from Benjamin, who once used it in response to a drunken rodeo whore. He squeezed her hand back. As much as he hated coming to these places, he loved the way her cares dropped from her face when they did, like snow from a cold January sky. A waitress in a black leotard and stiletto heels took their order and left.

"The help is so friendly," Fiona commented.

Woody grunted. He had hurt his back trying a position diagramed in a book Fiona had bought in Hollywood that afternoon. The *Camel's Suture* was the book's name. Or something like that. Woody was actually enjoying himself until the rope broke and he fell ass backwards over the bed. Fiona wanted to call a chiropractor but he put his boot down. It would have been too hard to explain. Seven Tylenols took the edge off the pain, but he doubted he could accommodate Fiona later that night. *Maybe,* he thought, *for once she'll leave me alone.* Their beers arrived. Woody sucked his down and ordered another.

"Pace yourself," Fiona said, "or I'll have to drive home."

That was his plan. Injured or drunk alone would not disqualify him from bedroom duties, but both together might. He wondered if he could fake the need for a body cast. Not permanent. Just a week or two to recover.

"There's so many young ladies here," Fiona said.

"It's amateur night," Woody said, "there's a sign over the door."

"I must have missed it."

"Ladies and gentlemen," the voice over the speakers said as the lights dimmed, *"time for our featured event!"*

"Hey," Woody said. "Isn't that Danny Carpenter over there at the bar?"

"On stage number one it's Sabrina!" A tall redhead strutted onto the far left stage.

Fiona did not look. "Can't be. He's shopping with Tiffy for a new dress."

"On stage number three its Amber!" A buxom brunette in a plaid skirt, parochial sweater, and bobby sox somersaulted onto the stage on the right.

"Nimble little vixen," Fiona said. "All those dance lessons are finally paying off."

Woody squinted at the bar. "Well, they must have found one, because that's Danny."

"And on center stage its Roxanne!"

Fiona looked over. "I believe you are correct. No wonder he would come to a place like this. He can't get a decent girl on his own merit."

Woody did not answer. He was distracted by the blonde approaching center stage. She wore a black leather skirt and a red spandex tube top. Silver studs ran the sleeves of her glossy black jacket. Black thigh boots shod muscular legs. She had chocolate eyes, strawberry lips, and breasts the size of softballs, though much softer and not as white. She slapped a riding crop against her thigh with a loud crack as she mounted the stage.

"I don't think that's the case," he finally said.

Fiona looked to center stage. "Oh my god."

A disco song began with a loud, thumping base. Tiffy removed her jacket. The skirt was next to go. When she hoisted the tube top over her head Fiona stood as if poked by a cattle prod and ran out of the club. Woody slowly finished his beer. Tiffy left the stage to fervent applause. Woody left ten dollars on the table, and followed Fiona outside. She was mute all the way back to the hotel. A valet took their car and they walked quickly to their bungalow. Fiona went into the bathroom and slammed the door. Woody undressed and got into bed. The bathroom door opened. For the first time since their first visit to the Hollywood Bar and Grill, Fiona wore a nightgown. She sat on the edge of the bed and picked up the phone.

"Who are you calling at this hour?"

"Hush," Fiona said.

Woody went into the bathroom. He brushed his teeth and threw water on his face. When he returned to bed Fiona was still on the phone.

"That's all right, Roy," Fiona said, "I just thought you should know what Danny was into before it was too late."

She hung up and dialed again.

"Who are you calling now?"

"Hush. William? Fiona here. I'm afraid I have shocking news. No, no, she's all right. No, she's not pregnant. At least not by Duncan, that is. Don't take that tone with me! Do you want to hear what I have to say or not? Fine. Are you sitting down?"

Woody covered his head with a pillow. But no matter how hard he held it to his ear, he still heard Fiona breaching the news of Tiffy's disgrace to William Bradshaw. His heart went out over more than a thousand miles of telephone wire to the man on the other end. He had never liked William Bradshaw for his blustering, bullying ways. He was proud of his concrete of all things. But Woody knew William Bradshaw would be holding his head in his hands and crying once the connection was broken. Despite his love for Fiona, Woody silently damned her for causing such pain. When she finally turned off the lights and sidled up to him, he pretended he was asleep, and for all her jostling he refused to give up the deception.

The painting was half finished when the last bottle hit the trash. Long after he had completed his twelve steps, Duncan would look back at the paintings from what he called his drunken period to see potential and talent and myriad mistakes. From his new found sobriety he would blame the alcohol instead of his youth, though in reality it was his experience that made the difference between then and then. Duncan put down his brush and took out his wallet.

"Beer run," he said.

Assan said, "It is after two. It is illegal to sell beer now."

"Well." Duncan put his wallet back. "Well, damn it."

"Nicely spoken," said Benjamin.

Assan stood. "But nothing prevents me from giving you a six-pack."

"I'll go with you," Benjamin said. "I feel like having a Slurpee."

"Get me a pack of Necco Wafers while you're at it," said Duncan.

"There he is," said Howard Lomo.

He and Leroy Kern sat in front of the hardware store in a faded blue sixty-six Mustang. Lomo had stolen it from the lot of a Vegas K-Mart after he busted out of the county lock up. Lomo had found an incarcerated vagrant of the same general height and build and, after determining the bum's release date, offered him a drink from a bottle of whiskey allegedly hidden in the laundry room. Once there, Lomo beat the man senseless. It was not as easy as he had hoped, as he earlier had to pop his shoulder back in himself, and the agony of the exertion had a detrimental effect on his stamina. He had exchanged identity wrist bands then stuffed the unconscious man into an industrial dryer. Hours later, when the vagrant's name was called, Lomo left through the front door. He had driven the stolen Mustang to their hotel room, where he found Leroy Kern watching a porno movie titled *The Bitches of Madison County* on pay per view. Kern had posted bail on his MasterCard. Lomo had been detained without bond due to the weapon found in his waist band and the violence with which he resisted apprehension.

You sir, the judge had said, *are clearly a danger to the community.*

"He ain't alone," said Leroy Kern.

"So what?" Lomo pulled a ski mask over his face. "No one else is going to get hurt." Lomo took his Beretta from the glove compartment and racked a round. "Unless they try to help that shit head."

"I don't like this."

"Shut up. Just shut up. Just shut up and sit there and keep the car running and when I come out be ready to go. Can you handle that?"

Leroy Kern did not like being bullied, but he was afraid of the man. Howard Lomo had not just crossed the line dividing good from evil, he had long jumped over it with wholehearted enthusiasm.

"Sure. I can handle that."

Howard Lomo got out and ran across the street. He paused outside the mini-mart and looked in. Benjamin filled a cup with cherry Slurpee from a machine opposite the door. A pack of Necco Wafers protruded from his back pocket. Assan was in back taking a six pack from the cooler. A dark-skinned kid stood behind the counter. No one else was inside. Lomo jerked the glass door open and jumped inside.

"Nobody move," he yelled. "This is a robbery!"

Benjamin turned and Lomo drew a bead. The glass door swung back and smacked Lomo hard in the ass. Lomo pulled the trigger, but his balance had been compromised. The round intended for Benjamin lodged in the Slurpee machine. Sticky red slush poured onto the linoleum. Assan dropped the beer and ran to the front.

"Abdul!" he yelled in Hindi, *"my equalizer!"*

Lomo turned to Assan. "What the hell are you jabbering about?"

Benjamin dove for the frozen foods.

"Oh no, you don't," Lomo said.

He fired another round. He had seen the result of Benjamin's proficiency with poultry in Leroy Kern's face. Abdul grabbed the Benelli Police Model semi-automatic twelve gauge shotgun with the pistol grip from under the counter and threw it to Assan, who caught it and racked a round into the chamber. It was an intimidating sound Lomo recognized from his police training. He turned. Assan lowered the weapon.

"Oh, shit!" Lomo said.

Assan fired. Abdul and Benjamin hit the floor. Lomo brought his arm up to shoot but when he pulled the trigger he noted his wrist ended in a bloody stump. His right hand twitched on the floor a foot from the Beretta. He screamed and picked up the hand and ran out the door.

Leroy Kern heard the shots with a peculiar combination of sadness and satisfaction. He did not object to the act, but he found the possible consequences repugnant. He resolved to detach himself from Lomo at the first opportunity. Leroy Kern put the car into gear when he saw Lomo run from the store, holding his arm to his chest. Assan stepped out the door and aimed the shotgun. Leroy Kern decided this opportunity was as first as any. He hit the gas. Leroy Kern was a block and a half away by the time Howard Lomo reached the middle of the street. Lomo held his detached right hand in his left and shook it at the vanishing Mustang.

"Come back, you asshole!"

Something hit Lomo in the back of his head. He looked down. A broken pack of Necco Wafers, thrown with Benjamin's usual accuracy, lay beside his dirty left sneaker.

"That's it," Howard Lomo said.

He put his severed right hand into his jacket pocket with his good left. He reached awkwardly behind his back and removed a second gun from his waistband. He turned. Benjamin and Assan stood at the sidewalk. Assan still held the Benelli, but Lomo no longer cared. He was dead anyway, he decided, and he was determined to enter hell dragging Benjamin by the hair with his one remaining hand. Assan lowered the Benelli. Lomo stepped past the center line into the path of a semi hauling portable dressing rooms to a movie shoot in Brentwood. The truck hit Lomo at an angle and threw him forty-five feet into a motorcycle parked in front of the Hollywood Bar and Grill, skewering him on a handlebar. Lomo blacked out. He woke to distant sirens and a tugging on his shoulder. The last thing Howard Lomo experienced in the land of the living was Sheila Rascowitz pulling his remaining hand, trying to remove him from the third Harley she had purchased in the last two weeks.

"Delaney," she screamed as she tugged, *"you're responsible for this!"*

But the clutch handle was caught in his ribs, and as he died reflecting on the ignominiousness of his predicament, all Howard Lomo could think of in a surprisingly clear way was that ultimately this strangely masculine woman was correct in her assessment of the situation.

Leroy Kern drove until the Mustang coughed and sputtered and finally expired on Angeles Crest Highway high in the mountains north of Pasadena. He turned off the headlights and put his head in his hands. His head hurt, his nose hurt, his neck hurt, his soul hurt. He did not know if Lomo had killed Benjamin before he died. He did not care. All he wanted was peace. Leroy Kern opened the glove compartment and reached inside.

Time to go, he thought.

He was reaching for a forty-four Smith and Wesson revolver that Lomo had stolen from a liquor store in Barstow along with three hundred and fifty dollars in traveling money. Lomo had tied up the manager, locked her in the stock room, and took a half gallon of Wild Turkey for the ride. Leroy Kern had seen him put the gun in the glove compartment. But that was before they opened the whiskey. Leroy Kern was passed out drunk when, somewhere past the California state line, Lomo stuffed the revolver in his belt as a back up to his duty weapon.

Leroy Kern panicked when he could not find the gun. He felt something cold and hard beneath an Auto Club Guidebook. He took it out. It was a small, white, glow-in-the-dark plastic Jesus with a magnet on the bottom, like the one that rode shotgun on his father's dashboard when he was a kid. Plastic Jesus shown ghostly in the night, arms outstretched as if to embrace Leroy Kern and head cocked slightly to one side as if to ask why. Leroy Kern clutched Plastic Jesus and cried. Years later, when he next met Benjamin at the First Church of the Evolutionary Jesus in Cheyenne, from the pulpit Benjamin would ask how Leroy Kern found Jesus and to the congregation's delight, Leroy Kern would tell the truth: *I just looked in the glove compartment, and there he was.*

Leroy Kern cried for an hour. Then he got out of the car. He placed Plastic Jesus on the Mustang's roof and closed the door. He walked down the mountain towards the lights of Los Angeles, looking back every few steps, until the holy glow of Jesus faded into the night behind him.

Fifteen

"How'd you do?" Danny asked.

He ached viewing the riding crop poking out of her bag. The memory of Tiffy on stage whacking herself with it sent his pulse galloping.

"I won, didn't I? That's one thousand. Another six fifty in tips. Plus," Tiffy almost squealed, "a man from *Playboy* wants to photograph me."

"That old line."

"That was no line. He gave me this." Tiffy took a card from her shirt. Sure enough. *Playboy Magazine.*

"Now what would your daddy say if he saw you in *Playboy?*"

"He's got a collection in the garage dating back to nineteen seventy three. He'd be a hypocrite to object."

"I thought I saw Fiona in there."

"Be quiet. What would Fiona be doing in a place like this?" She looked at her watch. "I got to go."

"Where are we going?"

"We aren't going anywhere." The cold night frosted her breath as she spoke. She unlocked the Cobra and got in. The engine started with a potent roar. *"You* are going home. *I* am going to meet the man from Playboy."

"How am I supposed to get home?"

Tiffy gave him a twenty. "Take a cab."

I've lost her, Danny thought as he watched her drive away. What he did not comprehend was that he had never actually possessed her. And worse yet, the stripping he had thought a lark had matured into a vulture, and Danny was incapable of putting either bird back in the cage. The message light was on when he returned to his room. He dialed zero.

"Your father called," the operator said. "He said it was urgent."

Danny hung up and dialed. His father answered and for five minutes Danny listened with only an occasional *yes sir* or *no sir*. He hung up and packed his duffel bag. He put on his jacket and put the duffel bag in the trunk of a taxi and rode to the airport. He exchanged his return ticket to

Cheyenne for the next flight to Denver. Fifteen minutes before his plane left, he remembered the Cobra. He ran to the rental counter and gave the clerk his contract. She punched keys on a computer and looked up.

"Your father called and said the car was stolen. We've notified the police. Is there something we should know?"

"Nope," Danny said, "that about covers it."

He reached the gate as final boarding was announced. He gave the attendant his ticket. She was a young black woman with bright brown eyes.

"Did you enjoy your stay in Los Angeles?" she asked.

"Some parts more than others."

He settled in his seat in first class. A stewardess approached.

"Can I get you anything? Some juice perhaps?"

"Double Dewar's, straight up."

Danny had never drunk whiskey before, but his father drank Dewars in times of stress. He downed the glass in one gulp and coughed violently.

"Are you all right?" the stewardess asked.

"I'm fine," he whispered when the fit finally passed. He held his glass out. "Another of the same, please."

"We've had a lot of calls since you moved in," Detective Randolph told Duncan. "This is the third dead body related to this address."

"I don't deserve credit for that drive by."

Randolph held up his hand. "Hell, it's not your fault. No one person could cause this much trouble."

Duncan looked at Benjamin but said nothing. Benjamin called a cab after the police left. He was off to see Angela.

"Near death makes me eager to propagate the Lonetree line," he said.

"Can we finish later?" asked Assan, "I have much cleaning to do."

The coroner took the handlebars from the bike when it proved too difficult to extricate Lomo, and now the bars rested with him in a body bag in the back of an ambulance. Sheila sat on the curb staring at her boots. Samantha pulled her to her feet, Sheila got on the bike behind her, and they rode off in tandem. Roscoe attached a hose to a spigot on the wall. He washed Howard Lomo's blood into the gutter and down the sewer and ultimately to the sea. Duncan returned to his studio. He picked up Cat and slouched on the couch. The phone rang. He decided not to answer but whoever was calling decided with more conviction not to hang up. On the eighth ring Duncan set Cat on the floor and answered the phone.

"Duncan?"

"Speaking."

A long pause, then, "you don't know who this is, do you?"

"I'm sorry, I don't."

"Jesus Christ! I didn't think I was that unimportant in your life."

"Tiffy!" Her habitually reproachful tone solved it. "How are you?"

"I've been a whole lot better."

"What's wrong?"

"Well, to start," Tiffy said, "I'm in jail. Think you could bail me out?"

Duncan almost did not recognize her when a deputy escorted Tiffy into the lobby. She had on the black leather outfit she had worn on stage hours earlier, minus the riding crop. She had left it behind when the deputies pulled her out of what they believed was a stolen car.

"Tiffy," Duncan said, "you look . . ."

"Beautiful?"

"Well, yes . . ."

"Sexy?"

"I guess . . ."

"Or maybe the word you were looking for was cheap."

Duncan did not admit it, but that was the second word he had thought of. The first was *wow*. Tiffy brushed by him. He followed her outside.

"See you Saturday, Roxanne," the deputy called after her.

Duncan opened Assan's mini-van. "Why did he call you Roxanne?"

"That's my stage name."

They drove north on San Vincente then turned left on Sunset.

"You're an actress now?"

"A stripper."

Duncan had not see that coming, though judging by her attire, he perhaps should have. He picked up his jaw from it's resting place on his chest and laughed.

"First grand theft auto, then stripping. You're a very bad girl."

"Always have been. You just never noticed."

Duncan pulled into the lot of the Beverly Hills Hotel. Tiffy got out.

"Walk me to my room," she said.

He took a ticket from the valet and followed. She stopped at a door surrounded by vines and ferns and struggled with the lock.

"That's just great," she said.

Duncan followed her back to the registration desk. She threw her key on the counter before a tall, thin man with watery eyes.

"My goddamn key doesn't work," she said.

"We changed the lock," he said with a gentle lisp. "It was Mrs. Delaney's wish." He rang a bell and a hop appeared. "Ms. Bradshaw's things please."

"Damn bitch," Tiffy said.

"That's my mom you're talking about."

She turned on him. "You don't miss much, do you?"

Duncan backed up. Last time Tiffy was this mad she punched him into a flower bed. Tiffy ripped open one of the bags the hop brought and threw clothing about until she came to her purse.

"It's all there, Ms. Bradshaw."

"It goddamn better be or I'll . . ."

"You'll what?" The clerk's lisp was gone and the teeth he showed were sharp and clean. "Call the police? Sure. You could explain to them about the white powder and marijuana in your bag."

Tiffy turned abruptly and left. Duncan picked up her bags and followed. They waited at the curb for their car. Tiffy turned back towards the lobby.

"Let it go," Duncan said.

The valet they called *Valentino* brought up the mini-van. Tiffy ignored him. Duncan tossed her bags in the back. *Valentino* stood in the driveway and made the sign of the cross as he sadly watched them drive away.

"Where to now?" Duncan asked.

"Your place."

"I don't . . ."

"Jesus Horatio Christ, Duncan, don't you fail me now! You're talking to the woman who took your cherry and screwed you for seven years straight, and if you don't think you owe me a little consideration you got another thought coming!" Tiffy gazed out the window. "It's not like I'm going to try to sleep with you."

"I didn't think you were," Duncan lied.

"Well, why not?"

"For one thing," Duncan said, "You don't want me anymore."

"Don't tell me what I want."

Duncan knew from past experience he could not win. He had learned long ago to pick his fights with Tiffy, and as soon as a situation demanded it, by God he would stand up to her.

"I'm pretty good, you know. Not at sex. I mean I am. But that's not what I mean. At stripping. I'm good."

"I bet you are."

"What the hell does that mean?"

"It means I bet you're good at it."

"As good as your girlfriend."

"How do you know about her?"

"Jesus Christ, what do you use for brains? Fiona brought me out here."

"Oh," Duncan pulled into Assan's parking lot. "I don't know how good she is. I've never seen her strip."

"You're kidding."

"Nope."

"Well you should," Tiffy admitted, "she's fantastic."

Duncan got out and put Tiffy's bags on the sidewalk. He went inside and gave Abdul the keys and bought a twelve pack of beer. He handed the beer to Tiffy and picked up her bags. She trailed him around the building and upstairs. He opened the door and followed her in. He dropped her bags, took the twelve pack, and headed for the refrigerator.

"What a dump," Tiffy said.

She spotted the painting of Pris on the easel. She sat down heavily. Duncan came out of the kitchen with two beers. He gave her one and sat on the floor against the wall.

"You okay?" he asked. "You look pale."

As she stared at the painting, Tiffy remembered a photograph her father had taken when she was nine. She was sleeping in that picture, her face framed by her long white hair, a smile on her face from a comfortable dream. Her father called her his angel, and he kept this picture in his wallet as proof should anyone deny his claim. She had never liked the picture, but now, looking at Duncan's painting, she realized there were worse things to be than somebody's angel. She would have cried had she been capable. Instead the emotions the memory evoked made her angry and spiteful.

"You want to see me strip?"

"I've seen it."

"I don't mean just taking off my clothes. There's more to it."

"Thank you, no."

"I wish you would cut this goody two shoes crap. I don't buy it. You know, I was sleeping with other guys when I was with you."

"I know now."

"I thought you did. I thought you just turned a blind eye."

"Nope. I would not have stood it."

"Oh no? What would you have done? What would you have said?"

"Goodbye, probably."

"Right. Like I believe that."

"I said it before I came out here, didn't I? And with less provocation."
Tiffy stood. "Do you mind if I put on some music?"

"Go ahead."

She took a compact disk out of her bag and put it in the stereo. A Latin band played a seductive, rhythmic cross of flamenco and jazz. She put the beer down. She picked up her bag and headed for the bathroom.

"I have to pee," she said.

She shut the bathroom door. She stripped and put on white panties, cotton socks, a white lace bra, a knee high plaid skirt, and a white silk blouse. She left the blouse untucked and unbuttoned. She turned off the light and opened the door. Duncan still sat on the floor across the room. She danced toward him, softly moving to the music. She swayed and thrust her hips and let her blouse fall naturally off her shoulders to the floor. She unbuttoned her bra and slowly opened it, unleashing the power and the glory of her magnificent chest. She thrust her nipples out as if to pierce his soul. She fell to her knees and looked into his face.

"I'll be damned," she said.

Duncan's arms were crossed over his knees and his head rested on his arms. He snored softly. Tiffy found a blanket on a shelf in the closet and draped it across his shoulders and knees. She sat half naked on the floor and watched him sleep. The anger had vanished. She did not know where it went. She just knew it was gone. She kissed his cheek.

"Good night, sweet Duncan," she whispered.

She turned off the light and undressed. She lay on the couch and pulled the sleeping bag to her shoulders. She slept and dreamed of two teenagers lying in a pasture's midnight grass beneath a summer sky, holding hands and watching shooting stars flame across a diamond studded heaven, burning their way into oblivion like a young woman's anger.

Hours later, Pris found Tiffy on Duncan's couch, naked after the sleeping bag had fallen to the floor. Duncan slept on the floor against the wall, still fully clothed. If he was down to so much as his shorts Pris would have walked away and never returned. But looking at him, she knew whatever he had done, he had done in kindness. She kissed his forehead. Duncan mumbled something that was probably her name. He opened his eyes and smiled when he saw her. He saw Tiffy lying naked on his couch.

"Pris," he said, panicked, "it's not what you think."

"Yes it is," she said, and she kissed him again. "And I love you for it."

Sixteen

Duncan was painting Roscoe and Sven when Misty came up. She collected empty bottles and got full ones from the refrigerator. She passed out beers and stood behind Duncan.

"That's better than the others," she said. "It's more natural."

Duncan stepped back. She was right, though he could not say why. The scene itself was unremarkable, just two men looking at television. He scratched his head with a brush. Three days he had vainly tried to paint them. The first day he posed them arm wrestling. But that just looked posed. The next day he faced them nose to chin (Sven was taller) looking belligerent. That just looked stupid. The third day he decided to paint when inspiration struck. But both were fidgety and they left prematurely to have a beer. Duncan had plenty in the refrigerator but they declined his offer. He had wondered if he offended them. Apparently not, as both returned that morning. And now they seemed happy watching professional wrestling on the television Benjamin had purchased the day before.

"Got tired of watching you paint," Benjamin explained when he brought the set up.

"Where's your girlfriend?" Misty asked.

"Which one?" Roscoe asked.

It pained Misty to ask the question and the answer, which reminded her two women remained queued before her, near collapsed her lungs.

"Pris," she finally said, "the other one is your ex-girlfriend, right?"

"That's right."

After Pris woke him that morning, he had draped the sleeping bag over Tiffy. She stirred at the touch of nylon, smiled, and introduced herself. Duncan watched nervously, but the two got along, and Pris suggested they go to breakfast. Duncan did not know if he was relieved or terrified. He thought he would make it until Tiffy suggested a threesome. He was halfway into a swallow of buttermilk pancakes. The ensuing coughing fit did not require a Heimlich. Pris smoothly declined while slapping his back.

Her refusal realigned his estimate of her sexuality to roughly eighty percent heterosexual.

"So," Misty persisted, "where is she?"

"I don't know. I haven't seen her for three days."

"Have you called?"

"I would have," Duncan said, "but she never gave me her number."

"Wouldn't matter," Roscoe said, "she doesn't have a phone."

"Everyone has a phone," Sven said.

Roscoe shrugged. "Pris doesn't."

"What do you want to see Pris about?" Duncan asked.

Actually, Misty did not. It was just an excuse to come see Duncan. And now, when asked, she was unprepared to answer.

"To settle a bet," she finally said. "I said Duncan could paint anyone to look sympathetic and Cassandra said there was at least one of three classes of people he couldn't." The conversation had occurred, though it involved no wager. "Child molesters, murderers, and personal injury lawyers."

"Why do you need Pris?" Sven asked, "Just ask Duncan."

"I don't know." Misty blushed. "Maybe someone close to you can know you better than you know yourself."

"He's already painted a murderer," Roscoe said. "Wilson did time for manslaughter. They charged him with second degree murder but he pled it down. And Peewee's done time for statutory rape."

"That shouldn't count," Misty said. "We all thought Amber was eighteen or she wouldn't have been hired."

"I don't care how old she looked, she was fourteen and built for sin and Peewee did her. He told the judge it was not right for a girl so young to have a body so old, but her daddy brought her to court in pigtails with an ace bandage around her tits and the judge slammed him."

"What about a personal injury lawyer?" Misty asked.

"I don't know," Duncan said, "I've never tried."

Roscoe stood. "I'll be right back."

Duncan kept painting. Something about the canvas bothered him, even though it was turning out as well as *Roscoe* and *Drive By,* though not as well as *Sleeping Pris.* Roscoe returned with a thin man in a rumpled suit with a crumpled shirt and a polyester clip-on tie with a spaghetti sauce stain near the knot. His dyed yellow hair had gray roots, and his small, red eyes were set so wide he could almost see inside his ears. He gave Duncan a business card. *Stuart Yog Esq.*, it said, *Divorce, Personal Injury, and Worker's Compensation on a Contingency Basis.*

"You must be Delaney. Roscoe told me what happened." He examined Duncan's face. "Healing nicely, I'm afraid. Did you take pictures?"

"Well, no. I painted a self-portrait though."

Duncan set the painting of Roscoe and Sven on the floor. He put his self-portrait on the easel. Yog studied the face on the canvas.

"Ok. Any idea who did it?"

"Yes, but no proof."

"Doesn't matter. Does he have money or insurance?"

"It was a she."

"Ouch. So much for your manhood. Sorry. Not so much jury appeal, but that's what we got. How is she set up financially?"

"Very well, I believe. But how can we prove . . ."

"Prove schmoove. We sue for a million and settle for whatever her insurance company is willing to pay. We never set foot in court and split the settlement fifty-fifty."

"But what if she didn't do it?"

"Who are you, Prince Valiant? Who the hell cares? As long as we can convince nine out of twelve citizens it doesn't matter if she did it or not."

"I thought a contingency fee was one third," Sven said.

"Half, third, who's counting? What do you say, sport?"

"Let me think about it."

"All right," Yog said. "But don't think too long." He squashed a small creature crossing the floor. "The cockroaches might get impatient."

"That was a spider," Misty said.

"Who the hell cares? It's still an insect."

"Actually, spiders are arachnids," Duncan said.

"You're too much," Yog said.

After Yog left, Roscoe said, "Well, what do you think?"

Duncan took the self portrait down and put the painting in progress back on his easel. "Cassandra wins the bet," he said.

They spent the rest of the night arguing over the relative worth of insects and arachnids. Duncan contended all spiders, save the poisonous varieties, were beneficial and should be spared. Misty dissented, maintaining that spiders were yucky. All agreed it proper to seek out and kill cockroaches while ladybugs should be granted life everlasting.

"Caterpillars are fair game," Roscoe said.

"But not butterflies," Sven said. "They are so beautiful."

Misty said, "Don't butterflies come from caterpillars?"

"Just kill the hairy ones then," Roscoe said. "And flies. I hate flies."

"Kill all the flies you want," Sven said, "but don't touch butterflies."

"All right, already! I said butterflies were okay."

"Wasps die," Misty said, "but bees live."

Duncan laughed. "And crickets must always be spared."

Roscoe looked confused. "Why?"

"Because they sing in the night."

Duncan was almost drunk, and the thought of crickets serenading the darkness seemed profoundly beautiful.

Roscoe stood. "It's late."

"It's only ten-thirty!" Duncan protested. "I'm almost done."

"I got to get back to the Hollywood. You with me, Sven?"

Sven rose. "Yes. I would like that."

"All right. I can finish without you."

After they left Misty asked, "How come you never come into the Hollywood?"

"I don't know. I guess I wouldn't feel comfortable there."

"Why not? We're all there because we want to be."

"Really. Did you grow up thinking, *gee, I'd really like to be a stripper?*"

"Of course not. And thanks for making me feel like dirt."

"That's not what I meant. You're there for the money, right?"

"Sure."

"Well, I don't want to support it."

"Oh, a feminist man." Misty nodded. "Feminist men just want to get laid." It was something she had once heard Sheila say to Pris.

"All men do. It's how you go about it that matters."

Benjamin came in an hour later when Duncan had regained most of his sobriety. He stood beside him and studied the painting.

"You never told me Roscoe was gay," he said.

"Say what?"

Benjamin pointed to the space on the couch between Roscoe and Sven. Roscoe gripped a beer in his right hand and Sven held one in his left. The hands between them were tenderly clasped.

"Oh my god," Misty said.

"Looks like he's a nickel short of a three dollar bill," Benjamin said.

Cassandra burst into the studio. "Duncan, come quick! It's Pris!"

"What's wrong?" Duncan's heart threatened to escape his chest via trachea. "Is she ok?"

"I don't think so," Cassandra said.

It was like he was back in the dream.

Everything was identical, from the steel pole impaling the raised stage to the small footlights, the mirrored walls, and the peeling veneer on the particle board tables. Pris stood on stage, her back against the mirrors, naked except for her black silk panties. Her blonde hair was loose and wild and she had a wolverine cast to her eyes. Her naked chest labored with each panting breath. She held a bloody, splintered chair leg. Stuart Yog lay on the floor by the footlights, a gash on his scalp running from forehead to ear and coloring his gray roots red. Roscoe and Sven stood on either side of Yog watching the stage. Sheila stood across from Pris, trying to calm her, but when she stepped closer Pris swung the chair leg towards her.

"I need a doctor," Yog moaned.

"Fuck you," Roscoe said.

"I'll sue your ass. I'll close this place down." He tried to stand. He fell back to his knees. "Someone call the police. That bitch nearly killed me."

"Fuck you twice," Cassandra yelled. "Asshole." She sat at the bar. "He tried to stuff a twenty down her panties. She told him to put it on the stage. You can't take money directly from a customer, you know."

"I did not know that," Benjamin said.

"That's solicitation. You can get busted for that. Anyway, this jerk puts the twenty back and takes out a hundred and jams it and his hand down her pants. Roscoe was in the john otherwise the prick wouldn't have tried it. So Pris slapped him and the bastard slapped her back."

Duncan nodded. "Which is when she picked up the chair."

"Uh huh. Smashed it over his head. Then she backed into the corner with the chair leg. No one can get close. We might have to call the cops."

"No police," Duncan said. He climbed onto the stage.

"I'm handling this," Sheila said, her eyes angry.

"How long have you been handling it?"

"A couple of minutes."

"More like ten," Yog said.

Roscoe kicked him. "Fuck you," he said.

Duncan said. "Let me try."

Sheila smiled. "Go ahead, hot shot. I hope she caves your skull in."

"Are you finally satisfied?" Pris said when Duncan approached. She swung the chair leg up and down her body. "To see me like this? Isn't that what you wanted?"

Duncan removed his jacket and stepped forward. "Not like this."

"Stay away." She brandished the chair leg. "I'll kill you."

"No, you won't."

He gently wrapped his jacket around her. She dropped the chair leg and sobbed. Duncan held her and buried his head in her hair. It was damp with sweat and faintly acrid.

"It's Bolo," Pris said.

"He's dead, isn't he?"

"How did you know?"

Duncan could not say Bolo predicted his own death in a dream. He tried a variation of the truth. "I can't imagine anything else could hurt you so."

Sheila glared at the man holding the woman she loved. The red fury she had felt towards Duncan was replaced by a cold rage tempered by her desire for Pris's happiness. She walked off the stage, pausing only long enough on her way to the door to army boot Stuart Yog in the ribs.

"Uhngh!" Stuart Yog moaned. "Won't anyone help me?"

Benjamin knelt beside him. He grabbed Yog's ear and pulled his head up. He held his Bowie knife to Yog's throat. Yog looked at the bright sharp blade with sideways eyes.

"Sure I'll help," Benjamin said. "I'll help you bleed to death if you don't shut up."

"Ok."

"And I don't want to hear another word about police or lawsuit. From you or anyone else. If I do, I hunt you down and kill you. Understand?"

"Jesus," Yog said, "there are witnesses here!"

"I didn't hear nothing," Cassandra said.

"Anything," Benjamin said.

"Whatever. What about you, Champagne?"

"All I heard was this jerk crying after he tripped and brained himself."

"Aw, Christ," Yog said. "I got the picture."

Benjamin sheathed his knife. He helped Yog to his feet. "Come on," he said, "I'll buy you a beer before you get the hell out of here."

"Can you drive me to the hospital?"

"Don't push it."

"You drive," Pris said. "I'm really tired."

Duncan opened the Cadillac and let her in. He slid behind the wheel and started the car. Pris only spoke to tell him which way to go. They turned onto a private road and drove through mossy gates onto a gravel driveway. He stopped before a big, Spanish style home with a red tile porch and a red tile roof. Roses climbed an arch around a tall wood door. Iron balconies framed two sets of French doors on the second story. A grove stood in the darkness west of the house. Duncan smelled oranges. Pris got out. Duncan followed her to the porch.

"Where are we?"

"Home. Bolo's home." She opened the door. "My home now."

She turned on the lights. A white couch sat on an oriental rug across from a granite fireplace with a black iron screen before it. A cracked leather armchair sat on polished hardwood beside the fireplace, a reading lamp behind it. Bifocals lay on a book on a table by the chair. Photographs of Bolo and a plain, dark-haired woman hung above the mantle. French doors led out to a fountain surrounded by green grass and yellow roses. An iron bench sat on old bricks facing the lights of Los Angeles.

"Would you like some tea?"

"Yes, please."

Pris smiled. "I'll be back in a minute."

Duncan moved the bifocals and picked up the book. It was an old, leather bound bible, in Italian. A photo fell from the bible to the floor. Duncan picked it up. It was of Bolo and the woman in the picture above the fireplace. A blond girl stood between them, a crowd behind them, and the mountain in the background made Duncan think of Disneyland.

"That's me."

Duncan put the photo down. Pris had changed into plaid flannel pajamas and had washed the makeup and the tears from her eyes. Duncan took one of the two tea cups she held. She sat on the big white couch.

"Could you make a fire?" she asked. "I want to watch something burn."

Duncan set his tea down. He moved the screen and wadded up newspaper he found behind the armchair. He laid the newspaper under an iron grate. A metal caddy held split wood beside the fireplace. He placed four logs above the newspaper. He lit the paper and replaced the screen. He picked up his tea and sat beside Pris. She stared at the photograph.

"I ran away to Hollywood after my dad died. I was fifteen and I didn't want to end up in a foster home. Guys on the street kept asking me if I was working. I didn't know what that meant until one asked me how much for a blow job and I ran like hell and hid behind a dumpster. I stayed there until I got so hungry my ribs jabbed my stomach and I crawled into the dumpster and ate leftovers and garbage. I was desperate and I didn't know what to do. The choices were starve or go to work. I decided to work."

"You don't have to tell me this."

"Yes I do." She sipped her tea. The green wood in the fireplace hissed and popped. "I approached the first well dressed, middle-aged man I saw on the street. I told him I would screw his brains out for twenty dollars.

"'I like my brains where they are,' he said. He smiled and I started to cry. He hugged me while I sobbed into his shirt."

"Bolo?"

Pris nodded. "When I stopped crying, his shirt was filthy where my cheek had been. I stunk, my clothes were dirty, and god knows why anyone would want to have sex with me let alone pay for it. He brought me here. His wife Maria gave me a bath and a room and told me I could stay as long as I wanted. She died from breast cancer the next year and then it was just me and Bolo. He kicked me out when I started stripping. He told me I could come back when I gave it up. But the money was too good. I couldn't make that much money any other way."

"What about modeling? Or acting?"

Pris smiled sadly. "I can't afford to be famous."

"Why not?"

"I'm too tired to talk any more tonight."

She set her tea on the floor by the couch then put Duncan's cup besides hers. She pulled his boots off and stretched him across the couch. She turned off the lights and lay beside him. She fell asleep in his arms, one layer of flannel and another of cotton and denim between them. Despite the absence of the possibility of sex, Duncan was almost as happy as he would have been if they were naked and joined at the pelvis. He fell asleep and dreamed of Christmas at the Circle D and a red-haired child playing in the snow beside a frozen creek and as he drifted further and deeper he wondered if the child was his or Sean's.

Seventeen

Fiona was sitting on the veranda enjoying the sun and a glass of freshly squeezed orange juice when the phone rang. Her heart skipped when Duncan said *mom*, but the ensuing words were gentle, and she dared hoped he had forgiven her attempt to buy off his harlot. She concluded her puppy dog of a boy was coming home with his tail sutured between his legs where it belonged. Woody returned shortly past noon. He had been at the beach taking the third installment of a five lesson surfing package. He wore a black wetsuit. His hair was damp and salty and hinted at ocean bleach. He leaned his chartered surfboard upon the wall outside the veranda.

"How was it?" Fiona asked.

"Flat," he replied, "I only caught a couple of waves. I got up once."

"Good for you."

Fiona followed him into the bathroom. Woody pulled his wetsuit off and stood under the shower. Fiona watched his ripcord muscles move beneath his skin as he lathered and shampooed.

"Duncan's coming over," she said.

Woody stopped shampooing. "Oh, lord," he said. "What is it now?"

"I think he's coming to say he's sorry."

He ain't the one who should apologize, Woody thought. He rinsed and stepped out of the shower and dried himself with the towel Fiona gave him. He put on a tank top and baggy shorts and rubber sandals. The tank top said *Hard Rock Café* across the back. Fiona had bought it for him. He shunned such shirts back home, but here it was his favorite.

"So we might be going home?"

The prospect appealed to him less than it did to Fiona. He had hoped to become a proficient surfer and to catch the *Tonight Show* live. And he did not eagerly anticipate the coming winter.

"We'll see," Fiona said. "Soon, I guess."

"Probably shouldn't push him too hard just yet."

"No, I think you're right. Was that a knock? That must be him."

150

Fiona opened the door for Duncan and stuck her head out. She looked both ways for Benjamin. But Duncan was alone and she shut the door and hugged him with a silent, grateful prayer.

"Hey, Duncan," Woody said, "care for a beer?"

"You got a cold one?"

"Nope." Woody picked up the phone. "But we got room service."

Woody ordered three. It was such a wonderful day Fiona allowed she would have one herself. She led Duncan to the couch and sat beside him.

"So you've forgiven your poor old mother?"

"I never begrudged you. And you're not that old."

"What mistakes I made were made out of love. But she was not the woman for you."

"That's for sure. Though I'm surprised to hear you say it."

Fiona sensed danger. "You *are* coming home, aren't you?"

"We've been through this mom. This is home now."

"I am confused. Didn't you just agree that girl was wrong for you?"

"Yes I did. I don't know why it took me so long to realize it."

"Uh oh," Woody said. "You think she's talking about Tiffy, don't you?"

"Well of course I'm not! I'm talking about that stripper."

"Then you won't much like what else I have to say. That stripper, as you call her?" Duncan stood. "We're getting married."

"The hell you are," Fiona spluttered after Woody revived her with an ice bucket of water to the face. "No son of mine is going to marry a tart."

In the interim between the faint and revival, room service had arrived with three beers. Duncan was one third through his when Woody emptied the bucket on Fiona's face. He would have revived her himself, but Woody seemed eager to execute the drenching. He stood by the bedroom door, the empty bucket in his left hand and a cold one gripped so tight in his white knuckled right that either the bottle or the bone surrounding it might break.

"She quit stripping," Duncan said.

Fiona took a deep drought of beer. "But she'll always have it in her past."

"Goddamn it, Fiona," Woody said. His face was red beneath the tan and his eyes were wide and angry. "That's enough."

"Woody," Fiona said dangerously, "last I checked you worked for me."

"Not anymore I don't."

151

He dropped the ice bucket and the beer and stalked into the bedroom. Duncan listened to drawers flung open and closet doors slammed. Woody emerged with his suitcase.

"What has gotten into you?"

"Fiona, I love you. Always have. But I'll be damned if I'll stand by and watch you let your son make the same mistake you made."

"You think marrying Sean was a mistake?"

"God, for such a smart woman you are dense. No, that was probably the best thing you ever did. Your mistake is not marrying me."

"You never asked!"

Woody set the suitcase down. "All right," he said, "I'm asking." He got down on one knee. "Fiona Delaney, will you marry me?"

"Woody, this isn't the time . . ."

"That's what I thought." He picked up the suitcase. "You've cheated on a dead man for twelve years. Correct me if I'm wrong, but your vows said, till *death* do you part. I believe you've fulfilled your obligations under the contract."

"Woody, what about Duncan?"

"He's a grown man!"

"He's my baby!"

"Don't look now, but your baby has grown up and you're all alone." He turned to Duncan. "Can I stay with you until I figure things out?"

"Sure. As long as you want. Benjamin's waiting in the parking lot."

Woody left. Fiona stood there, stunned and bereft, an empty space filling her chest and shrinking her heart into her bowels where it threatened to implode with fear and sorrow.

"We're getting married in Las Vegas tomorrow," Duncan said. "I'd like you there." He wrote the address on hotel stationary. "Woody's right. You should have married him long ago. Dad wouldn't mind."

Her son telling her how her dead husband would feel rekindled an angry ember. "How could you possibly know that?"

"I just know," he said.

Duncan followed Woody out the door. Fiona stood a long while holding her half empty beer. She heard the Purgatory Truck's distinctive roar fade in the distance. She went to the bedroom and sat on the bed. She finished the beer and dropped the bottle onto the carpet. Then, for the first time since Sean Delaney was transported into the hereafter courtesy of a ball of rapidly oxidizing jet fuel, she put her head in her hands and cried.

"She won't show," Duncan said.

He wore brown cotton pants, brown leather shoes, a tan linen shirt with a dark brown tie and his Stetson wedged atop his ears. The painting of Assan stood on his easel, and though he had finished it two days before, he nervously dabbed at it with a brush.

"You keep messing with that and you'll ruin it," Woody said.

Woody wore his Stetson, a white shirt with a silver and quartz bolo tie, his best blue jeans, a belt with a silver and topaz buckle in the shape of a charging bull, his finest boots with silver tooling, and a brave face to disguise his aching heart.

"Think positive thoughts," Sven said.

Benjamin carried a case of malt liquor into the studio and passed out sixteen ounce cans.

"I got the tall boys," he said. He popped one and drained a good portion. "Where's the bride?"

"She's not coming," Duncan said.

"Sure she is," Woody said. "She's got ten minutes."

Roscoe exited the bathroom. "Hey, give me one of those."

"Did you wash your hands?" Sven asked.

Roscoe returned to the bathroom. "It's like I got a new mother."

"You Americans," Sven said, "you are such barbarians."

Roscoe emerged from the bathroom wiping his hands on his t-shirt. "That's what you like about me."

"Are they gay?" Woody asked Duncan. "It's like they're married."

"Apparently so. Not married. Gay, I mean."

"Well, okay." Woody said.

Duncan did not know if that meant Woody approved or if he was simply acknowledging the confirmation of his suspicions. He returned to the couch and opened a beer. Misty carried a tray in from the kitchen.

"I could only find pop tarts," she said. "I've got raspberry, strawberry, and brown sugar and cinnamon."

She had cried for ten minutes after Roscoe told her the news of Duncan's impending nuptials. But she forced herself to stop, fixed her makeup, and marched across the street to congratulate Duncan with a kiss that burned her lips with restrained passion but barely left an impression on Duncan's cheek. Duncan took a raspberry pop tart.

"We brought crab cakes," Sven said, "but Benjamin ate them all."

"I couldn't help it. They're so damn good."

"She's not coming," Duncan said.

"Of course she is," Misty said, "she'd be crazy not to."

Actually, he thought, *she'd be crazy if she did marry me.* After thinking it over for a half day he knew marriage made no sense. What he knew of her hinted at an unpaved pothole of a road ahead. He did not dare estimate the chances this union would survive. But he did not want to spend his life wondering if he had let the best thing that ever happened to him get away.

Duncan had awoken at dawn and taken the Cadillac down the hill from Bolo's to a market on Ventura Boulevard. He returned to find Pris still sleeping on the couch. He knelt beside her and took a gilded plastic ring with a big glass stone from a bag. He had found it in the market's toy section and paid two ninety-five for it. She woke when he slipped it onto her left ring finger. She looked at the ring and then at him.

"What are you doing?"

"I'm asking you to marry me."

"Why on earth would you want to do that?"

He answered with a gentle kiss and when they parted Pris laughed and cried and Duncan did not know if he should be happy or frightened. She wiped the tears from her eyes and stared at the ring.

"It's so ugly, it's beautiful," she said.

"It's just temporary," he said. "Until I get you a real one."

"I don't want a real one." She kissed him again, longer and harder. She smiled when they finally separated. "Of course I'll marry you. Who else would be dumb enough to put up with me?"

Still, wide-ranging doubts filled Duncan as he stood at his easel enlarging Assan's nose. Every time his hopes dared fly, she ripped the wings off and sent his foolishly aspiring carcass to the rocky earth below. And with the stakes now greater and his hopes higher, he feared but was unprepared for the likely fall. Duncan jumped at a knock on the door. It was Assan and Angela. Assan studied the painting.

"My nose is too big," he said.

"Sorry." Duncan dabbed at Assan's face.

Angela threw her coat on the couch. "I got here as fast as I could," she said. "What's the big surprise?"

"Duncan's getting married," Benjamin said.

"That's wonderful! When?"

"Tonight," Misty answered. "In Vegas."

Duncan looked at his watch. "Assuming the bride shows up."

154

"Tonight?" Angela frowned. "I had plans for you tonight, Duncan, but this is obviously more important. I need your best painting."

"What for?"

"Never mind. It's a surprise."

"Well, all right." Duncan put down his brush.

"Is it finished?" Assan asked. "Can I take it now?"

"It's all yours. I hope it pleases your mother."

Assan took the painting off the easel. "I might get her a Rolex instead."

"You don't like it?"

"No, no! I love it. It will hang downstairs in my store. Thank you."

Duncan placed his self-portrait on the easel. "How about this one?"

"That's nice," Angela said. She flipped through his paintings and took out *Sleeping Pris*. "But this one is fantastic."

"It's not finished."

"Jesus, Duncan," Misty said. "It's perfect."

Roscoe said, "If you do any more to that you'll fuck it up."

"Well spoken," said Sven.

"All the same," Duncan said, "I choose the other."

"All right. I'll have a messenger pick it up tonight."

"But I won't be here."

"I'll stay," Misty said. "Somebody has to take care of Cat." She smiled to hide her splintering heart. "Besides. I hate Vegas."

Duncan's door slammed opened. Sheila Rascowitz stepped in. She wore black jeans, a black silk shirt, black boots, and a man's black tie. Her face was twisted and Duncan feared she was some evil harbinger ascended from hell to rip his chest open with her nails and extract his entrails with her teeth. Instead she stepped aside and allowed Pris to enter behind her. The skirt she wore was the color of fresh cream. Silk stockings wrapped her legs. She wore white leather pumps with one inch heels, a white silk blouse open to her sternum, and a linen jacket the color of her skirt. Her hair was loose and long and she carried a bouquet of small white roses and baby's breath.

"Holy Jesus," Woody whispered as Misty cried what everyone erroneously assumed were joyous tears, "it's an angel fresh from heaven."

Duncan was happy to stand there gazing upon her splendor until a nervous red-haired woman came through the door and broke the spell. Duncan embraced her and led her to Woody.

"Woody, I'm so sorry," Fiona sobbed.

"It's all right." Woody held her tight and kissed her forehead. "Everything's fine now."

Misty sat in the window stroking Cat for an eternity. She watched traffic stream below. In the hour since Duncan's departure she had cried herself out, and had ultimately conceded the futility of continued lachrymation. She set Cat down and replaced the self portrait on the easel with *Sleeping Pris*. She lay on the couch and stared at the painting. Cat climbed into her lap. She hugged him and decided to get a cat of her own.

"You're nice, but you're taken," she said.

She imagined herself in thirty years, corpulent in spandex and a low-cut blouse, tending bar in a strip joint, serving beers to equally obese bald men who favored girls young and beautiful over her, girls who ranged the stage like sex, but without the contact or the lubrication. She would leave the bar with a pocket half full of ones while the girls on stage departed with twice as many tens and twenties. She would drive a twenty-year-old Honda with bald tires to an apartment full of cats and a microwave. She questioned how she got here and how to get out. She fell asleep with Cat still on her lap.

Hours later when the messenger knocked, Misty stirred but did not wake. He opened the unlocked door and walked in. Angela had warned him of Duncan's odd living arrangements and said it was okay to do so. He stopped and stared at the beautiful girl sleeping on the couch. The messenger was nineteen and still a virgin. He had never seen anyone as lovely. He thought to wake her, but ultimately decided against disturbing such serene perfection. He helped himself to a beer and took *Sleeping Pris* from the easel. He shook his head. Two perfect females, one painter. Thinking to himself how some guys had all the luck, he left with the wrong painting, and thus sealed Duncan's fate.

Eighteen

Elnie Marcos was ordained a minister in the Church of Jesus, Philosopher in May 1987. Five feet tall and nearly as wide, she was a distant relative of the deposed Philippine dictator. She had received her degree from the Arizona College of Theology and Mortuary Sciences, a correspondence school and diploma mill run out of a post office box in Phoenix by a mortician who lost his license years before when he cremated seven corpses together and returned the bones of a seven-foot former pro basketball player to a carnival midget's wife. She spotted the mistake immediately, realizing the femur protruding from the ashes was too long to have grown inside her beloved. She reported the problem to the state board, and after a short investigation and a series of articles in the Phoenix Sun, the mortician found himself in need of employment. So he opened and operated his mail order university until he was arrested by Postal Inspectors and convicted of mail fraud in connection with a moderately successful Ponzi scheme. After that he ran his college from a federal prison cell.

Elnie knew nothing of her distant professor's travails. She studied the mail order materials he sent and consistently scored upper nineties on the tests she mailed back to Phoenix. Every student scored in the upper nineties but not every student knew their bible the way Elnie did. She took her degree and her vocation seriously, even if her school did not. Elnie tried to start several congregations, but the Church of Jesus, Philosopher was not a known or accredited sect, and after several aborted attempts, she went to work at the Bright Star of Light and Hope Wedding Chapel located five minutes from the Las Vegas Strip. She saved her salary and after six years of marrying on commission as many as one hundred couples per day she bought her employer out. She had married everyone from transvestite Elvis impersonators to ultra right wing white separatists wearing camouflage fatigues and carrying M-16s. The white separatists wanted a white male to wed them, but were unable to find a suitably racist minister who would allow loaded, fully automatic firearms in his chapel. They grudgingly settled for Elnie. She did not care who they were or what they believed. She was happy to unite them under the philosophical eyes of her Jesus. Even racist extremists were God's children, and when they robbed her after the ceremony and left her bound, gagged, but still alive, she thanked god, not for her life, but for the possibility of their redemption. So the only thing that struck her as odd when she married Duncan Delaney to Priscilla Nolan, besides how beautiful the bride and how nervous the groom, was how the maid of honor, a short haired masculine woman wearing black, kept looking at the best man, a long-haired Native American dressed in blue jeans and a long sleeved cotton shirt. The maid of honor never smiled, not once throughout the ceremony. If it was not such a happy occasion, as evidenced by the red-headed woman's tears and by the magnificently built blond man weeping into the bald biker's shoulder, she would have sworn the maid of honor begrudged the best man.

After the ceremony Elnie followed the menagerie from the chapel to the street. She lit a cigarette and watched the bride and groom get in an immaculate white Cadillac. The maid of honor got into a bright red truck between the best man and a lovely dark-haired woman. The groom's mother and a leathery cowboy got into a rented Lincoln. The tall blonde man, the biker, and the short Pakistani squeezed into the Lincoln's back seat. The Chapel organist joined Elnie on the sidewalk. He was once a replacement keyboard player and studio musician whose closest brush with fame was playing background piano on a Bobby DeLaRoy single in the early seventies. After that a bad cocaine habit sidelined him to Vegas house bands and even that did not last. He spent fifteen of the last twenty years on the street and would be there still if Elnie had not spotted him playing organ at the soup kitchen where she volunteered twice a month. The organist lit a cigarette and together they watched the party drive away.

"Circus must be in town," he said.

He crushed his cigarette and went back inside the chapel, where he spent the remaining five minutes of his break playing show tunes for a nervous couple from Omaha waiting to spend the remainder of their lives together.

Duncan sat on an absurdly comfortable couch in the suite Fiona had rented for him at the Mirage. He sipped champagne and watched Pris dance with Benjamin. Sheila stood by a window talking to Angela. Fiona and Woody snuggled across the room. Sven was making omelettes in the kitchen. Assan was downstairs playing blackjack with Benjamin's cousin April. Roscoe sat beside Duncan. He wore a too small t-shirt with a tuxedo silk-screened across the front. A fold of belly showed between hem and belt.

"Well," Roscoe said, "I guess you figured out by now that I'm a fagot."

"Yup," Duncan said. "When did you find out?"

"Long time ago. I just never admitted it to anyone. Never a reason to before I met Sven. Does it bother you?"

"Couldn't care less."

Sven came out of the kitchen carrying plates. "Dinner is served."

"That first night Sven took me to his place on the west side and made me an omelette. He's got a weight room and a tanning booth. I remember eating the omelette and thinking, *this is the man for me*. He's kind of vain, but he's a hell of a cook." Roscoe laughed. "I think I'll keep him."

Pris sat beside Duncan. "I want an omelette. Can I get you one?"

He smiled. "I'll have some of yours if that's okay."

She kissed him and left. Sheila left Angela and joined Duncan.

"Truce?" Duncan asked.

"Truce hell. You won the war."

She put her hand out. Duncan took it. Her grip evoked painful tears, but anyone watching would suppose they were letting bygones be.

"Listen to me, you little squid," she hissed through teeth clenched beneath a cordial grin, "if you hurt her, if you make her sad, if you *bore* her, I will hunt you and kill you and skin you and stuff you and hang you over my fireplace." She released his hand. Duncan felt the cool rush of blood returning to his fingers. "And just so we're clear on this: I look forward to you fucking up." She left to get an omelette.

"It's nice to see you two getting along," Pris said when she returned with a plate. "What were you talking about?"

Duncan took a bite of omelette. It was amazingly good.

"She just wanted to wish us luck," he said.

"I told you," she said when they were alone, "I won't be very good at this."

"Can't be worse than me." Duncan lit a candle by the bed.

"Tiffy seemed to think you were pretty good."

"How would you know that?"

"We talked at the restaurant when you were in the bathroom. She said you were the second best she ever had. She said you were clumsy at first but you improved with age."

"Who did she say was best?"

"Some valet. But since he's not here I was hoping you could teach me."

Duncan laughed and kissed her. "We'll learn together."

He turned off the light and took off his shirt. He got on the bed beside her and ran his hand up her arm to her shoulder. He kissed her again. When he tried to roll on top of her she stiffened.

"Not like that. Do you mind?"

"Not at all."

Pris undid his belt and pulled his pants and shorts off. She unbuttoned her blouse and dropped it to the floor. She pulled her skirt and her panties down and straddled him. She kissed him, her elbows at his ears and her breasts rubbing his chest. She moved her pelvis against his. He took her breast in his mouth. She stiffened, but as his tongue caressed her nipple she relaxed and said *uh-ngh-ah*. Duncan ran his hands from shoulders to her back and around her buttocks. When he stroked her inner thigh, she moved his hand away. Her hair glowed in the candle light as she took his penis in one hand and mounted him. He moved his hips up.

"Don't," she whispered.

He lay still. She moved up and down, her breasts bouncing slightly with the motion. Duncan felt tension in his groin but before he could ask her to slow down she sped up instead, arching her back, her hands on the bed beside his knees, and to Duncan's everlasting satisfaction her orgasm occurred less than two seconds after his. She sat up, her face twisted in what Duncan assumed was ecstasy.

"Oh god," she said.

"Was I that good?" he joked.

She put her hand to her mouth. She jumped off him and off the bed and ran to the bathroom. She slammed the door behind her. Duncan listened to her retch. He got up and stood beside the bathroom door.

"Are you ok?"

"Go back to bed," she said. "I'm fine. I'll be out in a minute."

He returned to bed. He listened to the toilet flush and the sound of brushing teeth. He listened to silence for a minute. Pris came out and turned off the light behind her. She lay naked beside Duncan.

"That's the first time I ever made someone vomit," he said.

She clutched him tighter. "It must have been the champagne."

"Do you want to sleep?"

"No," she answered. "I want to get this right." She straddled him again. "I've waited too long for this."

"Me too," Duncan said. He pulled her head down and held his lips against her ear. "A lifetime," he whispered.

Nineteen

You have sixteen messages, Duncan's answering machine said when he called from Bolo's Monday morning. The first was from the body shop, telling him his car was ready. The second was from Angela. "Look in the Calendar section of the Times," she said. "Your surprise is there." The remaining fourteen were hang ups. Duncan retrieved the paper from the lawn. The lead story in the Calendar section was titled, *LA's Hottest Artists, by Robert Armstrong.* Beneath the banner was a photo of *Sleeping Pris.* He sat beside Pris and put the paper on the table in front of her. She dropped her tea cup and it shattered on the floor.

"How did that get there?" she asked.

"Angela asked for a painting before we left. I chose my self-portrait. I guess they picked up the wrong one. Are you ok? You look pale."

"I'm fine." She picked up the paper. "This is a wonderful article," she said. "Listen: *One artist stands out. Duncan Delaney, a transplant from Wyoming of all places, paints like a cross between an urban Rembrandt and an underground Van Gogh.*"

He picked up the broken cup and wiped up the tea. He made pancakes while Pris read. He warmed maple syrup. He poured glasses of orange juice. She was still staring at the paper when he brought breakfast in. Duncan devoured his food. Pris sipped her juice and let her pancakes grow cold.

"Aren't you going to eat?"

She picked up the paper again. "I'm not hungry."

Duncan cleared the table. He took a shower and dressed and when he came out she still sat at the table in her robe looking at the newspaper.

"Can you give me a ride into town?" he asked. "I have to pick up my car and get my stuff from the studio."

Pris put the paper face down on the table. She looked up and smiled.

"Of course," she said.

Duncan had to wait an hour at the body shop while a worker reinstalled a backwards seat belt. When finished, the car smelled faintly of burnt insulation, but was visually perfect. Duncan paid his deductible and left. Misty was in his studio feeding Cat when he opened the door. Cat kept eating. Misty stood. She wore no make up and her eyes were puffy.

"Hi, Duncan. Congratulations."

"Hi, Misty. Thanks. Are you okay? You look like you've been crying."

"Allergies." She looked at Cat. "Doesn't seem like he missed you much."

Duncan laughed. "No, it doesn't."

He packed his things and put it all in the wagon. Misty was gone when he returned but Cat remained. He decided to drop his canvases off at Angela's before going home. He carried the paintings downstairs, put them in the car, then went back for Cat. He was halfway to the street when his phone rang. He remembered the fourteen hang-ups.

"Curiosity," he said to Cat as he went back to get the phone, "only kills your species."

"Duncan Delaney?" a man said when he answered.

"Speaking."

"This is Samuel Norris." His voice was deep and clear. "I saw your painting in the paper. I liked it very much."

"That one's not for sale."

"That's not why I called. I wanted to speak with you about Penny."

"Who?"

"The girl in the painting."

"Her name is Pris."

"No, it's not," Samuel Norris said, deep and clear as despair, "her name is Penny. I should know. I'm her father."

"Are you still there?" Samuel Norris asked after a long time.

"She said you were dead."

"I assure you I'm not." The humor in the voice eased Duncan's trepidation. "Though I understand why she said it." There was another long silence. "What else did she tell you?"

"Nothing."

"That doesn't surprise me. We didn't part on good terms. Though I am disappointed she changed her name. It would have been so much easier to find her if she had only kept her name." The voice was sad. "I wasn't the easiest father to live with. But I've changed. I'd like to see my baby again."

Duncan remembered dark nights lying in bed, staring at his ceiling, and wondering what might have been if his father had lived. Pris had six more years with her father than he with his, but could it have been enough? He could not imagine anything bad enough to preclude reconciliation and he further imagined a father would be the best of all possible wedding gifts.

"Listen," Duncan said, "I'm busy for another couple hours yet, but if you want, you can come by the house and see her."

"Are you her boyfriend?"

Duncan smiled. "Something like that."

"Will you be there?"

"I think I should be. At first at least." Duncan gave him the address. "It's one now. I should be home by four. What say you show up at five?"

"I can't tell you how grateful I am." He paused. "Could you do me a favor? Don't tell her I'm coming. I'd like it to be a surprise."

"Sure thing."

Duncan hung up. He picked up cat and headed downstairs. For the rest of his life he would remember walking down those stairs and thinking, *won't Pris be surprised.*

When Duncan came home, the Cadillac was gone. Cat jumped from the car and paced the gravel in front of the garage. Duncan looked at his watch. Three thirty. He hoped Pris would return before her father arrived. Next door, a gardener pulled the cord on a lawn mower. The engine started noisily. Duncan got out of the car. The gardener waved to him over the hedge. Duncan waved back and went inside.

The front door was open and the television was on. Duncan turned it off. A breeze ruffled the curtains through the kitchen window. Duncan smelled mower exhaust. He closed the window. He took a jar of mayonnaise out of the refrigerator, a loaf of wheat bread, and a tin of dolphin safe tuna. He made a sandwich, got a beer, and sat on a bench on the back porch and ate. The sun was hot against his forehead. He took off his shirt and went inside to fetch his hat. He opened the bedroom door.

A man lay on the floor by the bed, his pants around his ankles and his shorts at his shins. He looked to be fifty, thin with light blond hair turning gray, his face wet and red from a gash across his temple. Blood stained his shirt around five small holes. The man groaned and reached out with a bloody hand. Duncan stumbled out the door to the living room and seized the phone. It was dead. He raced through the house screaming her name into empty room after empty room. He sprinted outside and leaped the hedge into the neighbor's yard. He tripped and somersaulted across the grass. The gardener shut off the mower.

"Call the police," Duncan yelled. *"Policia!"*

Bolo's neighbor, an old screenwriter who retired when he could not adapt to computers, stuck his head out the door. "What's wrong?"

"Call the police!" Duncan yelled.

He leaped over the hedge and tripped again, skinning his back on the gravel where he fell. He stopped. With the lawn mower silent he heard the Cadillac rumbling inside the garage. He threw the garage door open. Blue fog spilled onto the driveway.

"That's dangerous," the old screenwriter called over the hedge.

"Call an ambulance!" Duncan screamed.

The Cadillac's top was up. A garden hose ran from the exhaust into a barely open window. Blue haze filled the car. Pris slumped against the seat with her eyes shut. Duncan pulled the hose out and tried the door. Locked. He broke the rear window with his fist and unlocked the door. The car's stereo played *Only Women Bleed*. He dragged her onto the lawn and laid her gently on the grass. She did not breathe.

The old screenwriter yelled, "I called 911."

Duncan forced his breath into her mouth. Her chest rose as his fell, fell as his rose. He felt a hand on his shoulder but he did not stop.

"Let me," the gardener said with a faint accent. "You're doing it wrong. I know CPR."

He pulled Duncan away. He pinched her nose and filled her lungs with his breath. Duncan staggered backward. There was blood on her t-shirt.

"She's bleeding!"

"That's your blood," the old screenwriter said. "Look at your hand."

Duncan slumped to the lawn and watched the gardener try to puff life into his bride's quiet lungs. A paramedic's truck pulled up. Two men in uniforms ran to Pris and the gardener. One ran back to the truck and grabbed an oxygen tank and mask. A fire engine stopped behind the truck and several men jumped to the curb. One came up to Duncan and looked at his hand.

"We need to take care of this," he said.

"Forget about me," Duncan yelled, "she's dying!"

Another fire fighter brought a first-aid kit up and opened it. He cleaned Duncan's hand and sprayed antiseptic onto the gashes. Duncan felt nothing.

"We'd just be in the way," he said. "They're doing all they can."

Duncan stared at the paramedics hovering over Pris. *Please god,* he thought. An ambulance pulled up, and then a police car. Two policemen got out. One entered the house. The other opened a notebook.

"What's the stiff's name?" he asked.

"She's not a stiff!" Duncan yelled.

"Whoops," the officer said. "Sorry, buddy. What's her name?"

"Pris Nolan. I mean Delaney. We were just married." He shook his head. "Or it might be Penny Delaney. Can't we do this at the hospital?"

The first policeman came out of the house. "Not until we get some answers," he said. He pulled Duncan's hands behind his back and cuffed him. "There's a gunshot victim in the house."

The two paramedics stood and went inside.

"Hey, what about her?"

"She's breathing," a fire fighter said. "She should be okay."

"Who's the guy inside?" the policeman asked.

"I don't know. I just got home. I found him in the bedroom. I found her in the garage."

The policeman took a driver's license out of an old brown wallet. "Name Samuel Norris ring a bell?"

Duncan wanted to vomit. "It's her father."

Two uniformed men put Pris in the back of the ambulance.

"They're taking her away!"

The policeman put down a portable radio. "Records say he's served time for manslaughter."

"I have not!" Duncan yelled.

"Not you, the guy inside." The other cop uncuffed Duncan. "You go with her. We'll send a detective to the hospital to talk with you."

Duncan put on a shirt and got in the ambulance with a paramedic. Pris lay on the gurney, silent and still, the oxygen mask strapped across her nose and mouth. Her hand was loose and limp but it was warm. The door shut and the ambulance lurched onward. The paramedic looked as young as Duncan, with a body built on exercise machines, and hair as short as Duncan's was long. He looked like a surfer. He smiled at Duncan.

"I think she's going to be okay," said the paramedic.

"You're lucky you didn't cut a tendon," the doctor said as he sewed a last stitch in Duncan's hand. He looked like he was two thirds through a thirty hour shift. He wound gauze about his knuckles and taped it in place.

"Can I see her?"

"They're very busy. You'd be in the way."

Duncan followed him out. An old woman with teak skin and dark brown eyes sat across the waiting room, holding a bible and staring at the ceiling. A young man, shivering in a blanket, sat near her. A younger woman sat by the shivering man, her arm around him. Duncan went to a pay phone. He put in a quarter and dialed. A machine answered.

"Benjamin," Duncan said at the beep, "Pris tried to kill herself." He started to cry. "I don't know what to do."

He left the name of the hospital and hung up. Fear rose like a bilious moon in his throat. He ran into the bathroom to a stall and vomited in the toilet. He rinsed his mouth and wiped his face. When he returned to the waiting room, the others were gone. He sat in a chair and picked up a magazine. He read for an hour and when he put the magazine down he could not remember a word of what he had read.

"Duncan!"

Angela and Benjamin ran down the hall. He stood and fell into Benjamin's arms.

"Easy," Benjamin said, "easy."

"Duncan, what happened?"

Duncan breathed deep. He released Benjamin and sagged into a chair. "I found her in the garage. She was in her car with the engine running."

"Oh, god," Angela said. "Why?"

Duncan knew why. It was his fault. He never should have given Samuel Norris their address. He should have trusted her and whatever reason she had for wanting her father dead. He never should have left Cheyenne. He never should have been born.

"Because of me," he said.

"Come on," Benjamin said, "Let's get some coffee."

Benjamin led Duncan to an empty cafeteria and bought two coffees. Duncan held the cup and felt its warmth seep into his blood. He sipped and the coffee burned his tongue.

"Careful," Benjamin said. "It's hot."

Duncan sipped again. The cafeteria door slammed into the wall with a metallic bang. Sheila Rascowitz burst into the room. She wore black leather chaps and a sleeveless leather vest. A fresh tattoo of a headless cat ran along her left arm. Her eyes burned like distant bonfires.

"You!" she yelled. "It's your fault!"

"I know," Duncan said. "I'm sorry."

"Sorry isn't good enough."

Sheila pointed a glove. Benjamin dove for the floor.

"Get down!" he yelled.

When the glove spit fire, Duncan realized it was not a glove after all. The first bullet pierced his shoulder, the second nicked his ear. A hammer hit him above his other ear. Detective Harkanian, sent to the hospital to question Duncan, opened the door to find him falling. He backed in dread and reached for his hip when Sheila pointed the gun at him. Duncan hit the linoleum. Benjamin tackled Sheila. He grabbed her arm and broke her elbow across his knee. She screamed and the gun fell from her hand.

"That's enough," Harkanian said.

Benjamin released her and her arm flopped uselessly to the floor. Benjamin knelt beside Duncan while Harkanian cuffed Sheila.

"Are you okay?"

It seemed like a stupid question and Duncan laughed. Benjamin touched Duncan's forehead and his hand came away covered with blood.

"I don't think so," he replied.

As his arms grew numb, Duncan wondered if he would dream. He hoped so. He wanted to see his father before he died. The ceiling grew black and fell down to meet him and he wondered no more.

The first thing Duncan saw when he opened his eyes were the flowers. The room was filled with bouquets of rainbow petals and a floral smell. He tried to sit up, but his head spun and he sagged back against his pillow.

"He's out of it," a voice said.

"Thank god," another replied.

He closed his eyes and dreamed he was with his father on the Circle D. Both were on horseback, the air was steam in their mouths, and Duncan knew it was that terrible winter's day in his youth. Duncan and Sean watched a jet fall from the clouds to crash on the range. Just before his father spurred his horse to the rescue, Duncan saw a parachute floating slowly down.

"Dad, look! You don't have to go this time!"

Sean smiled sadly and said, "if only it were that easy."

The pilot landed and put his hand on Duncan's shoulder. "He was a brave man," he said.

Sean reached the plane. "Only as brave as I had to be!"

The pilot waved and called, "thanks anyway, Mr. Delaney!"

Sean waved back and said, "don't mention it!" To Duncan he called, "always remember, she was a wonderful girl who loved you very much."

He climbed onto a wing and reached for the cockpit. The jet exploded around him, pummeling Duncan with metallic wind and thunder.

How pointless, Duncan thought in his dream.

"Not at all," the pilot said as he walked away from the burning jet. "He never knew I got out."

Duncan cried then, tears of relief that his father never knew the folly of his death and tears of pain at his last words.

"Look," a voice said, "he's crying."

"Do you think he knows?" another asked.

"How could he?" the first voice said.

He opened his eyes. Benjamin and Angela stood by his bed. They looked sad and worn. Woody and Fiona stood behind them. She turned her face into Woody's shoulder. Benjamin gently pushed Angela aside. He bent and kissed Duncan's forehead and grasped his good hand.

"Pris didn't make it," Benjamin said.

Duncan gripped Benjamin's hand with all his feeble strength.

"I know."

"The first bullet," the man with the stethoscope said, "passed cleanly through your shoulder. It did no lasting damage. The second sliced a piece off your earlobe. The third grazed your temple and fractured your skull, resulting in a hematoma that caused pressure on your brain. Which is why you were in a coma for two weeks." He smiled brightly. His name was Dr. Norbert Franklin, he was Los Angeles's pre-eminent neurosurgeon, and he was enjoying talking about Duncan's hematoma. "Any questions?"

"Tell me about Pris."

"I wasn't her doctor. That was Dr. Phillips."

"Could you tell Dr. Phillips I'd like to see him, please?"

Franklin hung Duncan's chart on the base of the bed and left. Duncan touched his skull. Half his head was bald. A bandage covered a hole drilled in his skull to relieve the pressure on his brain. He painfully swung his legs off the bed and stood. He shuffled into the bathroom and urinated. He flushed and rinsed his hands. He looked in the mirror. His face was thin and white, the hair gone from the left side of his head. *The last of the half Mohicans,* he thought. He almost laughed but then he remembered how sad he was. He limped back to bed. The door opened and a tall man came in.

"Here," he took Duncan's arm. "Let me help you."

Duncan got into bed. He felt horribly tired. The tall man opened the drapes. Duncan squinted against the light.

"I'm Dr. Phillips." He sat in a chair by the bed and wiped his glasses on his coat. "You wanted to see me?"

"I want to know about Pris."

Dr. Phillips breathed a ragged sigh. "We thought it was only carbon monoxide poisoning. We had her on oxygen. We expected her to open her eyes every minute. Then the police called and told us they found an empty Valium bottle in the car and we knew why she wasn't coming out of it. We pumped her stomach but it was too late. She never woke."

Duncan looked to the courtyard outside his window. Orderlies arranged children in wheelchairs in a circle around a brightly dressed clown. Two children were bald and one's arm was in a cast but the others did not look ill. The clown lost control of five juggled rubber balls that fell sequentially onto his head. The children laughed and clapped. Duncan looked away.

"This was in her pocket," Phillips gave him a folded note. "I should have given it to the police but in all the rush I never did. Just as well. She obviously meant it for you."

After Phillips left, Duncan held the paper to his nose. He wanted to smell her perfume but all he detected was Phillips' wool coat and residual exhaust. He unfolded the note.

Duncan, it said, *I'm sorry for the pain and grateful for your patience and love. Because of you, I was whole for a while. But I can no longer make love to you without thinking of him and what he did to me. I will always love you. But it just hurts too much.*

Duncan stared at the note until the children and the clown left and the courtyard beyond his window filled with shadows. Getting up was easier this time. He took off his hospital gown and dressed. There was a hole in the shoulder of his shirt, but it had been washed, and the blood was gone. He sat on the bed and pulled on his socks and tennis shoes. His shoulder was agony but he went on. He finished dressing, put the note in his pocket, picked up the phone, and called Benjamin.

170

Twenty

Duncan stayed with Benjamin and Angela. Fiona and Woody moved out of the hotel and into Bolo's with Duncan's permission. Both house and restaurant had passed from Bolo to Pris and were now Duncan's by virtue of his brief marriage. Fiona had herself declared conservator and took over the daily operation of *Café Bella* while Duncan was comatose. Her first management decisions were to hire Sven as omelette chef and Roscoe as bartender. Duncan approved because he liked Sven and Roscoe. Otherwise he could care less what she did with the restaurant.

The first morning out of the hospital he noticed how ridiculous he looked in the mirror, so he cut the rest of his hair. He wore baseball caps while his brain healed. He sat by Angela's pool for near a week, drinking an occasional beer and staring past the horizon.

Aided by Armstrong's positive review in the *Times* and the negative news of his shooting, his paintings had greatly increased in price. Angela and Benjamin practically lived in his hospital room that first week and she had no time to sell any. But she visited her office one morning and by the time she left she had sold two Delaneys for twenty-five thousand dollars each. The next day she sold three more at thirty thousand a piece. A Japanese investor offered sixty thousand for *Sleeping Pris,* but she intuitively refused to sell without Duncan's consent. The investor was lucky. Duncan woke and the price of a Delaney dropped to a paltry ten thousand.

"Too bad you couldn't have stayed in a coma longer," Angela joked one afternoon by the pool, "you would have made us rich."

"Relax," Benjamin said, "it's not like he's given up painting."

Duncan did not reply and that worried Angela more than anything.

Fiona and Woody visited every day, but Duncan was put off by her hovering, and he finally asked her to attend to the restaurant full time. It was what she wanted anyway. Duncan said she could have both restaurant and house, he wanted neither.

"You'll change your mind," Fiona said.

"Tell you what," Duncan replied, "I'll trade you both for the Circle D."

Fiona immersed herself in the restaurant and settled for telephonic progress reports. Duncan appreciated her solicitousness, but he preferred to be alone with his sorrow. But she persisted calling and one time foolishly commented, *God does things for the best.* Duncan hung up on her. The phone rang again and Duncan let it ring. The next time Fiona called, she carefully avoided speculating on God's intentions. One morning Detective Harkanian found Duncan by the pool. Duncan offered him a beer, and despite being on duty, Harkanian took off his coat and accepted.

"I would have come earlier," he said. "But Norris died a week before you came out of it and it kind of lost its urgency."

Samuel Norris, Harkanian told him, was indeed Pris's father, and a Pentecostal minister. He was a little man who used a big voice to inspire his congregation and browbeat his family. When Pris was twelve, she shot him in the back with a hunting rifle. The bullet made a clean hole in his shoulder, went through two walls, and lodged in the water heater. Despite losing a quart of blood, he survived. The water heater had to be replaced. Pris told the police she did it because her father had beat her mother longer than memory, and she wanted to make it stop. Despite her bruised face and body Shirley Norris denied any abusive behavior. Samuel was her sole support and often reminded her of it. He was also a respected preacher and community member who forgave his errant daughter at each of her seven hearings. The judge ultimately sent her to juvenile hall for three years. She was fifteen when she was released to her father's custody. The first night home, Samuel Norris looked at her matured body and raped her while her mother sat in the den knitting with the television on full blast so she would not hear her daughter scream. Pris reported the rape to a school counselor, who notified the police, but given her past behavior, nobody believed her, and she was returned home. She ran away that night. Samuel's soup was cold the next day, and he beat Shirley so badly because of it she ended up in the hospital for the week it took for her to die. Samuel pled guilty to involuntary manslaughter in a plea bargain and spent seven years in state prison. The police regretted dismissing Pris's story as a vicious child's lies. They searched but could not find her, which was unfortunate, as additional molestation charges would have sent Samuel Norris away for a much longer time.

"He would have survived," Harkanian said, "but someone got to him in the County U.S.C. jail ward. They beat him so bad we needed fingerprints to identify him. Couldn't have used teeth. Someone pulled them all out. Everyone on the ward said they were sleeping and didn't hear or see a thing.

"We found your car burning in your driveway the night you were shot," Harkanian continued. "Rascowitz must have gone there first. We charged her with attempted murder and arson. She's out on a half million dollar bail, so watch your ass." He stood. "We found Norris' gun on the floor of the Cadillac. It was a five shot Smith and Wesson. Close as I can figure it, he surprised her at the front door and forced her into the bedroom. She was beat up a little, not too bad, but she must have put up one hell of a fight." Harkanian said it admiringly. "She broke a chair over his head and got the gun. She shot the bastard five times. We figure she brought the gun into the car to . . ." Harkanian stopped. "Jesus Christ, I'm an insensitive pig."

"Go on. I need to know."

Harkanian sat down again and sighed. "She must have brought it into the car to shoot herself. But she had already emptied it into her dad. Maybe she thought it was a six shot. Maybe she thought she saved one last round. But . . ." Harkanian shrugged.

"Would you like another beer?"

"Sure," Harkanian said, "why not?"

Wilson and Peewee arrived on thundering Harleys that night. Angela tentatively let them in. Benjamin led them to the pool and got four beers.

"Sorry to hear about your lady," Wilson said. "She was beautiful."

"Did you hear about Roscoe?" Peewee asked.

"Yup."

"He took a different path," Wilson said.

"Where's Marco?"

"He's in County," Wilson said. "He got picked up by the Highway Patrol for possession of stolen bike parts."

"They beat him up bad," Peewee said. "Sent him to the hospital ward."

Wilson took an envelope out of his pocket. "Marco sent you this."

Duncan opened the envelope after they left. He expected to find more white powder, but instead he found a zip-lock bag with three human teeth: an incisor, a bicuspid, and a molar. Duncan looked at the teeth for a long time before he threw them over the fence and down the hillside.

Roscoe came by the next day with a small box. Inside were blonde baby hair, silver earrings, a folded paper, and a photo of Duncan and Pris taken at their wedding. Looking at the photo Duncan remembered another, the one of him and Tiffy taken at the rodeo. He compared Pris's smile to Tiffy's. He put the photo down. Pris won by a Cheyenne mile.

"Your mom found the box at the house," Roscoe said. "She asked me to bring it by."

"Thanks. How's Sven?"

"Aw, man, he's wonderful. He would have come but he said he would just start crying." Roscoe could not help smiling. "He makes me so happy I feel guilty knowing what you've been through and what you've lost."

"I appreciate it."

Roscoe hugged Duncan. "You have to let her go, man. We all do."

After Roscoe left, Duncan unfolded the paper. Written there were instructions on what to do after her death. It seemed she had planned this long ago. The only change on the note was at the bottom where she had directed where to spread her ashes. She had crossed out *ocean* and written *Duncan* and a question mark beside his name. He put the paper in his pocket. Benjamin came out and sat beside him.

"Think you could give me a ride?" Duncan asked.

After twenty minutes Duncan still could not find the grave, and he had to ask for assistance. A grave digger led him to the crest of a small hill overlooking the San Fernando valley. Her grave was among the first there, with a stone set in the grass. He had expected an upright tombstone, but the grave digger said those were not used much anymore.

"These make it easier for the lawn mowers," he explained.

Duncan sat by the grave. The grass was cool and moist and a breeze off the freeway rustled his emerging hair. *She Died for Love,* the inscription on the stone said. Duncan thought it true. He sat there for an hour thinking about the other reasons for her death until he saw Sheila coming. Even from a distance he knew it was her. Despite the knowledge he remained. He was too tired to get up and too hopeless to care. When she was twenty yards away, he lay across the grave. He closed his eyes and felt the earth's strength beneath him. A shadow passed over his face. He opened his eyes and sat up with difficulty when he heard her sobbing. Sheila sat a yard away, her right arm in a cast and her head against her left hand, her eyes wet and dull. A silver pistol lay on the grass beside her.

"I loved her too," she said. "Maybe more than you."

"Maybe."

He resigned himself to death. Here was as good a place as any and now was as good a time. Sheila picked up the gun and held it flat in her hand. She looked at it like it was an apple or a calculator or anything but a gun.

"I like the stone."

"I picked it out. Benjamin said it was okay with him."

"I'm sure she would like it." Duncan pointed at the gun. "What were you planning to do with that?"

"I don't know. Shoot myself. Maybe you."

"I don't think she would appreciate either."

Sheila stared at the gun. "You're probably right."

She laid the gun on the stone. She stood and walked away. Duncan sat there until the sun threatened to set. He picked up the gun and walked towards the cemetery office. On the way he passed an open, empty grave, raw earth beside it. He dropped the gun in the hole and kicked sweet, moist dirt onto it. He reached the office and asked for the manager.

"What can I do for you, Mr. Delaney?" The manager asked after Duncan introduced himself. He was a fat man with professionally sad eyes.

"My wife was buried here without my permission."

"I'm sorry to hear it. Do you find the accommodations unsuitable?"

"No, it's a nice grave as far as graves go. But it's not what she wanted. She wanted to be cremated."

The manager called for a file. He put on glasses and scrutinized the pages within. He looked up.

"The funeral was paid for by a Ms. Rascowitz. She paid for one of our eternity plots. I'm afraid we can't make a refund."

"I don't want you to. I want you to leave the plot the way it is. Stone and all. I just don't want her to be beneath it."

"I don't understand."

"Let's see if you understand this. Dig her up. Dig her up and cremate her. Then put the grave back the way it is now." Duncan was determined to follow Pris's wishes, but he wanted to leave a cenotaph for Sheila. "Call me when you're done and I'll pick up the ashes."

"This will be expensive," the manager said.

"I really don't give a shit," Duncan replied.

Duncan took a cab to his studio. He was thirsty so he went inside the mini-mart to buy a soda. Assan smiled broadly and hugged him. Duncan looked at the wall over the counter. His painting of Assan hung there. Duncan smiled despite himself.

"Nice painting," he said.

"Oh, yes. Everybody loves it." Assan frowned. "Except for one ugly woman with short hair who screamed when she saw it. For a moment I thought I would have to equalize her with my Benelli."

"Did she leave on a Harley?"

"How did you know?"

"Lucky guess."

Duncan paid for his soda and a candy bar and went upstairs. When he opened the door, he saw a woman sleeping on the couch with an orange cat on her lap and for one exhilarating moment he believed his life had been a nightmare from which he had suddenly awakened. But the woman stirred and he saw it was Misty. She sat up.

"Hi, Duncan. How are you doing?"

"They tell me I'll have good and bad days. Still waiting on a good one."

Misty looked down. "Your mom asked me to take care of Cat. Hope you don't mind."

"Not at all."

He had forgotten Cat in his grief. He felt guilty as hell. Cat rubbed his leg. Duncan smiled and picked him up and sat on the couch beside her.

"I saw our painting hanging in a museum the other day," Misty said. "Can you believe it? Some kid on a field trip says to me, *'hey lady, isn't that you?'* I'm there with Tommy Bertone. He plays guitar in a band called *Forced Entry*. He's kind of a jerk." Misty knew she was babbling but could not stop. "Anyway, Tommy doesn't like someone recognizing me and not him and the teacher leading the group asks me what you're like and Tommy says, *'fuck you lady,'* so I smack his face with my handbag and the guard throws us out. He left me in the parking lot but I didn't care."

Duncan smiled. "That sounds like fun."

"Yes, it was." Misty eyes were as brown as Tiffy's but where Tiffy's were hard Misty's were soft. "When are you going to paint again?"

"I don't know."

"She would want you to."

Duncan stood. "Come on. I'll walk you downstairs."

When they reached the street Misty got in her car and rolled down her window. "Can I come see you some time?"

"Sure."

"When?"

"I don't know. A month or two. I've got some things to work out."

"All right." She started the car.

"See you, Misty."

"Damn right you will," she said. She drove off.

Duncan went back upstairs and looked around. But there was nothing there he wanted anymore, only memories, and he kept those with him always. He called a cab and carried Cat downstairs to wait and he left the door open behind him.

Three days later the mortuary called. Angela was at the office and Benjamin was surfing with Woody so Duncan put on his jacket and his Stetson and carried Cat the three miles to Bolo's house. His mother had changed the curtains and pruned the hedges to let in more light. Pieces of Fiona's life now lay about, mail on a shelf by the front door, her reading glasses on the table where Bolo's had been. Bolo's pictures were gone from the mantle, replaced by Duncan's graduation photo and an enlargement of his wedding picture. Duncan walked through the house collecting his things. Hard as he avoided it he eventually came to the bedroom.

The blood was gone from the floor and the bedspread had been replaced. He emptied his clothes from the drawers and put them on the bed. He held one of her sweaters to his nose. He thought he smelled her in the fabric. But that hurt too much so he put the sweater back and took a suitcase from under the bed and packed it. He opened the garage door and put the suitcase in the Cadillac's trunk. He started the engine and put the top down. He pulled the car out of the garage and parked it in the driveway. He went back inside the house and found a piece of paper.

Gone to Wyoming, he wrote, *Love, Duncan.*

He stuck the note on the refrigerator and left the house, locking the door behind him. He got in the Cadillac and drove to Angela's office. She was out to lunch, but Marie was there, and Duncan retrieved *Sleeping Pris.* He put the painting in the back seat. For weeks after, Duncan slept every chance he had, hoping to see her in his dreams, but the harder he tried the less he slept and his dreams were devoid of her. One terrifying day he had to look at his painting to remember what she looked like. But that was weeks in the future and now he was just glad the painting was not sold.He moved Cat to the front seat. He drove to the cemetery and picked up Pris's ashes. He declined the decorative urn for an additional three hundred and fifty dollars. He got in the Cadillac and put the box of ashes on the floor. Cat sniffed the box once. He meowed sadly and fell asleep on the seat beside Duncan. Duncan put on his sunglasses and pulled down his hat.

Then he got on the 10 freeway and drove East.

Twenty One

On the clear blue Sunday of Duncan's twenty second birthday, Misty sat inside her BMW convertible outside the Circle D's gates. It had taken longer than anticipated to find her way there, but she had much to accomplish before making the journey. First, she quit working at the Hollywood, and with the money she had saved stripping, she had her breast implants removed. She felt good to have the foreign objects evicted from her interior and she felt better about herself for having abjured them. After the operation she was surprised by how little her chest shrunk.

"The implants burst long ago," the doctor explained. "Luckily they were of the saline variety. You must have grown some in the meantime."

She had developed in other ways too. After she recovered sufficiently from her operation, she dyed her hair back to its original brown, then went back to school to study for and receive her high school equivalency certificate. She was no brighter, but at least what light she now emitted illuminated a larger world, and as a result, she was far more confident. But confident or not, as she sat inside her car, she was nervous enough to vomit.

"It's okay," she told herself, "he's just a guy."

She drove the last half mile from the highway and parked outside a big white house. The Cadillac of Doom, open to the weather, rusted in front of a garage. All four tires were flat and the seats were torn and stained by the rain. She got out of her car. She wore the knee length skirt, white cotton long sleeved shirt, leather vest and boots she had purchased in Cheyenne hours before. Everyone at the store was so friendly and helpful that at first she thought they were mocking her. But a waitress treated her the same when she ordered a vegetarian omelette in a highway diner and she concluded that was just how people here were. And the fat man at the market with the cross around his neck and the tattoo of a snake on his forearm was positively helpful when she asked for directions.

She looked in the Cadillac. A key was rusted fast to the ignition. The car had not budged since Duncan parked it there close to one year before. He had opened the garage door vaguely intending to pull the Cadillac in and shut the door behind him with the engine running. But the car had died when he got back in and would not start though it had plenty of spark and enough gas and Duncan finally gave up and picked up Cat and brought him and the painting and the ashes inside. Misty turned away and climbed the front steps. Cat sat on a rattan chair on the porch, licking a paw and otherwise ignoring her. Misty ran her hand across his back. He purred once then went back to the paw. She breathed deep, stepped up to the door and knocked. When no one replied she looked in the window.

"God," she said, "what a pig sty."

A horse whinnied from afar. She turned. Duncan rode towards the house, an empty box under one arm and a sleeping bag tied to the saddle behind him. He had spent the last two days building a cairn at the site of Sean Delaney's death. That morning he had spread Pris's ashes around the rocks, finally releasing her and fulfilling her last wish as best he could. He spurred his mare when he saw Misty. He reined the horse in front of the house and jumped off.

"Hi," Misty said.

He hugged her. "I didn't recognize you at first. You dyed your hair."

"No," Misty said, "this is my real color."

"Well, it looks good." He tied the horse to the porch rail. "What brings you out here?"

"You invited me. Remember?"

"Of course I did."

Duncan set the box on the steps and slapped the dust from his pants with a glove. His red hair had grown back long below his Stetson. His beard covered most of his chin and some of his cheeks with a fine, red stubble. He had filled out since she saw him last. He was now lean bordering on muscular. He stepped onto the porch and opened the door.

"Come on in."

She followed him inside. The remains of meals lay on a table in front of the television. Magazines and books were scattered on the couch and on the floor before it. The carpet needed vacuuming and while the house did not exactly smell bad, neither did it smell good. Duncan removed his hat.

"Sorry about the mess. I wasn't expecting company."

"I should have called."

"I wasn't here anyway," Duncan said. He transferred magazines from chair to couch. "Make yourself at home. I'm going to shower."

Instead of sitting, Misty wandered through the house. One room contained an easel and twenty canvases stacked against a wall. All were landscapes of lonely, barren vistas. Another room was almost empty. *Sleeping Pris* hung without benefit of frame on the wall opposite the window. Misty shivered and closed the door. She went into the kitchen. Dishes lay piled in the sink and on the table. She looked at a postcard stuck to the refrigerator with a magnet. It was from the Hollywood Tropicana, and it depicted tanned, oiled women whose synthetic breasts strained the limits of string bikinis, except for the vaguely familiar blond girl in the center, a girl with chocolate eyes and strawberry lips, and breasts the size of softballs, though much softer and not as white. Misty turned the card over. *Thought you might enjoy this,* it said, *Benjamin.* She put the card back. A letter from the Los Angeles District Attorney's office lay on the table. She politely ignored it. If she had read it she would have discovered that Sheila, as part of a plea agreement brokered by a Los Angeles city councilwoman, had pleaded guilty to one count of aggravated assault and was placed on three years probation, fined five hundred dollars, and was ordered to serve four hundred hours of community service. What the letter did not say was that subsequent to the sentencing the councilwoman purchased three of Sheila's paintings at a substantial and deep discount.

Misty put on an apron she found on a hook. She filled the sink with hot water and soap, and spent the next fifteen minutes washing china and cutlery. Duncan found her there when he came out of the shower. His hair was wet and his freshly shaved skin was pink and soft. He wore a loose flannel shirt untucked over his blue jeans and his feet poked white and thin from the cuffs.

"You don't have to do those," he said.

Misty turned and scowled. "Jesus, Duncan," she said, the words opening a floodgate, "you need a woman around here!"

The dam containing his loss burst at last. He fell into Misty's surprised, soapy arms, his anguish flowing down his cheeks in salty torrents. He held her until his grief emptied its painful river into a thirsty desert, and past the dwindling desolation that remained he held her still.